What readers are  The House on the Lake

★ ★ ★ ★ ★

'I finished it in one sitting'
Julie, *Netgalley*

★ ★ ★ ★ ★

'Wow. From first word to last this fast-paced,
gripping story had me in its thrall'
Ceecee, *Netgalley*

★ ★ ★ ★ ★

'Another great read'
Pauline, *Netgalley*

★ ★ ★ ★ ★

'Emotional and extremely atmospheric . . . Highly recommended'
Samantha, *Netgalley*

★ ★ ★ ★ ★

'Oh, wow. From page one it pulled me in and didn't let go till the
very end'
Charlene, *Netgalley*

★ ★ ★ ★ ★

'I loved it . . . Great book – great, great, great!'
Gill, *Netgalley*

★ ★ ★ ★ ★

'Amazing read, I couldn't put it down and actually read it in one go!'
Hayley, *Netgalley*

★ ★ ★ ★ ★

'I wish I could give this more than 5 stars!'
Miriam, *Netgalley*

★ ★ ★ ★ ★

'Another gripping story from Nuala Ellwood'
Janet, *Netgalley*

The House on the Lake

NUALA ELLWOOD

PENGUIN BOOKS

PENGUIN BOOKS

UK | USA | Canada | Ireland | Australia
India | New Zealand | South Africa

Penguin Books is part of the Penguin Random House group of companies
whose addresses can be found at global.penguinrandomhouse.com.

First published 2020
001

Copyright © Nuala Ellwood, 2020

The moral right of the author has been asserted

The quotations from Nizar Qabbani's *Book of Love* are taken from an unknown translation

Every effort has been made to trace the copyright holders and to obtain their permission for the use
of copyright material. The publisher apologizes for any errors or omissions and would be grateful
to be notified of any corrections that short be incorporated in future editions of this book

Set in 12.5/14.75 pt Garamond MT Std by Integra Software Services Pvt. Ltd, Pondicherry
Printed and bound in Great Britain by Clays Ltd, Elcograf S.p.A.

A CIP catalogue record for this book is available from the British Library

ISBN: 978–0–241–98515–1

www.greenpenguin.co.uk

For Arthur and Nell

'I cannot think of any need in childhood as strong as the need for a father's protection'

– Sigmund Freud

Prologue

Blood.

That's all I can think about as I sit here huddled in the corner. I close my eyes but I can still see it, a dark crimson stain on the new-fallen snow.

His blood.

I get to my feet and look out of the tiny window. The snow is falling still. White flakes drift through the air, obscuring my view of the crag and the woods beyond. All is as it was and yet everything has changed. The landscape I once loved and treasured is now a warped one, with no beginning and no end.

It is rotten. All of it.

I have nothing left, I think to myself, as I close the window. Nothing except the terrible images that swirl round my head.

It's been four days now with no word. Any hope I had left in my heart is gone. I am alone, utterly alone.

I step back inside the room. My blankets are lying on the floor where I left them earlier. I have tried to sleep but it's no use. Every time I close my eyes I see his face and I'm reminded of what I've lost.

Love.

Family.

Home.

That was all I ever wanted. All I ever needed. I just didn't realize until it was too late.

I lift the blanket and give it a shake. Dust particles rise up into the air and I cough as they hit the back of my throat. Then I hear it. Knocking. It gets louder and louder and it takes me a few moments to work out that it's coming from downstairs. It's the front door. Someone is knocking on the front door. My heart lifts.

He's come back. I knew he would.

I run to the door, open it wide, and as I hurtle down the stairs I make a silent promise that from now on things will be better, I will be a better person. I won't complain or argue. I will be thankful for the family I have been given, for the person I love most in this world.

But it is a woman's voice that greets me as I reach the front door.

'Police. Open up.'

It's a sharp, menacing sound that seems to slice through the heavy wooden door as I stand trembling behind it.

'Stand back.'

There's a pause followed by an almighty thud as the door is broken down and two uniformed officers – one male, one female – rush towards me and grab me by my arms.

It happens so quickly I barely have time to catch my breath, though as they lead me outside I manage to catch a few of their words.

And then, in those final moments before they take me away, it all makes sense. The silence. The blood. The nightmares.

I realize what has happened.
It was me.
I killed him.

PART ONE

I

Lisa

9 December 2018

Joe's screams fill the car as we come off the motorway and make our way down a series of narrow and twisty country roads. I turn the radio up to its highest volume then grip the steering wheel, hoping that a bit of Little Mix might calm him down. I sing along too at the top of my voice and pretend that everything is perfectly normal, that we're off on a fun festive trip, my little boy and me. I try not to think about Mark and what he'll do when he finds out we've gone but his voice is everywhere. I can hear it in my head above the music, dripping with menace: *You silly fucking bitch. What the hell have you done?* I turn the music up but Mark's voice merges with it. Behind me, Joe starts wailing.

'Want Daddy. Want Daddy.'

My heart starts to pound, the familiar prelude to the panic attacks I've been getting recently. Turning the radio off, I slowly exhale, remembering the technique I learned at the mindfulness class they made me take.

In. Out. In. Out.

'It's okay, bubba,' I say as the pounding subsides. 'Mummy's taking you on a big adventure. We're going to the countryside where there'll be sheep and cows and lots of fun things, and we're going to stay in a beautiful house. You'll like it, I promise.'

I look at his face in the rear-view mirror. His big blue eyes are red and swollen with tears. His bottom lip quivers as he turns his head and looks out of the window.

'Come on, Joe,' I say, keeping my voice extra bright. 'Let's see if we can spot any sheep.'

But the fields on either side of the road are empty and a thick frost covers the hedges. There are no sheep, no horses, no sign of any life at all. A feeling of dread uncoils itself in my stomach as I drive through the desolate landscape. What the hell are you doing, Lisa?

Just turn round and go home, I tell myself. You don't have to go through with this. It's not too late. But then I remember Mark's face, the hatred contorting his features, and I think of the piece of paper, tucked away in my bag, with the directions to the safe place. I've kept it hidden all these months and now it's time to use it.

But as I drive I feel doubt creeping in. I had felt so certain when I set off but now all I can hear is my dad's voice, the voice of pragmatism and reason. 'Nothing comes for free, Lisa.' And part of me knows that is true. Have I made the biggest mistake of my life?

'Not want you. Want Daddy.'

Joe's voice interrupts my thoughts and though his words sting I know that I have no choice now. I have to do it. There is no other way.

I grip the steering wheel tightly as a road sign looms into view. Harrowby. I recognize the name of the village from the note. It sounds ordinary enough but as I take a left turn I see that the 'village' is nothing more than a cluster of decrepit terrace houses with smoke curling out of the chimneys. A grey mist hangs in the air as we drive past a pebble-dashed convenience store with a newspaper stand out front and a pub festooned with tired-looking Christmas decorations. An inflatable snowman floats ghost-like outside the front door. I shudder as memories of Christmas 2016 come hurtling into my head unbidden: the screaming, the blood – so much blood – and the fear that seeped into my bones as the horror of my situation became clear.

'Look, Joe, quick,' I say, pointing out of the window, in a feeble attempt to brighten the mood. 'See the snowman. Isn't he funny?'

'Want Daddy,' he screams. 'Where is he?'

It's ripping my heart. I want to shout at him, tell him that I'm his mummy, that I love him more than he will ever know. But that won't make any sense to him so instead I make some soothing noises then switch off the radio and turn on the story-time CD I bought yesterday. The opening bars of a jaunty tune strike up and then a soft male American voice begins the story of *Where the Wild Things Are*. It was my favourite book when I was a child and I'm hoping Joe will like it too. He has stopped crying at least.

'Is that better?' I say after a minute or two, keeping my eyes on the road.

He doesn't answer. He's lost in the story.

'Thank God for that,' I whisper, grateful for the silence.

We're on the edge of the village now. The sky is darkening and I blink as a boxy red-brick building comes into view up ahead on the right. Drawing closer, I see the words ALL HALLOWS painted in black letters on a wooden sign and a man standing outside the church.

9

The vicar. I catch his eye as we pass and a chill flutters through me as I remember the last time I was in a chapel, my arms covered in bruises. I blink the memory away and concentrate on the road ahead. The satnav had told me to follow the road out of the village for three miles, though the words on the note are etched on my memory. *The lake will appear right ahead of you. It's impossible to miss.*

The hills rise up on either side, closing in on me like the folded pages of a pop-up book as I follow the narrow road. The sky is dark grey now. Night is coming. There are no houses, no people. No cars pass by. My chest tightens with dull panic and I can feel it rising in my throat. I focus on the soft voice on the CD, describing the wild things roaring their terrible roars, and suddenly I'm six years old again, curled up on the sofa next to my dad as he reads to me the story of a young boy who sailed away.

The memory calms me and I sit up straight and focus on the increasingly bumpy and potholed road. And then, as we reach the crest of the hill, it appears in front of me: a wide expanse of black water. As I draw closer, a dark shadow seems to rise out of the lake and slowly take form, and I see a tall, black stone building with barred windows. This can't possibly be it, I think, pulling up by the lake. It looks like a prison or one of those asylums they used to lock people away in back in Victorian times. And it's clear nobody has set foot in it for years – it's almost completely falling apart. I take the note out of my handbag and read, praying that I've taken the wrong turn.

I look out of the window. There's a sign next to the door but the light is fading and I can't see what it says. I fold up the note and put it back into my bag.

'Two minutes, Joe,' I say, turning round to look at him. He's fast asleep, his ragged old toy rabbit pressed to his pink cheek.

Careful not to wake him, I gently open the door and step outside. The air is cold and there's a biting wind. I button up my padded coat and walk towards the building. My stomach twists when I think about that last conversation with her. Everyone said she was unhinged. What if this is all some sick joke?

There's a broken jetty on the edge of the lake. An old rowing boat bobs beside it, rocking from side to side in the breeze. *Thud, thud, thud*. The noise makes my skin prickle and I hurry towards the house.

It's bigger up close, an intimidating bulk that looms above me like a great ship. The windows are dark and caked in mud and there's a thick wooden door straight ahead of me with a heavy brass knocker in the centre. The sign I saw from the car is thick with dirt and grime. I step forward and wipe it with the back of my hand then read the name, written in what looks like a child's handwriting.

Rowan Isle House. This is it. This is the house.

I half walk, half run back to the car. Thankfully Joe is still fast asleep in the back. I open the door on the driver's side and slump into my seat. I should just turn on the engine and get the hell out of here. That would be the sensible thing to do. But then I think about what I've done and how angry Mark will be. I can't go back there.

Not to that hell. I try to think of other options. Hotels. B&Bs. But that's a short-term solution and with the cost of rooms my money would run out after a few days. I have no option. No other way out.

Then I twist round in my seat and look at my little boy sleeping, his soft, fair eyelashes peeking out from behind a curtain of golden curls. I love him so much it hurts. I'm his mother and I have to keep him close, have to protect him now.

2

Soldier

Rowan Isle House, 2002

This will be my first entry in this book. I've been given it to record my progress as an elite soldier. You may think that if I'm a soldier then I must live with other soldiers in a camp or out in the desert where people drop bombs. But I'm not like other soldiers. For a start I'm not a grown-up, I'm a girl. I have black hair and black eyes and I live in a big old house that looks out on to a lake. It's not a pretty house, not like Misselthwaite Manor or Green Gables, the houses that I read about in the books I get from the mobile library. It doesn't have clean white shutters or fancy furnishings. It's a dark house with old wooden beams and stone floors. We don't have much furniture either, only the very basics. But then Sarge says that's all we need.

Sarge is my dad but I call him 'Sarge' because that's what he was when he was in this thing called the SAS. His real name is an OFFICIAL SECRET, though I've told him that I'm good at keeping secrets and I won't tell.

Anyway, where was I? Oh yes. The house. Well, I've lived here all my life so it's all I've ever known. And even though I like reading about pretty houses in my library books I wouldn't swap this one for the world. It may not look like much but we make it cosy, especially in the winter when Sarge brings out the old animal skins. I like sitting in front of the fire with the skins across my feet while Sarge reads me my favourite book: *The Wind in the Willows*. Those are the best times. When it's freezing out and we're warm inside listening to the tales of Ratty, Toad, Mole and Badger, my best friends. How can you be friends with them, you may ask, when they're not real? But, you see, that's the thing, Sarge makes them real, and has done since I was small. When he's reading the bits with Badger he puts on his glasses and makes his voice all low and serious, and in my head I can see the old badger as clear as anything. I see him with a book in his hands because he's clever, Badger, or 'well read' as Sarge likes to put it.

For Toad, he sits up straight and puffs his chest out. And I giggle because he's not Sarge any more, he's that silly Toad strutting about Toad Hall or zooming through the country lanes in his fast little car. 'Beep, Beep,' shouts Sarge as he sits in his chair holding a pretend steering wheel. 'Out of my way!' And then, like magic, I'm out there on the open road with him, feeling the wind in my hair, even though I've never been in a car in my life.

Like I said, Sarge makes everything seem real.

It's not just stories and soldiering though. Sarge also makes sure I get what he calls a 'proper education'. By that he means learning about the things that matter, the things that will help me when I'm grown. Sarge says that other children go to school to learn what the government wants them to know. It's how they control them, he says, how they keep people in line, so they don't ask questions or start revolutions. I'm not sure what a revolution is, though Sarge says it's about time this country had one.

Anyway, Sarge has taught me well. I know my times tables and I practise my maths when I sell the eggs that our chickens lay. We set up a little stall out front and put a sign by the gate that says FRESH EGGS FOR SALE. We sell them for £2 a dozen which Sarge says is a bargain. I'm in charge of serving the customers because Sarge doesn't like talking to people so I get to work out how much change they need and things like that. Sarge says I wouldn't learn how to think on my feet like that in a classroom.

Sarge taught me to read when I was three. I love reading. Besides soldiering, it's my favourite thing to do. When I read it feels like travelling all over the world when I haven't even left my room. Just by opening up a book I can be taken away to America or China, India or Africa, and when I've finished the story it feels like I've actually been to those places, like I can feel the hot African sun on my skin or the smell of the spices in an Indian market. I told Sarge how I felt and he said that the world is a dangerous place and it's best that we stay put. I know he's right but I secretly wish I could feel the real African sun or take a dip in the River Ganges. One day maybe.

For now, Sarge says that we're safe here in this house. That as long as we stick together no one can get to us. The people in the village are dangerous and to be avoided. I have seen them with my own eyes, seen how they look at us. Once we went into the shop because Sarge had got some money from selling a sheepskin and he wanted to put up a notice on the board telling people that there were more for sale, but as soon as we got in there the woman who runs it tried to get us out. She told us that it was too expensive to put a notice on the board, then she stood with her hands on this machine that Sarge told me was called a till, something that holds money in it. 'She thought we were going to rob her, the stupid woman,' Sarge said to me when we were on our way home. 'Doesn't she know that we have everything we need?' That was the last time we ever went to the shop. And after that we set up our egg stall with our own little box to hold the money. Sarge said our eggs were fresher than the rubbish you got in the shop and he hoped that woman never had a day's luck in her life. I agree with him because the way she looked at us that day wasn't nice. It made me feel like we were bad people, me and Sarge, and we're not. We're good people. We're just not like them.

Anyway, I can do what I like in the house, though the upstairs is out of bounds as Sarge says the flooring up there is old and rotten and we don't have enough money to get it fixed. It's dangerous to walk on, he says. I had a peek up there once, though, when I was small, and the stairs were so loose and wobbly I was scared I'd fall so I came back down again pretty sharpish. I'm allowed to play out the back where we have a garden that looks out on to the woods and hills, though I'm only allowed to go to the woods when Sarge is with me. That's a rule. And we don't go to the village much. But I'm not too fussed about going there anyway, not after what happened in the shop that day, and, besides, there's so much to do here. Even when it's freezing out I can find things to occupy me here in the house and if he sees me looking idle Sarge will set me a task, like polishing our boots ready for manoeuvres the next day or loading then unloading the rifles. You have to be prepared for anything. That's what Sarge says.

And today I got a taste of that; of how it feels to be a proper soldier. It's my birthday today, my eleventh birthday. Now normally, on my birthday, I would start knitting a pair of socks for the cold months. Sarge forages the wool from the briars around the sheep field. He wraps it in string and brings it to my room with a tray of homemade oat biscuits and a glass of goat's milk. That's what he's done every birthday since I was five and I first learned to knit.

But this birthday it's different. Instead of wool I got this book and Sarge said that I must write in it every day, that it's a logbook, something every good soldier needs. He also said that today is a very important day, a day I'll remember all my life.

And he was right. It was a good day. Because today I made my first kill.

It began when it was still dark out. Sarge woke me earlier than usual, about 4 a.m. There wasn't even time for a kit inspection because he said we had to hurry, that this was the best time to do it. You've got to catch them when they've just woken up, he said. Catch them unawares.

I wanted to stay in bed. It was freezing out and I didn't want to go off into the woods. Plus it was my birthday and usually Sarge lets me sleep late on my birthday. So I pulled my doss bag over my head and told him to go away. That was a bad move. I knew, even before the words had left my mouth, that he would have me for insubordination, birthday or not. He didn't say anything though. And that is always a bad sign. I heard him storm out of the room.

After a minute or so I looked out from under the doss bag and saw him standing above me with a bucket of water. Before I could dart back under, he threw the whole lot over me.

The cold felt like tiny knives stabbing me all over. I screamed and jumped out of bed. Sarge said it was a lesson learned. That being tired was not an excuse. That in his big war he'd had to walk across the desert for six days with next to no sleep. And that he hadn't been able to stop because he had a mission to carry out, that people had depended on him. 'I never want to hear you say you're tired again,' he said. 'Do you hear me?'

I said I heard him loud and clear. He looked at me for a moment or so to check that I meant what I said, then he left me to get dried and dressed.

Ten minutes later I was following him across the moor towards the woods. It was pitch black out. Sarge was holding his rifle in the crook of his arm as he walked. I could see the metal glinting in the moonlight. I knew that if I kept my eye on that shiny light then I wouldn't lose sight of him. I wasn't scared. Not at that point. Even though I could hear noises, I knew it was just the sounds of the woods: the creatures that don't go to sleep in the night, that prowl around in the bracken looking for food. And I could never be scared of them. Their noises make me feel safe.

There are other noises too, the ones I can't hear but Sarge can. The screams and shouts of people that he says have followed him from the desert. Sometimes he shouts back at them, other times he puts his hands over his ears and screws his face up really tight. I know never to talk to him when he hears those noises but I make sure I stay by his side so he knows he's safe, that he's not alone.

I imagine some people might feel sorry for me. Living out here with just Sarge for company. I know how we live is different. It's different from the people I read about in the library books – those people live in big fancy houses with servants or in sweet little cottages with pretty curtains at the window, with mothers who bake cakes and sing the kids lullabies at night. And it's different from the way Sarge lived when he was little – in a thing called a bungalow in a place called Middlesbrough which Sarge says is to the east of here – and it's different from the dead mum in the desert who lived in the blazing heat and shared food round a big table like in her photograph.

But I wouldn't change it. Not for anything. And though we live far away from other people, I never feel lonely because actually this place is full of life. Even at four this morning, though Sarge and I were the only humans walking out, I could feel the others all around me. I'll try and describe it like I'm back there in the woods. There's a noise that sounds like *tickety-tack*, *tickety-tack*. That's the skylark. It sits up at the top of the beech tree, like some kind of general giving orders to his army. Then as you go deeper into the woods there's a rustling of leaves and a scratching of claws. That's the foxes nestling down to sleep in the hedgerow. There are two of them. A dog and a vixen. He's a big brute, always wild-eyed and snarling, but she's little and quite tame. She comes up to the house sometimes at twilight. Once she came right up to the door while I was peeling veg for tea. She looked so thin that I felt sorry for her so I held out a bit of potato peel and she came up and took it from my hand. She has kind eyes, that vixen. Amber eyes. Like the dead mother in the desert.

Anyway, I'm going off on one, as Sarge says. Talking about foxes when I should be making a record of the very important thing that happened.

It went like this:

After I heard the foxes we walked on another few metres, into the deepest part of the woods. Sarge was up ahead, then he stopped suddenly, turned to me and raised his gun. Just a tiny bit, but enough so I could see.

His face was all pearly white in the moonlight and his eyes were fixed on me.

'Ready?' he said.

I wasn't ready. I was terrified. My legs felt all wobbly and I thought I was going to be sick. Sarge knows me better than I know myself and he could see I was scared. He lowered the gun and walked very slowly towards me.

Then he placed the gun on the ground and knelt down in front of me. His face looked softer.

'Look at the sky,' he said. 'What do you see?'

I did as I was told. A white circle hovered above the woods like a giant face.

'All I can see is the moon,' I said.

'That's right,' said Sarge. 'The moon. And do you know something?'

His voice was so quiet I had to lean in to hear.

'The moon isn't afraid,' he said. 'Do you see?'

I'd never really thought about the moon having any kind of feelings but I nodded my head.

'That moon up there,' he said, looking up at the sky, 'it keeps beaming its light, stronger and brighter, even though it's out there all alone in that vast sky. Do you understand?'

'I think so,' I said.

'You've got to be like the moon,' he said, picking the gun up from the ground and handing it to me. 'You've got to be strong and bright and brave.'

I took the gun in my hands.

'Now,' he said, getting to his feet. 'I'll ask again. Are you ready?'

'I'm ready,' I replied. But my legs were shaking.

'Keep your nerve,' he said. 'And remember what I told you.'

The dark was lifting as we walked on and I had to blink so my eyes could get used to the speckly light. I could sense Sarge walking behind me steadily but I kept my eyes to the ground, watching for movement. My ears felt like they had been carved open. Every noise, even just the snap of a twig or a flutter of wings in the trees above me, sounded like an explosion.

Sarge and I know the layout of the wood so well we could walk through it with our eyes closed. But this morning everything looked different. Or maybe it was me who had changed. Sarge says eleven is a good age, the age when you see the world for what it is.

And what I saw in that moment was our target.

She appeared from nowhere. She had a plump body with dirty brown hair and her eyes were black. She looked up at me. I stopped. Deadly still. Behind me I heard Sarge take a breath. He didn't speak but I heard his voice in my head telling me what to do.

'Hold the gun firm but gentle. Like an honourable man's handshake.'

I can tell you now that it isn't easy to do that when you're shivering with cold and fear but I kept my eyes on her and steadied myself.

'Get into firing position.'

I tucked the gun into my shoulder and kept my eyes on the prize. Then I pressed my cheek against the stock. I could hear Sarge's words in my head.

'Take off the catch and keep your eyes open.'

I knew what would come next. The loud bang. And when you know that's coming all you want to do is close your eyes, block it out. I could feel mine going but I forced myself to keep them open.

'Keep the target in sight.'

I stared down at her. She could sense something. Her eyes moved fast from left to right. Then her body went all frozen, like one of the ice statues in my *Narnia* book. I heard Sarge whisper behind me.

'On a count of three.'

Taking a deep breath, I started to count.

'One.'

I curved my finger back towards the trigger.

'Two.'

My heart was beating so fast it felt like it was going to burst out of my chest.

'Three.'

The noise was so loud it almost knocked me off my feet. I staggered backwards and swung the gun round.

Sarge ran towards me and grabbed the gun.

'Jesus, be careful, child,' he shouted. 'That's a weapon in your hand, not a toy.'

For a moment I forgot where I was. The noise of the gunshot was ringing in my ears and I went all dizzy. Then I saw Sarge heading towards her so I pulled myself together and followed him into the clearing.

'Did I . . . did I get her?' I said.

Sarge was crouched down near where she fell, but his long woollen army coat was blocking my view of her.

'Sarge? Did I get her?'

He turned round and my heart sank. I recognized the look in his eyes. Disappointment.

He shook his head.

'You shot her in the legs,' he said. 'You've paralysed her but she's still alive.'

'But she can't be alive,' I shouted.

It didn't make sense. I'd followed Sarge's instructions to the letter.

'It's okay,' he said. He said this in a nicer voice because he could see I was upset. 'This was your first time. It takes practice.'

'What shall we do with her?' I asked.

'She'll need to be put out of her misery,' he said. 'She won't survive out here with this injury.'

'Okay,' I said. 'Do what you need to do.'

Sarge looked at me then and shook his head. His face was hard again.

'No,' he said. 'This is your kill. You have to finish it.'

Of course I was scared but I thought of the moon all alone up there in the vast night sky and I thought of Sarge trampling through the desert on next to no sleep and then I thought for a second or two about the dead mum in the desert and the vixen with the amber eyes but I put those two out of my head. Then I bent down and wrung her neck, just like I'd seen Sarge do with the chickens we keep in the garden.

When it was over we walked without speaking back to the house. My hands were stained with blood and the air around us smelt like meat and metal. When we got to the door, Sarge patted me on the shoulder and told me I'd done well.

We cooked the rabbit that night. Sarge said it was my birthday feast. He'd made some home brew and he poured a glass for the two of us. Then he raised his cup in the air and said, 'To the victor the spoils.'

Sarge says the meat will last us for five meals. The bones will then go into a stock for soup that will feed us for another five.

'Survivors' is what Sarge calls us. The two of us out here on our own, facing down the world and winning. And today I felt like a winner when I carried that rabbit home. I did me and Sarge proud.

3
Lisa

I sit for a minute and try to gather my thoughts. Behind me, Joe snores gently. I look at the time on the dashboard clock: 4.00 p.m. Soon the light will be gone altogether. And exploring that house in the dark doesn't bear thinking about. I take my dad's torch out of the glove compartment then open the car door and make my way back towards the house.

As I grip the torch in my hands and shine its reassuring light ahead of me, an image of my dad walking through Highgate Cemetery flashes before me, his long black coat trailing behind him. He would take me to the cemetery at twilight on Halloween to 'get into the spirit'. I smile as I remember his round pink face peeking out of the hood of his coat as he stood by the statue of Karl Marx. 'You're about as scary as a wet lettuce, Frank,' my mum would giggle as he came down the stairs in his Halloween get-up. And she was right. But that didn't matter to Dad. What mattered was making every occasion special for me, whether that was Halloween or Bonfire Night, Christmas Day or my birthday – each one was to be treasured and celebrated. When you're loved as much as I was as a child you feel invincible, like the horrors of the world will never find you. You're protected.

If only Dad were here now, I think to myself as the torch illuminates the front door, he'd know what to do. He always knew what to do.

The door is covered in dirt and cobwebs. Following the instructions from the note I turn the handle and push against the heavy wood with my shoulder. It eases a fraction but it's stiff and heavy. The cobwebs cling to my skin like that sticky weed that used to grow in my parents' garden back in Highgate. I wipe my hands on my jeans then push at the door some more until finally, with a sharp creaking sound, it yields.

As I stand there, looking into the darkness, a strange sensation comes over me. It's like tiny needles piercing my skin. I squeeze my eyes shut and make a silent wish that all will be okay, that nothing terrible will greet me on the other side. Opening my eyes, I look into the blackened doorway. The silence is suffocating. I should get the hell out of here right now. Drive Joe away from this. But where would I go? There's no option. I take a deep breath, glance quickly behind me to check that the car is still there, then slowly step inside.

The smell that hits me is a fetid, animal scent, a mix of shit and straw. I close the door behind me then see that there are two bolts on the back, one at the top, the other on the bottom. The sight of those bolts reassures me somewhat. I can lock the door and hide in here, hide from Mark and all my troubles.

Shining the torch ahead of me, I can see that the walls of the hallway are covered in faded yellow wallpaper with the ghost of a flower pattern just about detectable. I scan the walls for a light switch but there is nothing.

Pointing the torch to the ceiling, I see that there are no light fittings. My stomach twists as I walk on, trying to contemplate spending the night in this house. My feet make a rustling sound and when I look down I see that the stone floor is strewn with what looks like straw or grass. It smells raw and pungent, like silage. How could anyone have lived in this way, I ask myself, as I lift the torch back to shoulder height and point it ahead of me.

There are three doors leading off the hallway, one in front and one on either side of me. I open the door on the left and step into what I reckon must be a living room of some sort as I can just make out the shape of a sofa under piles and piles of rubbish. As I step closer I see that the 'rubbish' is in fact a collection of yellowing newspapers. I pick one up and look at the date: 7 September 2003. The year my dad died. A shiver flutters across my chest as I read the date again, remembering the pain and sadness of that year, then I drop the paper back on to the floor.

There is a fireplace beyond the sofa. As I scan it with my torch I can see that the mantelpiece is cluttered with bits of paper and ancient bottles of antiseptic. Above it is a set of antlers that have been nailed to the wall. They loom out at me ominously. I look down at my feet. It looks like they have been bound in barbed wire but it's just the twisted shadow of the antlers. To the left of the fireplace are three rickety-looking shelves, piled high with paperback books. I can just about make out some of the titles: *The Science of Animal Husbandry*, *A Farmer's Almanac*, *The Turn of the Screw*. I pull this one out, remembering it from my A-level English class, and open it up. Inside is a library sticker with a return date stamped on it: 10 January 2005. Long overdue now. The covers are dusty and yellow, and a sour scent hangs about them, like cat pee. I close the book, put it back on the shelf, then slowly make my way out of the room.

I stand in the hallway and try to think straight. I need to find some kind of normality: a bathroom, a kitchen. I try the door straight ahead of me and as I open it I instinctively put my hand on to the wall to locate a switch but, again, there isn't one. I step inside and point the torch ahead of me. There is a huge wooden table in the centre of the room. Like the mantelpiece in the living room, its surface is piled with junk and clutter. There are empty food cans, old newspapers, bits of wool and twigs. A flash of colour catches my eye and I bend down to take a closer look. It's a red ribbon, the kind I used to wear in my hair when I was a child. I pick it up and rub it between my finger and thumb. It's velvet. I stare at the ribbon, wondering how something so pretty has come to be in the midst of all this junk. Then I coil it round my wrist and tie it in a knot.

I lift the torch and direct it at the far wall, desperately trying to locate something, anything, that resembles a modern amenity – a washing machine, an oven – but there isn't even a sink. Shining the torch to the left, I see a black metal contraption wedged against the wall. It has ornate tiles on the front of it with blue figures painted on them. There are various knobs and handles on the top of it, though I have no idea what it is. I've never seen anything like it before.

Next to it is a glass door. Wiping my hand across the grimy glass, I see that it leads outside. I try the handle.

The door is locked. I shine the torch up and down its surface then notice a bolt at the very top. I slide it across and pull the door open.

Standing on the wooden step, I look out on to an expanse of purple wilderness. The hills, which seemed to close in on me as I drove here, now look like sleeping giants, their peaks arching towards the grey sky. A dry-stone wall dissects the field beyond the house, framing a square patch of land. There are wooden canes sticking out of the ground and what appear to be, in this fractured winter light, the remains of a vegetable patch. The rest of the garden is cluttered with wire cages. I take a deep breath then grimace. Even out here in the open the air is putrid. I turn to go back into the house but something catches my eye; I look closer. There's something poking out of one of the cages. I walk towards it. It's a tail of some sort. Orange and wiry. A fox's brush? A memory of Highgate Cemetery at twilight and the cries of the foxes that would nest in amongst the gravestones flashes across my mind then disappears. I flick the brush with my hand and it falls on to the ground, sending up a flurry of tiny flies into the air. Definitely a fox, I think to myself, but as I glance back at the cage my heart flips inside my chest. There, lying on the bottom of the cage, grey and mottled, is a skull.

I stagger backwards then run back to the house, yanking the glass door so hard it almost falls off its hinges. Back through the stinking mess, out of the front door and past the lake.

When I reach the car I have to lean against the bonnet to catch my breath. A couple of moments later I open the passenger door and I am greeted with the sight of Joe, red-faced and screaming.

'Shh,' I whisper, trying to keep the panic out of my voice. 'It's okay, baby. Mummy's here.'

He looks at me with terror in his eyes.

'Want Daddy. Want Daddy now.'

I don't know what to do. I can't take Joe into that place when he's in this state. Think, Lisa, think, I tell myself. Then I remember the shop in the village. I'll drive there, get some food and provisions, and give myself time to put together a plan.

Joe's screams intensify on the short drive into the village. Not even a replay of *Where the Wild Things Are* will calm him down. As he thrashes about in his car seat I try to remember all the things they taught me in parenting class when Joe was first born; the stacks of literature we were supposed to read with headings such as 'Surviving the Terrible Twos' and 'Gentle Parenting Tips'. But the skills I was meant to hone in those years were thwarted by the horrible situation I was living through.

How can you apply gentle parenting when you're trapped in a toxic environment? How can you survive the terrible twos when you're only just managing to keep going yourself? Still, the guilt at the years I've wasted living in fear gnaws at my insides. I glance at Joe in the rear-view mirror, his face wet with snot and tears, and I make a promise that I'm going to make up for all of it.

When we reach the village I swing the car into a space outside the pub. Someone has placed an unlit cigarette in the inflatable snowman's mouth. I'd laugh if my situation weren't so dire.

I unclip my seat belt, open the door and step out into the freezing air. When I open Joe's door he lets out an ear-splitting cry.

'It's okay, Joe,' I say, leaning across to unfasten his belt. 'We're just going to have a look in the shop.'

He shakes his head violently from side to side.

'Not want to go shop. Want Daddy.'

'Come on, darling,' I say, trying to keep the agitation out of my voice. 'I'll get you some sweets. What about some nice chocolate buttons, eh?'

'No,' he yells. 'Want go home. Want Daddy.'

He thrusts himself forward in the seat and smacks me right in the eye. The pain shoots up my head and my patience snaps. I look at my little boy, his face red and contorted with rage, and all I see is Mark. It's then that the anger and frustration I've been holding in for the entire journey comes tumbling forth.

'Your daddy's not here,' I yell. 'Do you hear me? He's not here and he's not going to be. Now stop being such a naughty boy.'

He falls silent then looks at me for a moment. I unhook the belt on his car seat but as I lift him out of the car he starts wriggling and squirming in my arms. His hands, balled into fists, hammer at my chest and it's all I can do to keep him steady.

'Hey, are you okay?'

I turn to see a man standing next to the inflatable snowman. He's in his early thirties by the looks of it, broad-shouldered – 'stocky' as my mum would have said – with dark eyes and close-shaved chestnut hair. He's got one arm folded across his chest and in his hand is an unlit cigarette, presumably swiped from the snowman's mouth. He frowns as he watches me.

'I'm fine,' I say, hoisting Joe on to my hip and trying not to make eye contact with the man as I step on to the pavement.

'You sure about that?' he continues, pausing to light the cigarette.

I nod my head briskly.

'Haven't seen you before,' he says, narrowing his eyes. 'You visiting?'

'Something like that,' I say. 'Sorry, I'm in a bit of a rush.'

I turn and make my way to the shop, Joe hanging angrily off my hip.

'Well, nice to meet you,' calls the man from behind us. 'Whatever your name is.'

I shudder. Why do men do that? Yell after you. Invade your space. Demand you tell them your business. What gives them the right?

As we reach the shop I put Joe down then arrange my hair so that it falls across my eyes. I need to make myself as respectable as possible. I push the door open and my heart lifts as I see a lottery machine, a cashpoint, a display of gluten-free bread. Things I've taken for granted after years of living in a big city. Comforting ordinariness. It's strange but even though I was only in that house for a few moments it felt like I'd slipped through some weird time portal, as though real life had ceased to exist.

There's a woman sitting behind the counter reading a newspaper. She's in her fifties and has a mop of curly greying hair. She looks up as we enter, gives me a cursory glance over her cherry-red spectacles, then returns to her reading. Good. The less attention I draw to myself the better.

I take a wire basket from the stack by the door and make my way over to the fridges. I have no idea what I'm supposed to be buying. Food. That's it. I pick up a pack of fresh chicken breasts and I'm about to put them in the basket when I remember there is no oven in the house. I put them back then move on to the chilled ready meals. There is a selection of pre-packed sausage rolls. I choose a handful of them and put them in the basket. I hear Mark's voice in my head: 'You're not giving our son that processed rubbish, Lisa.' But Mark's not here and I have brought our son to a house in the middle of nowhere with no running water and no bloody oven. A sausage roll is the least of our worries.

'Shall we get some juice?' I say, turning to Joe.

He is making a low humming noise.

'What kind would you like? Apple or orange?'

I hold up two cartons but he just shakes his head.

'Come on, Joe,' I say, crouching down so I'm at his level. 'Tell Mummy what you'd like to drink.'

He scowls then lifts his hand up. I go to grab his wrist before he can hit me again but he quickly yanks it away. A clawing dread rises up my chest as I put both cartons of juice into the basket. Every part of me wants to shout for help; to alert someone to the predicament I'm in. But I know if I do that then Mark will find us and I can't risk that happening.

I move around the shop adding cleaning fluid, sponges and bin bags to the now overflowing basket. It's more than I need but it's reassuring to see the familiar items. For just a few moments I forget about the house and focus on being an ordinary mum.

When I get to the counter the woman folds her newspaper and puts it down. She doesn't speak, which I'm grateful for, just scans the shopping and puts it into carrier bags for me. While she does that I cast a glance at the headline on the newspaper. *Nothing yet.*

Still, it's only a matter of time. My heart starts to palpitate. I need to get away from the village now. He could be anywhere. He could be closing in.

'That's £22.80 when you're ready, love.'

I look up at the woman. Her accent is soft and warm, and for a moment I feel like telling her everything that's happened, ask her to help, to take me and Joe to her nice, cosy cottage and give us hot tea and toast. But instead I distract myself with separating the plastic ten-pound notes that have unfurled out of my purse and landed on the counter like those fortune-telling fish you get in Christmas crackers.

I hand three of them to the woman and as I'm waiting for my change I turn to check that Joe is okay. But he's not there.

'Joe?' I call. 'Joe. Where are you?'

'Are you all right, love?'

I hear the woman's voice behind me as I rush up the drinks aisle, frantically calling his name.

'Joe! Where are you, baby?'

I reach the third and final aisle and there's no sign of him. The room shrinks around me and I feel my legs giving way. This can't be happening.

'Lost someone?'

I look up and see the man from outside the pub standing there. He's smiling at me.

'My little boy,' I say, staggering towards him. 'He's run away from me and I –'

'He's over there, love,' says the man, pointing at the door. Joe is standing by it, looking sheepish.

'Oh, thank God,' I say, running to him. 'Joe. You naughty boy. You mustn't run off like that.'

Then I compose myself and turn back to the counter. The woman looks at me sympathetically as I approach.

'I think he were looking at the comics,' she says warmly. 'My little grandson loves them too.'

'Yes,' I say, my heart still fluttering with shock. 'I just . . . lost sight of him.'

'Well, no harm done, eh? Here's your change, love,' she says, handing me a five-pound note and some coins.

'Thank you,' I say, hurriedly putting the money into my purse.

'You from London?'

It's the man speaking. I turn round.

'It's just I recognize the accent,' he says, coming towards me. 'I used to have a cousin who lived in Brixton.'

I shake my head then turn back to the counter. Grabbing the bags of shopping, I make for the door, taking Joe's hand. I've drawn too much attention to myself. I need to leave. Now.

'You here for long?' calls the man.

I don't reply. Instead I start to run. I hold my breath and don't dare release it until I've reached the safety of the car.

4

Soldier

A New Year and whole new start for me. Forget Christmas, I just had the best present anyone could have given me because today Sarge told me that I'm finally ready to embark on the 'big' mission. This is an important one because, if I pass, Sarge says I'll advance to the next level and become Soldier Number 1.

Sarge and I have been planning this mission for the last few months. Every day the two of us have gone up to the hills for what Sarge calls RECONNAISSANCE AND INTELLIGENCE GATHERING. We even worked on Christmas Day. I wasn't too happy about that but Sarge soon put me right. 'A day is what you fill it with, my girl,' he said. 'You have to be alert and vigilant no matter the day's name. Never forget that.'

I told him I understood. And I did. I'm eleven now. Old enough to not need presents and all that. Though I did feel a bit sad when I woke up on 25 December and saw there was no knitted sock at the end of my bed. For as long as I can remember Sarge has left that sock there on Christmas Eve and it's always filled with the same things: a tangerine, six hazelnuts, a mince pie (baked by Sarge) and a pair of gloves to see me through winter. But since my birthday Sarge has changed. He treats me differently.

He's been listening to the news lots on his old portable radio. Sometimes at night when I'm lying in bed I can hear voices through the wall talking about someone called George W. Bush and the War on Terror. This George person seems very angry with terror and it seems to make Sarge angry too because he shouts at the radio whenever George is mentioned.

Sarge says I'm old enough to be a proper soldier now, to find out about the evils of the world and fight back at them. The first step towards that is to listen carefully and concentrate on the skills Sarge is teaching me. 'The game playing's over,' he said. 'Now it's time for the real battle to begin.'

We've started by making my very own ghillie suit. This helps to disguise you from the enemy so that if they look your way they just see a mound of grass, not a person. Sarge has taught me how to make one using one of his old army boiler suits and some fishing net. Sewing the suit is quite tricky because the net is coarse and keeps slipping out of the needle but Sarge has made it fun by singing rude songs that he learned in the army. I can't write down the words as they are very naughty but the way he sings them, with this silly pretend posh accent, makes me laugh so much I get the hiccups. This morning I got them so bad I almost messed up my stitching.

Sarge stopped then and got me a glass of water. When he came back his face was all serious and he said that there was a reason why we were doing what we did, that there was still a battle to be won. He told me some more about his big war then. He said that if he did it again he wouldn't be fighting the Iraqis. Instead he would take his gun and wave it in the face of George Bush and his '~~reetarde~~ retard son' and ask them to fight like soldiers. Sarge calls them criminals. He thinks they should be in jail and that it's their fault that he shouts in the woods and that I have no mother. He looked away as he said that and changed the subject. Talk of the dead mother in the desert always makes him sad. I wish he would tell me more but he won't. My whole life he's told me exactly three bits of information about her.

1. That he met her in the big war.
2. That she came from a place called Baghdad.
3. That she died in the desert.

All the other stuff I know about her comes from my head, from the stories I told myself after seeing the photo of her. I found it one day a few years back when I was bored and wanted something to read. The library van hadn't been because it was snowing out so I had a look through the books in Sarge's room. One of the titles caught my eye because instead of words it was just squiggly shapes. Sarge told me later that this was Arabic, the language of my mother, and that the squiggly shapes were the title of an Arabic poem. I opened up the book to see if there were any English words inside, and I saw that Sarge had written in the pages of the book, next to the squiggly poems. I felt a bit funny then because some of the words he'd written were sad and I thought it best if I didn't read them so I closed the book, but when I did the photo fell out. There were three people in it, all sitting round a table: an old man with a crinkly face and a grey beard, a plump, smiley, middle-aged woman in a long red dress and, in the centre of the two, a young woman with dark hair. When I looked closer I felt all funny because even though this was an old photo and the people in it were wearing strange clothes, the woman in it looked like me, just a bit older. She had my thick black hair, my weird eyes that turn from black to yellow-green depending on the light and the same brown skin. I'd never seen anyone else who looked like me before. Sarge has fair hair and pale skin, the people from the village are all pale or pink, even the characters in the books I read are too. But it was more than that. The girl in the picture had my face.

The photo was all glossy and it slipped through my hands. It fell to the floor face down and when I picked it up I saw there was writing on the back. In black ink someone had written:

Our love
Has no mind or logic
Our love
Walks on water.

Like the picture of my mother, those words have been saved to my memory. They were the strangest, most beautiful words I'd ever read. The idea of love being something outside of a person, of having a mind of its own, was something I'd never imagined before. I sat for a bit reading the words over and over again and wondering who had written them, because it wasn't Sarge's handwriting. But then the door burst open and he came storming in and grabbed the photo from my hands.

I'd never seen him so angry. He told me that I was a snoop and a thief and if he ever caught me going through his things again he'd put me in solitary. I tried to tell him that I wasn't snooping, I'd just been looking for a book, but he wouldn't listen. He took the photo and hid it somewhere. I never saw it again.

Not that it mattered. I didn't have to see the photo. If I closed my eyes I'd see her face, her warm eyes and those beautiful words. I didn't need Sarge to tell me that the girl in the photo was my mother. I knew it in my heart.

Anyway, for now I must put all thoughts of the dead mother in the desert to the back of my mind and concentrate on the new mission Sarge is planning. He hasn't told me when we're going to do it, just that I should expect it very soon. He's not going to give me any warning so I will have to be prepared and on guard at all times. But, like Sarge has always told me, being prepared is part of being a soldier, it's what makes the difference between victory and defeat, life and death. I've got a lot to prove to Sarge after what happened with the rabbit. I have to show him that I have what it takes to be an elite soldier. When the time comes for this mission, I'm going to make sure that I'm ready.

5

Lisa

It's getting dark when we arrive back at the lake. I turn off the engine and sit for a moment. I think about the evening ahead of us. The lack of light switches in the house means I now face a whole night sitting in total darkness with a child who is already restless and scared. I toy with the idea of sleeping in the car but that would leave us even more vulnerable and exposed.

I look out of the windscreen. The sky is grey and leaden. A shaft of evening sunlight illuminates the house, making it look, for just a moment, quite beautiful. I notice the chimneys for the first time, three tall brick rectangles poking up to the sky, and the ornate cornicing round the windows. It reminds me of the pictures I used to do at primary school. The teacher would ask us to draw our homes and I would pretend I lived in some impressive stately pile with pillars and gates and peacocks in the garden. I remember my teacher's face as I handed the drawing to her, a look of puzzlement as she tried to equate the modern first-floor flat she knew we lived in with the ornate palace I had created on the paper. I sit for a moment, the smell of chalk dust and pencil shavings in my nose. Then the sky shifts, the light dulls and I pull myself together.

'Come on, Joe,' I say, unclipping my seat belt. 'Let's go and have something to eat.'

He is sitting rigid in his seat, his eyes fixed ahead of him. 'Joe?'

He doesn't respond. A sick feeling rises in my stomach. I would rather he shout and scream and yell for his daddy than stay silent and motionless like this.

I get out of the car and open the back door. He doesn't move.

'It's okay, baby,' I whisper, leaning across to unclip him. 'I know you're tired. Mummy's going to make us some nice food and then we'll get some –'

The blow comes out of nowhere. I stagger backwards, cupping my cheek in my hand. Joe is still staring straight ahead, his tiny hands clenched into tight fists. My face throbs.

'Joe,' I say, trying to keep my voice calm and steady, 'that was very naughty of you to hit Mummy but I know you're tired and hungry. Why don't you come with me and we'll go get some food?'

I hold out my hand towards him. It's shaking. Why am I so terrified? He's a three-year-old boy. My boy. But the situation I've fled, the anxiety and fear, mixed with this wilderness I've dragged us both to, have cast a sinister light on everything. Even Joe. The person I love most in this world.

I stand like that for a minute or so and then out of sheer desperation I find myself resorting to bribery of the worst kind.

'Joe, if you come inside with Mummy I promise we'll go and see Daddy.'

As soon as he hears that word his head jerks towards me. The look of hope on his tiny face breaks my heart but I have no choice. I have to get him out of the car. I can deal with my promise later.

'Daddy,' he says, stretching his arms towards me. 'We go find Daddy.'

I don't reply, just lean across and lift him out of the seat, cursing myself.

'Mummy needs to get some things from the boot and then we'll explore the nice house,' I say, placing him on to the grass and taking his hand. 'It's going to be such a fun adventure.'

I hear him mutter something about 'Daddy' as I open the boot and take out the shopping bags and our luggage. In the corner of the boot I spot my dad's old toolkit. Dad was a firm believer in being prepared for every eventuality. Unlike me. I reach for it and tuck it under my arm. 'Thanks, Dad,' I whisper, though I know if he were here he'd laugh at the idea of me attempting to use a toolkit.

I close the boot then take the bags in both hands.

'Right, Joe,' I say, my voice sounding unnaturally bright. 'Follow Mummy. This is going to be a real adventure.'

I hear his little footsteps behind me as we make our way to the house and for a moment I tell myself that maybe this might all still turn out fine. But when we reach the door and I set down the bags and take the torch out of my pocket the sense of unease returns.

I open the door and wedge the luggage into the entrance. Then, taking Joe's hand, I switch on the torch and begin to navigate the dark corridors.

'Where's Daddy?' he says, his voice echoing against the empty rooms. 'You said we see Daddy.'

I don't answer. Instead I hold the torch ahead of me. It casts twisted black shapes on the walls. The smell seems worse than before. I try not to think about the cages and the skull.

I decide that the room to the left of the corridor will be the best place to settle Joe. It seemed the only one with a modicum of normality about it. I push the door open and stare into darkness.

'Daddy in here?'

'It's a special place,' I tell him, pointing the torch into the centre of the room. As well as the bookshelves there's a large sunken sofa, an armchair covered in blankets and a low, round, wooden table. 'We're going to have a big adventure here.'

'Don't like it. I want to go home. Where's Daddy?'

'Shall we have a picnic?' I say, realizing how ridiculous this sounds. 'I got you some lovely things from the shop. Why don't you sit here and I'll get everything ready.'

I lift him on to the sofa, but instantly he starts to struggle.

I run my hand along the sofa and feel the dampness.

'Okay,' I say, taking one of the cushions and placing it on the floor. 'We'll have our picnic down here. It will be even more fun.'

'No,' he cries, kicking his legs out. 'Want to go home.'

What the hell am I doing, I think to myself as I try to wrestle my little boy on to the cushion. Just go home. But I know what will happen if I do that. A punishment much worse than anything this house can throw at me. So I take a deep breath and crouch down in front of Joe, speaking slowly and calmly.

'Listen to me,' I say, remembering what the counsellor told me about keeping eye contact, not an easy thing to do in semi-darkness. 'Everything's going to be all right. Mummy just needs to get ready and then we're going to have some dinner. Remember Max's dinner in the story?'

'Still hot,' says Joe.

His face softens and my heart aches. I hate myself for putting him through this.

'That's right,' I say, stroking his arm. 'Max had a big adventure just like we're going to have but he still had to come back and eat his dinner. And, yes, it was still hot. Well remembered.'

'We have dinner with Daddy?'

'Why don't you sit here on the cosy cushion,' I say, 'and Mummy will see what we've got to eat.'

I don't know whether it's fatigue or hunger or both but he does as he's told and sits on the threadbare cushion, lifting his knees up to his chin.

'Good boy,' I say, stroking his soft hair. 'Mummy loves you very much, you know that?'

He doesn't answer. I stand up and scan the room, pointing the torch at every surface. In this light the antlers above the mantelpiece look even bigger than they did before, like the beast they once belonged to is somewhere beyond the wall waiting to smash through. I move the light on to the top of the mantelpiece, wondering as I do why anyone would keep bottles of antiseptic lined up on there. And then I see, tucked behind the bottles, three large candles. I pick them up. Their wicks are intact.

'Look what I've found,' I say to Joe, placing them on the table. 'Candles. Shall we light them?'

Joe nods his head. I get a flashback to his three-month birthday, back when I would celebrate the seventh of each month, the day he came into the world. I remember the caterpillar cake bought from M&S and the three candles wedged in the thick chocolate icing. Mark said I was foolish for wasting money on a cake when Joe wasn't even old enough to eat solids. But I'd wanted to make every seventh special, that's how much the day meant to me, how much I loved my baby. And it was worth it to see his little face when I lit the candles, his eyes sparkling as he watched the flames dance. A few months later it would all change.

I blink away the memory then dig in my pocket for my lighter. Despite several attempts to give up, I still can't do without the odd cigarette. In fact, right now I could smoke a whole pack, if only to calm my nerves. But, on my meagre wage, cigarettes are an expense I can't justify these days.

I line the candles up along the table then carefully light each one. Once they catch, the room lifts. I look at Joe. His face is glowing.

'Look at that,' I say, standing back to admire the light. 'Isn't it pretty?'

Joe stares at the flames, his tired eyes mesmerized.

'Right,' I say, taking the carrier bag that I left by the door. 'Let's see what goodies we can find.'

We're so hungry and tired we make our way through two large sausage rolls each (though Joe just eats the sausage and hands me the pastry), a family bag of crisps and two cereal bars. Joe's eyes are growing heavier. I will have to put him down to sleep. I decide we'll stay in this room tonight. There will be bedrooms in the house somewhere but I refuse to go looking while it's dark. Further exploration can wait until morning.

Instead I take the remaining cushions from the sofa and place them together on the floor. Then I scoop the heavy blankets from the armchair and bring them to where Joe is lying. The blankets smell of damp but they'll be warm. That's all that matters for tonight. Joe is asleep now. I ease him up on to the line of cushions and drape one of the blankets over him, tucking it round his chest.

Then, blowing the candles out, I wrap the remaining blanket round myself and lie down on the floor next to Joe, placing my hand on his chest. We've both got our winter coats on but it's still icy cold, even with the added layer of the blanket. As I lie here, I try to ignore the noises that are filtering through the window; the screeches and cries of wild animals, the wind battering against the panes. Instead I try to focus on the gentle sound of Joe's breathing, the beat of his heart against my hand. And as I try to block out the immediate fear, that of the unknown, I think of the other fear, the monster I am running from. *Please let this be okay*, I whisper to myself, *please let us be safe*. But when I close my eyes all I can see is his face.

6

Soldier Number 1

Rowan Isle House, January 2003

I did it! Today I finally reached the next level of my training. Sarge has given me a smart new uniform with a badge on the sleeve and said that from now on I can call myself Soldier Number 1.

It's such a great feeling to have passed the test but, my goodness, that mission was tough, the toughest thing I have ever had to do.

It took me a while to finish off the ghillie suit but a couple of days after New Year it was finally ready. The next morning Sarge appeared at my door and I knew it was time. We went up to the top of Harrowby Crag, both wearing our ghillie suits, and got into position. Sarge said he was to be the spotter on this mission. He had already ~~reckied~~ reccied the area and ~~gajed~~ ~~gagied~~ gauged the shooting parameters. That is very important, he said, as a misfired shot could be the difference between life and death. We dug the hide, then once we were inside Sarge gave me the gun and told me to keep my target in focus. I did as I was told. When I saw the target move into view I put my hand on the trigger and prepared to fire. But at the last moment Sarge put his hand on mine and whispered to me that we'd had enough for now and that tomorrow we'd be hitting that target for real.

I was a bit disappointed that I wouldn't be getting the chance to carry out the mission that day, but after all that preparation I didn't want to let Sarge down, so I was up and dressed by the time he knocked on my door at 4 a.m. this morning. After kit inspection we marched single file out of the house. The air smelt of fire and Sarge said it was the residue of the fireworks that the idiots had let off in the village to bring in the New Year. I liked the smell of it though and I'd also liked seeing the fireworks from my window on New Year's Eve. The colours were so beautiful, it was like the sky was alive. I didn't tell Sarge that though.

When we got outside I went towards the gate as I thought we'd be going straight to the crag but Sarge walked in the other direction, towards the lake, and started to untie the boat.

I ran after him and asked, 'What's all this about, Sarge?'

He didn't answer. Didn't look at me either. I get nervous when Sarge goes quiet like that. What usually follows is him shouting up at the sky, kicking out at nothing, cursing the American murderers. I could feel a funny lump in my throat but I swallowed hard and tried to stay in position as Sarge tried to untie the boat from the dock. When the rope finally came loose he looked up at me, his face all screwed up and sweating, and told me to get in.

'But I thought we were going up there,' I said, pointing up to the crag behind him.

Sarge's face changed then. His eyes got all wide and he balled his hands into fists.

'One more word and I'll have you for insubordination.' He was yelling really loudly and spit from his mouth went flying into my face. Then he got even angrier. 'You think you have the right to question the word of your superior? You fucking little shit. Get in that boat and await your orders or you'll be spending the rest of the week in solitary.'

I got such a shock then because Sarge doesn't swear like that unless he's talking about George W. Bush. He'd never spoken to me like that before. Not even when I'd broken the door of the stove that time and the house filled with smoke. But I was a kid back then and he treated me like one. Now I'm eleven he treats me like an adult, like one of his men, and it's hard to get used to. So when he yelled like that I was in such shock that my legs wouldn't move. I just stood there staring at the water, trying to stop myself from crying.

It was a cold day and the lake looked a funny grey colour. Sometimes, when Sarge and I go out in the boat and the sun is shining, I see little shapes rising up off the surface. They look like tiny dancing fairies spinning and twisting in the air. I've come to know them as the lake sprites and when I go to bed at night I open my window and say goodnight to them. Sometimes I hear them giggling and other times I can hear them whisper to each other. They are very mischievous little things. I wished they would appear as I stood there looking out at the lake this morning but all was silent and the only voice I could hear was his.

'I said get in that fucking boat.'

He grabbed my arms and dragged me to the water. I'd been in that boat hundreds of times but now as I stood looking at it bobbing in the water I felt scared.

Then suddenly I wasn't on land any more. Sarge had pushed me into the boat. He got in next to me, grabbed the oars and started to row.

'What are we doing, Sarge?'

I knew he wasn't going to answer. Not with his face the way it was. He was muttering under his breath too, something about death and bones. He kept repeating it over and over again. Death and bones. That's all it was. Death and Bones. I wanted to make him stop, get him to focus on our mission. He'd been so happy yesterday, all excited about what was to come. But last night when I walked past his room on my way to bed I saw that he was reading that book, the one with the squiggly words. He always goes strange after he's read that book, like he's in the worst mood ever, and now he was back to muttering to himself. But I didn't dare say anything, not while he was like that. Instead I sat holding on to the side of the boat and watched as he steered it into the centre of the lake.

He let go of the oars then and I looked up at him. The next thing I knew his hands were round my neck. I went to scream but my voice was trapped in my throat. I tried to prise his hands off but he was too strong. Then, suddenly, he picked me up and threw me into the water.

I tried to grab hold of the side of the boat but he kept pushing it away from me. I could feel my head going under the water. I kicked my arms and legs until I came up but soon the water was back over my head. I was going to drown. I was sure of it. But why wasn't Sarge helping me?

'Please, Sarge,' I gasped, spluttering and coughing up water. 'Please!'

But he didn't answer. He just sat in the boat and stared at me as I flapped my arms and tried to keep my head from going under again. Then suddenly he put his arms out towards me. I lifted mine up for him to take but instead he grabbed me by the collar of my uniform and plunged me under the water. Within seconds he'd lifted my head out again. But then he repeated it again and again and again. I couldn't breathe. I swear I thought I was going to die. I couldn't scream or beg him to stop because every time I came up for air he'd plunge me under again. I don't know how long this went on for but just when I thought I couldn't take it any more, he stopped.

I held on to the boat trying to breathe, no idea what would happen next. Then he looked at me like he'd just woken up from a dream. All of a sudden he was Sarge again. 'Come on, love,' he said, his voice calm and normal. And he lifted me out of the water into the boat.

I couldn't speak. Just sat shivering while he rowed us back to shore. 'Pleased to tell you that you've passed the first stage of this section of training,' he said as he helped me out of the boat. 'Now it's time for the next stage. The part we've been working towards.'

He pointed towards the crag.

'But . . . Sarge,' I said, my teeth chattering. 'I . . .'

I couldn't get any words out. I was so cold. So scared.

'The target is on the move,' he said, walking ahead of me towards the crag. 'We have to locate it and get into position.'

I just stood there, shivering uncontrollably. 'MOVE!' he yelled. So I followed him.

It was difficult to climb in wet clothes and I could feel myself slipping as we got to the higher part of the crag. I wanted Sarge to help me, to lift me on his shoulders like he used to when I was little, but he didn't even look back at me, just kept on striding ahead. It was at this point that my head began to clear and I tried to make sense of what had just happened on the lake. Why had he done it? Why had he changed the plan? Why did he look surprised when he pulled me out of the water? Still, I knew that it wouldn't help to ask these questions of Sarge while we were in the middle of the mission so I followed him obediently and kept my mouth shut.

When we reached the hide Sarge knelt down and located the rifle and binoculars. He handed me the gun then put the binoculars to his eyes.

'We're set,' he said, lowering them. 'It's all down to you now.'

I got into position and tried to raise the gun but my arms were hurting from struggling in the water. I put the gun down and rubbed them. They felt sore and hard but I knew I'd have to ignore the pain and get through this test otherwise Sarge would be even more angry. I could see the target wandering in and out of view. I could hear Sarge's words in my head as I picked up the gun, my arms throbbing with pain, and got ready to fire. 'You'll know as soon as you pull that trigger if it's a hit or a miss.' I thought about the last time. The rabbit I left half alive with its leg hanging off and the look on Sarge's face when he turned to me and said, 'You haven't killed her.' And I told myself in those few seconds that I had to do it this time. I had to make the kill. I widened my eyes, kept them fixed on the target, then on a count of three I pulled the trigger.

This time I was ready for the explosion, though it still made my ears ring. I heard the thud of Sarge's footsteps running down the crag towards the target. I staggered out of the hide and made my way to the edge. When I looked down I saw Sarge waving his hands at me. Beside him on the ground lay a bloodied ewe.

'You've done it,' he cried, his face beaming. 'You've made your kill.'

And he looked so happy, the lines had gone from his face, and his smile was so wide that, in spite of everything, I felt happy too. I ran down to join him and together we hauled the ewe back to the house. After we'd skinned and butchered it, Sarge sat me down and told me that I'd passed to the next level, that I was now Soldier Number 1. Then he sat in his chair and read one of his books, the one about the old man who lived in the woods, and I sat in mine and drank hot milk. And when I looked at Sarge he seemed so peaceful that I knew I was doing something right.

When Sarge had gone to bed I took the cups into the kitchen. I was just about to blow the candles out when I heard a scratching at the back door. My first thought was to go get Sarge but then I remembered that I was Soldier Number 1 now and I had to be brave so I went to the door and opened it a fraction. The first thing I saw was a pair of eyes, then the outline of a long nose, and all my fears fell away. It was the vixen. I opened the door wider then crouched down and stroked her rough fur. She's such a gentle thing despite her sharp teeth. 'Are you hungry, girl?' I said to her. 'Shall I get you some supper?' She looked up at me and her eyes were so soft and kind. I went back into the kitchen and sliced some of the leftover meat into a bowl then took it out to her. She ate it in no time and it was then I noticed how thin she was. It had been a bad winter and food will have been hard to come by. 'Don't worry,' I said, stroking the top of her head. 'I'll make sure you get a good meal. I won't let you starve. I promise.' I don't know whether she heard me because as soon as the meat was finished she scarpered back down the garden.

Now that I'm in bed I feel better. Sarge and I have eaten well and so has my lovely vixen. And I have become Soldier Number 1. For those things I should be grateful. So I'm going to forget about the water and the death and bones and all the horrid things that happened today, and just focus on the good. Sarge says I did well and that is enough for me.

7

Lisa

10 December 2018

I wake with a dull pain in my right arm. Something is pressing into my skin. I turn over and the pain subsides. As I come to I look down to see that I am lying on my phone. Instinctively I go to check my messages but when I hold it to the light I see it has no signal.

And then I remember where I am. The clutter on the mantelpiece is casting a shadow on the wall, turning the bottles of antiseptic into rows of toy soldiers looming over the room. I clutch my phone like it's a weapon that can somehow protect me as the events of the past twenty-four hours return in fragments. I see myself, red-faced and frantic, running down the drive-way, bundling Joe into his car seat. I see my gloved hands clutching the steering wheel on that interminably long journey from London, Joe screaming his head off in the back. I see the house rising out of the lake like some mythical creature in the dusk and a shiver slices through me.

I need to shake this feeling, need to think clearly, work out what to do next. I look down at my phone again. The lack of signal makes me uneasy but then I tell myself that at least this way Mark will be unable to trace me. To him, to the outside world, I have fallen off the radar, ceased to exist. Once, that idea would have terrified me. Now I feel reassured by it.

I put the phone back in my pocket and sit up. Joe is sound asleep on the cushions next to me. Sharp winter light is streaming through the bare windows, highlighting the grime and dust that covers every surface in the room.

I remember the cages and the skull, the kitchen with no amenities, and my heart sinks. I'd been so exhausted last night, so desperate to dissolve into dead sleep, the precariousness of the situation hadn't really registered. Now as I stand here looking down at my little boy, his chest rising and falling, the reality of what I have done, what I have brought my child into, begins to sink in.

I pick up the blanket I slept in, fold it carefully and place it on the armchair. It smells of mould and animal dung. God knows what I inhaled as I slept in it last night. I glance at Joe. He's swaddled in another filthy blanket, his blond curls matted to his forehead. What kind of a mother does this? I ask myself. Who would bring her child into this? He should be waking up in his own bed, with his spotless Mr Men quilt and cuddly toys standing guard about his head. In an hour or so he'd be at nursery, making paper chains for Christmas and playing with his friends. Now he's lying in some dump.

'I just wanted to keep you with me,' I whisper to his sleeping form. 'I'm sorry, baby. I'm so sorry.'

My eyes fill with tears as I think about what I've run away from. The twisted feeling in my gut every single day, those four walls, with their exotic-bird-printed wallpaper, bearing down on me, his voice telling me what I'd done wrong that day, how he could have done it better. He could always do it better. 'Lisa, are you actually that stupid?'

I exhale slowly, try to expunge his voice from my mind. I have to keep busy, I tell myself, or I'll drive myself mad. I bend down and pick up last night's empty crisp packets and sausage roll wrappers and put them into the carrier bag. Tying the handles together, I step quietly out of the room and head to the kitchen.

My dad used to say that things always looked better in the daytime, that the sunrise brought answers to problems that seemed insurmountable in the middle of the night. I think of his words as I step into the kitchen that, in the morning light, doesn't seem quite so terrifying. I put the bag of rubbish on to the table then take a good look around. There are jagged wooden shelves running along the wall that look like they've been fashioned out of an old tree branch. Like the mantelpiece, they are laden with clutter. There's an assortment of tins and boxes, old candles, paintbrushes and more bottles of antiseptic. I see the words 'Powdered Milk' written on the front of one of the tins. Taking it down, I read the label: 'Best Before 01/08/2003'. Fifteen years out of date. My stomach twists as I look at that year. The year of my dad's death. That's the second time I've been confronted with it since I arrived here. It seems to be mocking me.

'Don't let the dark thoughts in,' I mutter to myself as I put the tin back on to the shelf. 'Keep focused and clear.' I make my way to the back of the kitchen where the odd contraption I noticed yesterday sits. I realize it must be a stove, though it juts out at all angles, like someone's

58

cobbled it together from bits of old scrap. There's a flue with a ledge running across the bottom on which sit a black cast-iron kettle, a two-handled heavy-set cooking pot and an old-fashioned iron. There is a door in the bottom that I presume is where the wood goes but when I try to open it I find it's wedged shut with grease.

I take a deep breath and try to contemplate living in this place over the winter with no form of heating. I've got to get that stove to work. But how the hell do I do that? As I stand looking at it I hear Mark's voice in my head again, what he said to me the night we had Beth and Harry over for dinner. I was pregnant with Joe and suffering badly with morning sickness. Mark had invited our friends over at short notice. I usually wouldn't have minded. I'd known Beth since I was eighteen. We'd met during the first term at university and had quickly become inseparable. Back then I was a bit of a party girl, always up for a glass of wine and a night of clubbing. To outsiders I must have looked like I didn't have a care in the world but Beth soon saw through that. One night, over a bottle of Merlot in the cheap Italian bistro that served plates of pasta for five quid, I told her about my dad's death and she opened up about losing her mum to cancer when she was five. We swapped our sob stories and formed a bond that remained unshakeable for two years. Then I met Mark and the friendship took a back seat. I could tell Beth didn't like him but I told myself she was envious, that the fact I'd found someone as attentive as Mark while she worked her way through a series of one-night stands trying to find the 'one' had made her resent me. How wrong I was. I remember her face that night as she sat watching

Mark criticize me. She knew. She'd known all along. Why hadn't I listened to her?

Mark seemed oblivious to Beth's dislike of him. Probably because he barely spoke to her. What interested him was Beth's new husband, Harry. Harry was a solicitor, specializing in property law. As an estate agent and would-be property developer, Mark saw Harry as someone who could be of use. This is what he based all his friendships on: whether or not the person could be of use. As for me, I was his fragile flower, the person who made *him* feel useful, feel in control.

That evening he persuaded me to cook a roast. He knew I was a lousy cook at the best of times let alone when I was struggling with nausea but he said that as it was my friend – Beth – who was coming I should be the one to cook. 'A roast chicken's nice and simple, Lisa,' he'd said, opening up the cookbook. 'All you have to do is follow the instructions.' And I did follow them, right to the letter, but it was still a disaster. The chicken was raw in the middle, the vegetables were overdone, the gravy stuck to the bottom of the pan. The thing is, I'd always associated roast dinners with my dad. He'd loved to cook them, delighting in the ritual of prepping the meat and the vegetables then gathering round the table to eat and chat. After he died my mum couldn't face Sunday lunches so the tradition ended along with our happiness. As I grew up I avoided eating roast dinner altogether because of those memories, because of the happiness I'd known and lost.

I remember the look on Mark's face as I sliced the chicken and a load of blood poured out on to the plate. He looked mortified. Beth and Harry looked awkward too but Harry tried to lighten the mood. He said it happened to him all the time when he cooked chicken. 'They're a bugger to get right,' he laughed as he dialled in an Indian takeaway for us all. Beth nodded at me and mouthed, 'Are you okay?' I'd smiled brightly, rolled my eyes and said I wouldn't be giving Nigella a run for her money any time soon. But inside I was screaming. I'll never forget Mark's words as we waved Beth and Harry off at the end of the evening. They have stayed with me ever since and each time I think of them they take on a new meaning. 'Well, that was a bit embarrassing, wasn't it?' His breath reeked of beer and Chicken Madras. 'I don't know. You just haven't figured out how to be a grown-up, have you, Lisa?'

Looking at the stove with its seemingly unfathomable parts, I tell myself that no matter how difficult this becomes, no matter what I have to face, I'm going to prove Mark wrong. I'm twenty-eight years old, not some silly child.

I stand up straight and try to imagine that I'm sensible, grown up, that I know what I'm doing, but then I'm hit with a smell so pungent it almost takes my breath away. Putting my hand to my mouth, I see that to the left of the stove is a small alcove. The foul smell seems to be coming from that direction. Holding my breath, I step inside it. There's a tall wooden box in the middle of the space. As I approach I see there's a hole in the top and an old rusted bucket to the side of it. It can't be. But as I peer inside the hole my fears are confirmed. This is the toilet.

I retch and stagger back through the kitchen and out into the hallway. I stand looking at the two doors that lead off to the left. I open the first one and step inside. The smell is different here, a sweet, musty scent that reminds me of a perfume my mum used to wear when I was a child. She used to douse herself in it and Dad would tell her she smelt like she'd 'raided the perfume counter in Selfridges'. Dad meant it as a joke but Mum used to get upset. Any little comment like that would set her off. She would sulk for hours and Dad would try to coax her with freshly baked biscuits or suggest we all go for a nice walk on the heath. But once my mother got into a bad mood there was no shaking her out of it. I push my parents to the back of my mind as I look at the room I've entered. The bare walls are painted a pale-blue colour, like a hospital waiting room. It's empty except for a pile of sheets and blankets in the corner. I step towards them tentatively. There could be rats or mice under there. Or worse.

I prod the pile of blankets with my foot. Thankfully there's no sign of life. I breathe out. Every nerve in my body is on edge. I crouch down to see if any of the blankets are salvageable. They don't smell as bad as the ones in the living room. I lift the top one off and see a khaki sleeping bag beneath. I lift it up and press it to my face. It smells of damp and must. Then I hear an ear-piercing scream.

Joe.

I drop the sleeping bag and run to the living room. He's standing in the doorway, his face red and swollen with tears.

'It's okay, Joe,' I say. 'Mummy was just in the kitchen.'

But he's inconsolable.

Then I notice the dark patch on his blue joggers.

'Oh, darling, it's okay,' I say, taking his hand in mine. 'Let's go and get washed.'

As soon as the words are out of my mouth, it hits me. There is no bathroom, no proper toilet or bath or shower. I have fresh clothes for Joe and a couple of packets of wet wipes in my handbag but he's going to need a proper clean and the only source of water is the great bloody lake out the front.

'Hey,' I say, crouching down so my eyes are level with his. 'Would you like to play a game?'

He shakes his head furiously.

'Come on,' I say, scooping him up into my arms. 'It'll be fun.'

'Not want game,' he shouts, smashing his fists into my shoulder. 'Want Daddy. Want to go home.'

Unable to withstand any more punches, I put him down then go and retrieve my suitcase from the entrance. Luckily, I packed some towels in case there weren't any here. Little did I know they would be the least of my worries. I pull out a large bath towel and a flannel.

'Right,' I say, returning to the living room. 'Let's get those wet clothes off.'

He folds his arms across his chest as I try to wrestle the sodden joggers from his legs. Once he is undressed I wrap the towel round him, tuck the flannel in my pocket and lift him into my arms.

'Okay,' I say, my back straining under the weight of his rigid body. 'Let's go and play the splish-splash game.'

I open the front door. Thankfully, the sun is out, though the air is chilly. I pull Joe towards my chest as

I head for the lake. Mark would go mad if he knew what I was about to do. But I can't see an alternative.

'No,' shouts Joe as we reach the water's edge. 'Want to go home. It's cold.'

I look at the water. Just a few days ago I was sitting in a warm house planning Christmas. Now I'm contemplating plunging my child into a freezing lake in the middle of winter.

I dip my hands in the water. It's icy cold. There's no way I can put Joe in there. So instead I take the flannel, soak it in the water then squeeze it tight.

'Right, let's get you clean,' I say, holding Joe close to me and removing his towel. 'I wonder if Max saw a lake when he visited the wild things. Can you remember?'

Joe doesn't answer, though he screws his face up and lashes out with his fists as I wipe his body with the flannel.

'There. All done,' I say, wrapping the towel back round him. 'That wasn't so bad, was it?'

I stoop to pick him up and, as our eyes meet, I see fear in his eyes. But it's not the water my little boy seems to be scared of. It's me.

8

Soldier Number 1

Rowan Isle House, September 2003

I feel bad because I haven't written in this journal for such a long time, though the truth is I haven't felt like there was much to report and what's the point of a journal if it's full of boring stuff. But when I saw it on my shelf this morning I decided it was time to start writing again. Maybe if I do that then the exciting stuff will start to happen.

Sarge hasn't given me any missions to carry out for months, not since the last one. Instead I've been carrying the bulk of the housework which I don't really mind but can get rather tedious. I try not to think about what happened on the lake because when I do my heart goes all shaky. Sometimes I have nightmares that I'm under the water and Sarge is holding me down. But in the nightmares he doesn't pull me out, he lets me sink and I go down, down to the very bottom of the lake where everything is black. I wake up feeling all sweaty and breathless but I never tell Sarge about the dreams. I just get up and get on with things because that's what a good soldier does.

Right now it's harvest time, always a busy few weeks for Sarge and me. Still, despite the hard graft it's my favourite part of the year. After months of living off oatmeal and boiled water with a bit of meat every now and then the thought of fresh vegetables makes my mouth water. For weeks I've been dreaming about the crunchy orange carrots with their parsley-like stems that I'll pull from the earth, their sweet smell filling my nostrils as I shake the soil from them and place them in my basket. The green peas that I'll pop out of their pods with the back of my thumb, and the sharp white onions that smell so good when Sarge roasts them round a saddle of rabbit. I feel hungry just thinking about it, though Sarge says only some of the produce will be for the pot. The rest will be sold and the money will see us through the winter.

Today was the start, and we spent hours digging up potatoes and carrots and picking green beans. Sarge put me on to scrubbing the potatoes and bagging them up. It was a dull job and I told him I'd rather dig up the rest of the vegetables but he told me that part of being a good soldier is learning to put up with boredom. 'War's not always about action,' he told me. 'It's about standing in the scalding heat for hours on end, repeating the same task over and over again, scrubbing your boots until you can see your face in them. Once you can cope with boredom then you're ready to fight.'

It's annoying that Sarge has kept me away from soldiering these last few months. Instead of heading up the crag together or into the woods rabbiting, he's declared that I need to be in the house more, to help with the cooking and cleaning and gardening, make sure the stove's got enough wood and the bog's slopped out. I don't mind doing all that but I'd much prefer to be out hunting with Sarge. He goes into the woods alone now and he stays out much longer too. One time he came back with blood all over his face and I was ~~freting~~ fretting he was injured or something. But it wasn't his blood, it was the blood of the rabbits he was carrying under his arm. It wasn't like Sarge to make such a mess. He always makes a clean kill and he's proud of that fact. I wanted to ask him how he got the blood on his face but he had that look, the one that comes over him when he hears the voices, so I just stayed quiet and set about skinning the rabbits.

Being stuck with the chores made me feel like I'd done something wrong, that I wasn't cut out to be Soldier Number 1 after all, but when Sarge said that thing today, that boredom is part of being a soldier, I understood what he'd been doing all these months. I've still been in training, I just hadn't realized it. So now I feel better. It doesn't matter that I'm bagging spuds rather than doing target practice, Sarge still believes in me and he has a plan. And that, for me, can only be good news.

Anyway, when I'd finished bagging and pricing the veg, Sarge handed me a stack of cardboard boxes and told me to go and collect the eggs from the cages. I don't really like this job as those chickens can be ~~vishous~~ vicious. When I was a kid one of them pecked a hole in my sock and made my ankle bleed. Sarge used to go out and collect the eggs after that because I was too scared. But today he asked me to do it and I knew it was another test that I had to pass so I took the boxes, opened up the latch on the first cage and carefully stepped inside.

They made such a racket, those chickens, flapping their wings and shrieking. I tried to grab the eggs as quick as I could before I got pecked but that only made them go even more crazy. I just wanted to get out of there but I knew Sarge was watching from the back door so I took a deep breath and stepped across them. They all went running towards the back of the cage then, like a big ball of feathers, leaving the rest of the cage clear. One of the chickens was dead. It was lying at the front. Its legs and body were in the cage but its head had been pulled out of a gap in the wire and was all mangled. It didn't scare me. Dead chickens are a regular part of life. I just knew that we needed those eggs to sell so I kicked the dead chicken aside and collected the rest.

When I'd finished I closed the cage and went over to tell Sarge what had happened. His reaction wasn't what I was expecting. Instead of shrugging it off like he usually did, he got mad as anything and started raging about the 'bloody foxes being the ruin of him' and how he was going to set a trap that night for them. I thought of my friend the vixen with the eyes like the dead mother in the desert and I went cold. I don't care about a dumb chicken or a rabbit or a dozy old sheep getting killed, but the vixen is different. If she died, I don't know what I'd do. I didn't tell Sarge any of this because I didn't want him to think I was getting soft. But I started to put a plan together in my head.

Early evening we set up the produce out the front. Sarge says that's the best time to do it as folk are on their way home from work and they're hungry. But in the end the only custom we had was from the vicar. He pulled up in his shiny red car at about 7.30, just as I was about to put the stall away. Sarge must have seen him coming because he came out of the house and asked the vicar what he could get him. He bought a few bags of veg – carrots and potatoes – and a dozen eggs. I was watching him while Sarge bagged the stuff. He was an odd-looking fella. Very short with narrow shoulders and pale-blue eyes that looked like the glass china Sarge brought from the bungalow in Middlesbrough. They were cold eyes and looking at them made me feel cold too. He didn't speak much, just muttered and handed over his cash. As he scurried back to his car, I realized what he reminded me of. With his cold eyes and his white collar he was the spit and double of a wood pigeon.

I was about to share this observation with Sarge when he suddenly spat on the ground. 'Scum,' he muttered, shaking his head. 'Scum, the lot of them.'

Here was my chance. As we cleared away the produce I asked him why he dealt with the vicar, why he took his money, if he hates religion so much. He stopped for a moment, frowned, wiped his forehead then looked at me. 'I've got nothing against taking his money,' he said, fixing me with that glare he usually keeps for staring at a target. 'In fact, it makes a change for folks like us to get something out of the likes of him. It's usually the other way round.' I asked what he meant and he started going on again about how when he was little he was sent to a Catholic school where he was taught by priests. He said every last one of them was a sadistic bastard. But he was tough too and he could handle that. What he couldn't handle were the weekly visits from the parish priest. Every Saturday morning he'd come downstairs and see Father Hugh sitting in the kitchen drinking tea and eating cake with his mother. Cake they couldn't afford but his mother always got in to keep up appearances, Sarge said, to make the priest think that they weren't like the rest of the people on the street, the ones with dirty windows and dog shit in their yard, that they were good people, respectable people, who kept cake in Tupperware boxes and drank tea out of china cups. The priest would ask how they were doing – Sarge and my gran, it was just the two of them because my granddad had died when Sarge was five – and he'd make out like he cared. He'd listen to my grandmother's complaints about the condition of the houses round about and say how wonderful it was that Sarge was doing so well at school. But then just before he was leaving he'd casually mention the little matter of the church roof that needed fixing or the Christmas boxes for the elderly that needed filling, and if Gran had a bob or two to spare it would be gratefully received. Sarge said they had no money whatsoever to spare. They were poor. Dirt poor. But the priest played on her good nature, told her that all the parishioners were pitching in, made her feel guilty. 'Cos that's what they do, lass,' Sarge said as we lifted the trestle back into the house. 'They play on your conscience.' And my gran would fall for it. She'd go to the little teapot she kept on the dresser and take out her last couple of bob to give to the priest. Then she and Sarge would live off bread and marge for the rest of the week.

'They have no conscience,' Sarge said. 'Parasites, the lot of them. That's why I have no problem taking their cash off them now.'

He spent the rest of the evening ranting about the church and hypocrisy and illegal wars, then he started talking about the desert. 'There was all this blood. It was everywhere,' he said, his eyes glazed with beer. That bit startled me because he had never said it before and I wondered what he meant. Had he killed someone? But I knew not to question him when he was in that mood. Also, though I feel terrible saying this, I wanted him to be distracted. While he was talking he drank three large tankards of home brew that I kept on refilling for him. I knew that if he kept thinking about the vicar and the war and kept drinking more booze then he'd forget about the foxes. And I was right. When he finally stumbled off to bed I went to the back door to look out and there were no traps, just a calm, still autumn evening. But I did see my vixen. She was standing in the shadow of the house up by the side, and she was looking at me so intently, so peacefully, like she knew what I'd done for her, like she knew I was her friend.

9
Lisa

Think, Lisa, think, I tell myself as I pace around the musty living room. You've made it here. Now what?

I stand at the grimy window and look out at the lake, remembering her words.

If you ever need to get away, the house is yours. It's peaceful there. Safe.

Yet I feel anything but safe. I feel like any moment now he's going to knock on that door and find us. Even standing at this window I feel exposed, though I know that it's impossible for him to know where I am. I've made sure I haven't used my bank card, relying instead on the cash I've been saving these last few months, withdrawing ten and twenty pounds here and there so the police wouldn't be able to track my bank card here. I had planned this escape down to the very last detail yet the one thing I couldn't have predicted was that the safe house she promised me would be like this. Why did she tell me to come here, knowing the state it was in? Was it a trick? No, I can't allow myself to think that. She's my friend and she protected me when I was at my most vulnerable. She would never lead me to danger. I have to believe that. I have to trust that I have made the right decision. For both our sakes.

I step away from the window and look at Joe. He is sitting on the pile of cushions in the living room, his knees pulled up to his chin, his eyes fixed on the floor in front of him.

He hasn't spoken a word in over an hour.

I've tried to coax him out into the garden to play, told him that if we're lucky we might see some animals, but he's not interested. It's like he's shrunk inside himself. The silence unnerves me so I fill it by singing a song my mum used to sing when she was doing the housework, an old Irish folk tune that my grandmother had sung to her when she was small. But I don't get as far as the first chorus before Joe starts banging his fists on the floor and shouting at me to stop.

I look at my red-faced, angry child sitting on a pile of rags in this broken-down house and I feel tears pricking at my eyes. Maybe it was the song and the memory of happy times with my mum. And I realize I'm everything Mark said I was: a girl who never grew up, who never learned how to do what adults do. 'For fuck's sake, Lisa, you can't even change a light bulb.' I put my hands to my ears to drown out his voice as if he's here in the room and not in my head.

When I take them away, Joe is still screaming. Why can't he just be quiet for five minutes? Why can't he just stop? Then I look at him and all my rage ebbs away, leaving me with an overwhelming sense of love, so powerful it feels like it might rip me in two.

Pull yourself together, Lisa, I tell myself. He's a child, *your* child, who is miles away from home and all his comforts. He's confused and hungry and cold. And even after

73

everything, Mark's still his dad, of course he's going to be asking for him. I need to step up now and start being a proper mother. Wiping my eyes, I locate the shopping bags that are lying crumpled by the door and dig around inside, trying to find something that could constitute a healthy breakfast. I'm relieved to see that despite my manic state yesterday I still managed to put some fruit into the basket. I take a tangerine from its mesh bag and begin to peel the skin.

'Look what Mummy's got,' I say, holding up the fruit for Joe to see. 'Lovely tangerines.'

'Father Christmas been,' he says, staring at me with wide, watery eyes.

'Not yet,' I say, my stomach sinking at the mention of Christmas. 'But he'll be getting ready. The elves will be working round the clock to get all those presents finished in time.'

'That,' he says, pointing at the tangerine. 'Father Christmas?'

And then I get it. I know what he's talking about. He's referring to something I thought was lost for ever, a memory I'd tried to resurrect. When I was young my parents would fill a long red knitted stocking with nuts and sweets, a small present and a tangerine. Then, when they were sure I was asleep, they'd tiptoe into the room and hang it on the end of my bed. All my big presents would be downstairs in the living room round the tree but that red stocking was the first thing I saw when I opened my eyes. It was the first taste of the magic that lay ahead that day, the promise of what was to come. I'd wanted to carry on the tradition when Joe was born but Mark couldn't understand the idea of having fruit and nuts as presents, he dismissed it as '1980s North London hippy nonsense', so Joe's first Christmas had consisted of expensive, educational toys, all chosen by Mark. The next Christmas was the toughest of my life. I don't know how I got through it. But despite my heartache I still made sure, with some help from a friend, that Joe got a stocking with a tangerine. Nothing, not even Mark, was going to stop me doing that. The fact that Joe remembers warms my heart. I did do something right, after all, I think to myself as I peel the fruit and feed him it, piece by piece. No matter what Mark says, I did do something right.

When Joe is finished I wipe the sticky sweet juice from his mouth with my hand.

'Was that nice, beautiful boy?' I ask, rubbing his soft skin.

He nods his head.

'Where's Daddy?' he says, his eyes boring into mine. 'Is he coming?'

'You'll see Daddy in a little while,' I say, the lie sticking in my throat. 'But for now, you and I are going to have a little explore. Come on.'

I scoop him into my arms, step over the carrier bag that is spilling out half-eaten packets of crisps and empty juice cartons, and head into the hallway.

The smell of damp and must is overpowering, much more so than it was last night. There is green mould pock-marked along the walls and a thick dust covers the floor like a carpet. It rises up into the air as we walk then hangs suspended in the sunlight. Joe starts to cough and I pull him closer to me. We reach the bedroom I was in earlier.

The door is still open but we don't go in. I am determined to find one room that is at least halfway habitable. We walk to the end of the passage and in the gloom I can make out the shape of a staircase.

'Baby, I need you to stay here for two minutes while I go to find a nice bed,' I say, placing Joe down at the foot of the stairs. 'Is that okay?'

He looks at me with a frown then points at the stairs.

'Daddy up there?'

'No, darling, Daddy's not up there,' I say, trying to keep the exasperation at bay. 'But there might be some-where for us to sleep.'

'Not tired,' he says, shaking his head furiously.

'No, not now,' I say, looking up at the stairs where a shaft of light has illuminated a circular plume of dust that hangs suspended at the top of the banister like a halo. 'For later, when it's bedtime. Now be a good boy and stay there while I go and have a very quick look.'

As I climb the stairs I see that the light is coming from a tiny skylight in the ceiling, but as I turn the corner and step on to the landing I'm enveloped in a darkness so thick it almost takes my breath away and an icy chill rip-ples down my spine. A voice, deep and low, whispers inside my head: *You shouldn't be here.* And it is right. There is something rotten and unpleasant up here, something I can't quite place, though I know I need to leave it well alone. Gripping hold of the banister, I slowly make my way back down the stairs. When I reach the bottom, and Joe, I lift him in my arms and hoist him on to my waist.

'Want to get down.'

The force of Joe's voice startles me.

'Let me go,' he cries, pounding at my chest with his fists.

'Sorry, baby,' I say, easing him on to the ground. 'Mummy was just . . .' I can't explain it. I reach out to take his hand. 'Stay close to me and we'll see if we can find somewhere to put our things.'

He stamps his feet and scowls at me. I take a deep breath, then take my hand away and walk back down the passage, passing the open door of the bedroom. I can hear Joe's footsteps on the stone floor behind me as I stop outside the door at the end of the passage, close to the entrance hall. I try the handle and it opens immediately. I put my hand out behind me to keep Joe back, not sure what I'm going to confront.

It's very dark in the room and it smells of stale moth-balls. Stepping carefully inside, I can make out the frame of a bed in the centre. I approach it and see that the bed is covered in animal skins. It looks disgusting but I need to see if it can be slept in. I fold back the sheets. A cloud of dust rises, catching in my throat. This is old dust, ancient body particles. I try not to think about the person who once slept here, clothed in animal skins.

Yet to my relief I see that the mattress is clean and soft, and the animal skins, though not what I'm used to, will at least be warm. We can sleep in here tonight. I replace the skins then look around the room. There's a shelf on the wall beside the bed. A set of beads is threaded across it. I look closer. It's a necklace made of tiny pearls. It looks out of place in this house, a piece of beauty and femininity among the animal skins and the stench and the dirt. Next to the necklace is a metal candle holder, the candle long since melted, and a small leather-bound book. I take it down from the shelf and open it. It's written in what looks like Arabic. As I turn the pages I see that someone has added little pencil drawings alongside the printed words. Foxes and birds and faceless women.

'Daddy,' says Joe behind me. 'We go find him now?'

'Not yet,' I say as I push the skins to the edge of the room with my foot. 'We just have to be here for a little while longer. We need to sort out this bed and make things habitable and then . . .'

I stop and turn to look at him, through the fog of dust, and my heart hurts. He is standing in the doorway, his hands clasped in front of him. He's still a baby, not even four years old yet, and I'm expecting him to understand things that even adults can't.

'I'm sorry, Joe,' I say, placing the book back on the shelf. 'Mummy just wants to make everything perfect for you and –'

My words are interrupted by a banging noise. It's coming from outside.

'Daddy,' cries Joe, his eyes shining.

My body goes rigid. It can't be. He can't have found us. Not here.

'Shh,' I whisper, scooping him into my arms and edging out of the room into the passage.

'Is it Daddy?' he says, his voice bright. 'Has Daddy come?'

I want to put my hand over his mouth, keep him quiet, but if I do that he'll get hysterical.

The banging starts again. Three loud thuds. It's then I realize it's coming from the front of the house. I hold my breath for what feels like minutes but can only be a few seconds, my mind whirring with panic.

If it's him, what will I do?

'Want to see Daddy,' says Joe, wriggling and squirming in my arms. 'Let me down.'

I squeeze him closer to my chest, muttering prayers under my breath. But holding Joe tighter just makes him more agitated. He breaks free of my arms, kicking me in the stomach as he descends to the floor.

'Ow,' I cry, doubling over, and he makes a run for the door.

The pain winds me. My eyes sting with tears but I have no time to think about it. I have to get Joe away from that door.

I stagger after him. If he opens the door then it's all over.

'Daddy,' he shouts, banging his fists against the door. 'Where you?'

I stand in the hallway unable to breathe, waiting for Mark's reply. But all is silent. The banging has stopped. A few moments later I hear footsteps and the sound of a car door closing. As the engine starts up my body starts to loosen. He's leaving.

'Daddy gone?' says Joe, turning to me with tears in his eyes.

I stand for a couple of seconds, waiting. When I'm sure the car has gone I rush to Joe.

'It's okay, Joe,' I say, taking his hand. 'Everything's okay.'

'No,' he screams, shaking his head furiously. 'Don't want you. Want Daddy. I hate you.'

He yanks his hand away from mine and starts pounding the door with his fists.

'Want to see Daddy,' he cries. 'Daddy's outside. Want to see him.'

'Joe, calm down,' I say, guiding him away from the door. 'Daddy's not there. Look, I'll show you.'

I pull back the bolt. The door is stiff and I have to yank it open.

'See,' I say to Joe. 'There's no one there.'

I quickly usher Joe back into the house but as I close the door I take a tentative look over my shoulder. All I can see is the lake and the gate and the blur of the road, yet somehow I can't shake the feeling that someone is out there, watching me.

IO

Soldier Number 1

Rowan Isle House, July 2004

Right. This time I promise I'm going to write in this journal and not just put it away in a drawer like I did last time. It's been nearly a year. But then not much has happened that would be worth writing about. In fact, there have been times when I've been so bored I've felt like screaming. I'm supposed to be in training to be a soldier, one of the elite, but I've done nothing but gardening and housework for almost ten months.

Again.

I thought by now I'd have had another mission to complete but there hasn't even been so much as a whisper of one.

I know Sarge has his reasons for the whole boredom thing. It's a test that I have to pass just as much as the active missions but it's been so long since I held a gun I'm scared I've forgotten what to do, or worse still, that I've lost my nerve. But so far, despite my protesting, Sarge shows no sign of budging.

He's been acting weird the last few days too, which isn't helping. Like this morning, for instance, I was mopping the floor in the Mess and he came and stood by the stove. He didn't say anything, just stood there with his arms folded across his chest, looking at me. I thought he was about to tell me off for something so I stopped what I was doing, propped the mop against the table and asked him what I'd done wrong. He was quiet for a moment then he smiled and said, 'You haven't done anything wrong, pet.'

I was taken aback then. First, cos he called me pet, not Number 1, and he hasn't done that for a long time, and second, because he sounded so sad. I'm used to Sarge's moods. I've lived with them all my life so I have a good idea of them, how they alter and shift like the sand in the desert. There are the angry ones, the excited ones, the broody ones. Those ones are the most worrying for me cos he just goes inside himself like a hermit crab, sometimes for days on end, and I'm never sure when he's coming back. When he does snap out of it he's always altered, like he's left a bit of himself behind wherever he's been.

But today's mood was different. I'd never seen him like that before. He was sad, but not in a brooding way. It was like he wanted to open up, to share whatever he was feeling inside.

I couldn't concentrate on the mopping while he was standing there looking at me so I left the mop against the table and went to go out to the garden to collect some eggs. But when I got to the door Sarge put his hand out and told me to stay. His grip was so tight I knew I'd have to do as he said so I moved the mop and sat down at the kitchen table. Sarge stayed where he was, leaning against the stove.

I looked up at him as if to say, 'Come on then, what do you want to talk about?' but instead of giving me a list of instructions like he usually does he smiled and said, 'You're so much like your mother.'

His eyes went all watery then and for a moment I was scared. I'd never seen Sarge cry and I'm not sure I wanted to. He's always in control and that makes me feel safe. Crying is weakness. That's what he's told me since I was a little kid. If a soldier cries, he's lost it. Sarge didn't look like he'd lost it though. And I liked the fact that he had mentioned my mother. He never talks about her usually, and I've always been scared to, especially after what happened when I found her photo. He'd got so angry then that I reasoned it was best to just keep her in my head.

So this morning when Sarge started talking about her I didn't know what to think. At first I thought it was another test so I was careful how I reacted. But it soon became clear that he was being sincere. After a while he sat down at the table next to me and I plucked up the courage to ask him about my mother. There were so many things I wanted to know: what did she sound like, what did she smell like, what was her favourite food, her favourite colour? But in the end my question was a simple one: what was her name?

Sarge frowned at first and I thought he was going to tell me to shush but instead he put his head in his hands, stared straight ahead and started to speak, as if he was talking to some invisible person, not me.

He told me that my mother's name was Noora. I liked it immediately. It sounded like a whisper, or a fairy's sigh as Sarge used to call whispers when I was a kid. I rolled her name up and over my tongue until it became as familiar as the face in the photo. He said he'd met her in the big war, said she'd been hired by something called the UN to help the soldiers understand the Arabic words that the enemy were using. I asked if she knew how to use a gun and he said she didn't have to; that words were her weapons. I wasn't too sure what that meant but it sounded like she had a good mind. I wanted to ask Sarge about those words on the back of the photo and whether she had written them but then I remembered how angry he'd been that day so instead I asked him what she was like. He smiled then and I was relieved because every question was a potential explosion. She was kind and gentle, he said, with these amazing eyes that changed colour as you looked at them: first brown, then hazel, then amber. Sarge's voice went quiet as he described her skin. It was warm and soft, he said, and it smelt of orange groves and sugar, and when she smiled it felt like he'd come home.

His eyes went all glazed then and I knew I should have kept quiet but my eyes had turned to water too and there was a question burning inside me that I had to get out.

'How did she die?'

He flinched at the words, it was like I'd smacked him in the face. Then, without looking at me, he pushed the chair back, stood up and walked into the garden.

I sat by myself for a bit, turning over in my head all the new things I'd learned about my mother. Then I heard a loud bang outside and my heart leapt inside my chest. I jumped up and ran out back.

The first thing I saw was an empty cage lying on its side by the door. Sarge must have picked it up and thrown it. Then I saw him. He was standing by the boundary wall, looking out at the woods. I walked quietly towards him, hoping that when he turned round he wouldn't have that look on his face, the one that comes when he's hearing the voices.

But when I reached him he started to speak and his voice wasn't angry at all.

'Look at those trees over there,' he said, pointing his finger in the direction of the woods. 'You know your granddad told me that the bark of most trees in Northern Europe was adapted to withstand attacks by elephants.'

'Elephants?' I said, trying to imagine one of those creatures stomping through Harrowby Crag.

'Yes, elephants,' he said. 'They used to roam these parts before the Ice Age. Hippos too. Imagine that, pet?'

I tried to, but the thought was as crazy as trying to imagine my mother anywhere but the desert, or me and Sarge anywhere but here.

'Funny, eh?' he said, shaking his head. 'How things survive. Now the elephants are gone, the danger's gone, but the trees are still protecting themselves. It doesn't make any sense.'

His eyes got all red then and I realized that he wasn't talking about the trees any more or the elephants or even the dead mother. He was talking about himself.

11

Lisa

Two hours later

I sit at the kitchen table looking at the dark screen on my phone. The battery is now completely dead. Without my phone I have no way of calling for help, no link at all with the outside world. In my head I try to plan out a crude escape plan. If someone broke into the house and attacked me then I would need to get out fast. And to do that the back door would have to be unlocked. But then it would depend where I was and how they had got in. My agitated thoughts fizz back and forth inside my head like a Catherine wheel.

The most important thing, I think to myself as I step out of the kitchen and go into the bedroom where Joe has finally settled on the newly discovered bed, is to keep my boy beside me at all times. That's all that matters. Kneeling by the side of the bed, I watch as his chest rises and falls, his long eyelashes touching his cheek like spider's legs, and my eyes fill with tears. It shouldn't have had to come to this. I'm his mother. I carried him inside me for nine months, felt every wriggle, every kick. His heart had beat in time with mine as he lay on my chest that first day and I'd held his fat little hand and promised him that I'd be there for him for ever. He's part of me. Without him I'm just a vessel floating through the world without an anchor.

I stand up and adjust the covers then, as Joe gently snores, I explore the room a little more. The windows are shaded with thin, yellowed nets that give the room an eerie glow. I run my finger along the top of the window and release a cascade of dust. Coughing, I step away from the window and go to the wardrobe, a dark wooden hulk that stands opposite the bed and looks, in this light, like the hull of a ship.

Opening the heavy door, I cough again as more dust fills my lungs. Behind me, Joe stirs. I turn and watch him. He's lying on his back, his eyes fixed on the ceiling. Then he closes them, turns on his side and starts to snore again. I swallow my cough down and turn back to the wardrobe.

Through the murk I see a row of camouflage-patterned overalls hanging from the rail. There must be a dozen of them. To the left are a couple of shelves. On the top shelf sits a pair of shiny hobnail boots, man size. There's a strong smell of mothballs in here and it sticks to the back of my throat. I can't breathe. I need air. I go to close the wardrobe but as I do I notice a mirror running the length of the inner door. As I step closer I'm shocked to see a strange face looking back at me. Pale with blackened eyes and shorn dark hair. It looks spectral, monstrous. But then I realize with despair that I'm staring at my own reflection.

I think back to three days earlier. Holed up in my rented room, I'd set to work transforming myself with the help of a boxed hair dye and a pair of cheap scissors. The new start had to be just that. I could leave no trace of the woman who had existed before. She was gone. In her place was a dark-haired, responsible person who was heading to a house in the countryside for a nice break with her sweet little boy. As I look at this new person I see Mark standing behind me as he used to when we were first married and I would brush my long blonde hair in our immaculate bathroom. His hand resting on my shoulder, watching my every move. 'Promise me you'll never cut your hair,' he'd whispered, his mouth so close to my ear that it made me shiver. 'Promise me you'll always be mine.'

The memory of that moment strengthens my resolve. I'm not under his control any more. I got away from him. I close the wardrobe then go to the window, pull aside the net and look out. It's getting dark now, though without my phone I have no idea what time it is. The hills in the distance change shape as the light shifts and for a moment I stand mesmerized, a strange sense of peace descending on me, loosening my muscles. I turn from the window and go to gently wake Joe. If he sleeps too long now he'll be up all night.

He scowls as he comes to, then yawns and rubs his eyes.

'Daddy come?' he says, looking up at me.

The peaceful feeling dissipates when I hear that. No matter how much I try to tell myself that I've done the right thing, Mark is still Joe's dad and he misses him. I can't change that.

'No, Daddy hasn't come,' I say, lifting him off the bed. 'It's just us two for a little bit. But we're going to have a lovely holiday. I promise you that, Joe.'

I need to think about dinner, I realize as I make my way to the kitchen, Joe trailing sleepily behind me, and

I'm going to have to brave the lake at some point and give myself a wash. There's a sour scent emanating from my armpits and I feel itchy and unpleasant. I've never gone more than a day without having a shower and I feel wretched.

My mind is so preoccupied with these thoughts as I enter the kitchen that at first I don't hear the back door opening. But then I look up and see a dark figure standing in front of me and I scream.

12

Soldier Number 1

Rowan Isle House, July 2004

Reverend Carter came to buy eggs this morning. He's not a regular customer, it's been ages since he last came, so I was surprised to see him. It was just me manning the stall because Sarge had gone off to set traps in the woods. I didn't tell the vicar that though. That kind of talk would get us into trouble. So when he asked if I was by myself I told him Sarge had some business to attend to. I liked how that sounded as I said it. It sounded like we were important. The vicar didn't seem too impressed though. He just nodded his head then smiled this weird smile.

While I was boxing up his eggs he started asking me questions. Like how old I was and what subject I liked best at school. I told him I didn't go to school and when I said this he put his hand on his chest and said, 'Oh dear, my poor girl.' I told him I was fine, that I didn't need school, that Sarge had taught me how to read and write and count, and that he was training me to be an elite soldier. I also told him that Sarge said schools and churches were 'the mouthpiece of the powerful and corrupt' and that he was bringing me up to rebel against all that.

When I said this his face went pink and I thought he was going to drop the eggs I'd just handed him. But instead he put them back on the table then came round to my side and kind of grabbed my hand. I was a bit startled because no one except Sarge has ever touched me like that. I tried to yank it away but he gripped tighter and said that I had to understand that you can only find the truth through Jesus, that rebelling against Jesus was evil, that what Sarge was doing to me was evil. He asked me if I would like to go to the church one Sunday and find out what the truth was all about. I was about to answer him when I heard someone shout. When I looked up I saw Sarge coming towards us with two rabbits slung over his shoulders.

'Oy,' he shouted, his face all red and sweaty. 'What the hell do you think you're doing?'

The vicar pulled his hand away and walked back round to the front of the table. He said, 'Hello, sir', which seems like it should be friendly but it sounded nasty. Sarge stood right in front of him and asked him again what the hell he was doing. The vicar told Sarge that he was shocked to hear that I wasn't enrolled in school and then he repeated his offer to have me come to church so that I could find out the truth about Jesus.

When he said this Sarge's eyes bulged out of his face and I thought he was going to explode. He grabbed the vicar by the shoulders and marched him to his car, yelling for him to 'get the hell off my land'. Then he called him a word I've never heard of. Pervert. The vicar looked all flustered when Sarge said this and his eyes darted from side to side as if he was checking to see if anyone had heard. But there was no one about. The road was empty of cars. It was just us three and the birds. When the vicar got to his car, he pushed Sarge off and kind of squared up to him. I came out from behind the table so I could hear what he was saying. He said, in this really quiet voice, that this may be Sarge's land but the woods were not, 'And there are prison sentences for poachers.' He nodded his head towards the dead rabbits that were still hanging from Sarge's shoulders. Then he got in his car, slammed the door and drove away.

'He forgot his eggs,' I said. But Sarge didn't hear me. He stormed into the house, dropped the rabbits on to the kitchen table and told me to go get my gun. At first I was scared he was going to follow the vicar and do something stupid but when I came back out with my gun he told me that it was time. I was finally going hunting again.

But it was all wrong. The way we stormed towards those woods. That wasn't how you approach a kill. There was no planning, no preparation. That's what I told myself afterwards anyway, when Sarge marched me back to the house in disgrace.

This is what happened. We hadn't even reached the centre of the woods when Sarge ordered me to get down. There were a couple of scrawny old rabbits nibbling the grass up ahead. They weren't fit for the pot and their fur was all matted so wouldn't be of use to us. I told Sarge we were wasting our time, that he'd done the hunt for the day, that we should shelve this and head back. But he just glared at me and pointed at the gun.

I did as I was told, picked up the gun, got down on the ground and aimed at the rabbits. They carried on nibbling their grass, oblivious to the danger they were in. I cocked the gun and pulled back the trigger. But then something strange happened. As I lay there on the ground I felt myself rise out of my body. It was the weirdest feeling. I tried to pull myself down, tried to keep my eye on the rabbits, but it was impossible. The world began to wobble. There's no other way of describing it. The trees swayed in front of my eyes even though there was no breeze and as I tried to focus I saw what looked like a huge elephant weaving in and out of the trees. I heard Sarge mutter something behind me and I blinked. The elephant disappeared. The trees stopped swaying. The rabbits were still there but the moment was lost. I couldn't do it. I threw the gun to the ground, startling the rabbits who went scurrying off into the bushes.

Sarge grabbed me by the scruff of the neck and hauled me to my feet. Picking up my gun, he thrust it into my arms and marched me back to the house, ranting and raving all the way about my lack of commitment, my laziness, how I'd just 'buggered up' any chance of progressing to the next level. 'You'd rather listen to Jesus freaks than your own father,' he yelled as we emerged from the woods. 'That's what happened. That nutter filled your head with his nonsense and you lost your focus.'

He went on and on but I wasn't really listening because up ahead, standing next to the trestle table, was a girl. She was about my age, maybe a little older, and she had long hair, as white as snow, tied up in a ponytail. As we got closer I saw that she was wearing a school uniform, like the ones the girls wear in *Malory Towers*. Hers was green with a yellow tie.

When she saw us coming she stepped forward. Sarge stopped ranting and folded his arms across his chest, his usual defensive pose when faced with strangers.

'Hello,' she said, and her voice was all light and breathy, like Ratty or Darrell Rivers. 'My name's Isobel. My father sent me to collect his eggs. He forgot them earlier.'

I went to speak but before I could get the words out Sarge put his hand on my shoulder and told me to get inside. 'Straight to your room,' he hissed. 'After what you just did in the woods it's a grounding for two days. Got it?'

I didn't want to go inside, and I certainly didn't want to be grounded for two days. I wanted to stay out here and look at this girl with her pale skin and white hair and eyes the colour of the summer sky. But I knew there was no point arguing with Sarge. Once he makes his mind up, that's it. So I nodded and made my way into the house. As I passed her, the girl smiled and I caught her smell. It was sweet, like the violets that grow in the woods in springtime. The smell stayed in my nostrils for the rest of the day and even now as I sit in my room writing these words I can still smell it. It's like nothing I've ever smelt before, certainly not in this place that only ever smells of animals and boiled cabbage and carbolic soap. No, Isobel's scent is new and clean. It's how I imagine heaven smells, though I won't ever let Sarge hear me say that. 'Religious nonsense,' that's what he'd think. I'm getting to the end of the page now so I'm going to finish here then make up my bed on the floor. Being grounded used to be the thing I dreaded the most but tonight I'm almost thankful for being alone. It means I can think about her. About Isobel.

13

Lisa

'Who . . . who are you?' says the woman at the door, looking just as scared as I feel. 'What are you doing here?'

She's about my age, perhaps a little older, and is wearing a long black coat with a fur collar. Her hair is long and white blonde, her face thin and deathly pale.

'I'm just staying here for a few days,' I say, my hands still trembling from the shock.

She looks at me for a moment with her head to one side. Her mouth is a slash of blood-red lipstick. I reach for Joe's hand and pull him to my side.

'Staying here?' she says, frowning. 'Just the two of you?'

'Yes,' I say tentatively. 'Just the two of us.'

'No one else?' she says, putting her hand to her chest. 'You're sure there's no one else?'

'I'm positive.'

She nods her head.

'Okay,' she says, exhaling. 'I'm . . . I'm sorry to have bothered you.'

We stand awkwardly for a few moments. My heart is still pounding wildly because for just a second, when I'd walked into the kitchen and seen the dark shape, I'd thought it was Mark standing there. I'd thought he'd found me.

'I should go,' she says, turning to leave. 'I'm terribly sorry for disturbing you. I saw the car earlier . . . but there was no answer when I knocked on the door . . . I thought you were . . . It doesn't matter. I'm sorry.'

'It's okay,' I say. 'I just got a bit of a shock.'

The more I look at her the more normal she seems and I realize just how jittery and on edge I am.

'Have you brought Daddy?'

I look down. Joe is standing next to me, pointing at the woman.

She smiles then and her face softens.

'No,' she says. 'I'm afraid not.'

I lift Joe up and place him on the table next to the box of toy animals I brought with us from the house. He picks up a plastic tiger and waves it at the woman.

'How old is he?' she says, turning to me.

'He's three,' I reply. 'Four in April.'

'He's lovely,' she says, smiling at him. 'You're very lucky. Anyway, I really must go. Again, I'm very sorry for disturbing you.'

'Want picnic?'

I turn round. Joe is waving a plastic spoon at the woman.

'You have picnic with me?'

She laughs and shakes her head.

'That sounds lovely,' she says. 'But I really must be going.'

'No, stay for picnic,' cries Joe, banging the spoon on the table.

'Joe,' I say, taking the spoon. 'Don't be naughty.'

But I can sense that he's getting restless and I can't face another tantrum.

'Look, would you like a cup of tea?' I say, reckoning that if this woman stays for what Joe thinks is a picnic I might just be able to avoid him having another meltdown. 'I think Joe would like that.'

She looks like she wants to get out of here fast.

'Yes. Stay for picnic,' says Joe.

This seems to melt her. She smiles again then closes the door.

'Okay,' she says, coming over to the table. 'If you're sure it's not too much trouble.'

It's then, as I watch her sit down next to Joe, who is sitting on the table with his legs dangling over the edge, that I remember we have no running water or electricity. How the hell can I make her a cup of tea?

'So, you're here on holiday?' she says, looking up at me as I stand impotently by the stove.

'Er, yes, of a sort,' I say. 'More like a . . . a retreat.'

She nods her head, though she looks unconvinced. She's obviously wondering why any mother in their right mind would bring their child to this ramshackle house in the middle of winter for a break.

'You have picnic,' says Joe, holding the spoon to her mouth. 'Nice soup.'

'Oh, yummy,' she says, pretending to have a taste. 'Tomato. My favourite.'

'Not tomato. Chicken,' says Joe, pointing the spoon at her again. 'Have more.'

I watch as she takes another pretend spoonful then decide to come clean.

'Look, I'm ever so sorry but I can't actually make you a cup of tea,' I say awkwardly. 'There's no water or electricity here. The, um, letting company didn't say.'

'I thought so,' she says, looking around the kitchen. 'To be honest, I can't imagine anyone letting this place out to holidaymakers in this state, let alone a young mother and child.'

'It is rather . . . basic,' I say, watching as Joe chews on the toy spoon.

'That's an understatement,' she says, shaking her head. 'I've lived in the village all my life and the previous owners were – how can I put this politely – a little eccentric.'

'It's been pretty scary, actually,' I say, glad to be able to admit it to someone at last. 'The lack of . . . well, anything really.'

'I don't doubt it,' she says, her eyes widening. 'I don't know what this holiday firm is thinking, letting you stay here with a young child.'

She gives a little shiver as she says it and the relief I was feeling at her presence turns into unease.

'What do you mean?' I say. 'Is there something I should know about this place?'

'No,' she says, smiling at Joe, who is holding the spoon out for her again. 'Nothing like that. It's just, well, it's not exactly kitted out for modern living, is it?'

'It's not,' I say, feeling tired suddenly.

'How long have you been here?' she says, looking down at the stone floor. There's a dark stain that I've convinced myself is some kind of animal's blood.

'Only a couple of days.'

She looks up at me as I answer and her expression changes. It feels like she can see right through me.

'That's a long time to be without heat or water,' she says, her eyes still fixed on me. 'And with a little one too. It's a disgrace.'

I give a little shrug and avert my eyes from her gaze, feeling guilty. There is no holiday lettings organization, just a crudely drawn map and a person with good intentions. Though I'm becoming more unsure of those intentions with each passing minute.

'Look, let me help get the stove working at least,' she says. 'You can't be without hot food and water in this weather.'

'Oh, that would be great,' I say, my shoulders lifting. 'If it's not too much trouble.'

I have never felt more grateful to another human being as I do right now. The loneliness of the last few days has felt like a cancer eating into my flesh, my bones, right down to my core. If Joe hadn't been here with me, to battle me and smack me and demand I take him back to Daddy, I would have doubted I even existed.

'It's okay,' she says, getting up from the table. 'You've got a child. It's the least I can do.'

She smiles and walks across to the stove.

'Now do we have matches in this place?' she says, looking around.

'No,' I say. 'But I've got a lighter. Will that do?'

'It should be okay,' she says, opening the door of the stove.

I grab the lighter from my bag and hand it to her.

She takes it then quietly sets to work. I stand by the table and watch, reassured not just by her company but because there is something about her brisk, no-nonsense manner that reminds me of my dad. When I was a child I would follow him as he fixed things around the house – broken shelves, spent light bulbs, cracked pipes – safe in the knowledge that nothing bad could happen when I had my dad to look after me. I haven't allowed myself to think about him much over the years, it was too painful, yet these past few days he is everywhere. I recall Mark's words when I came out of the doctor's three weeks after Joe was born: 'If you're not careful you'll end up like your father.' He said it in such a throwaway manner that I couldn't work out whether it was a statement or a threat.

'There we are.'

She stands back from the stove as a warm glow spreads through the kitchen. The woody smell reminds me of my parents' kitchen in Highgate. A cosy, enveloping scent that always made me feel warm and safe. The memories of family suddenly become too much and I feel my eyes begin to water. Blinking the tears away, I smile at the woman, who is standing next to the stove, her arms resting on the kitchen counter.

'Thank you,' I say, bending to scoop Joe into my arms. 'You don't know how grateful I am, really.'

'It's not a bother,' she says with a shrug. 'Like I said, I couldn't let that little boy stay here with no warmth. I'm so sorry, I haven't even asked your name.'

'It's Lisa,' I say. 'And this is Joe.'

'Well, it's nice to meet you,' she says. 'My name's Isobel. Isobel Carter.'

14

Soldier Number 1

Rowan Isle House, August 2004

Sarge hasn't been the same since that day with the vicar. I try to ask him what's the matter but he just shakes his head and marches off into the woods, night after night, and doesn't come back until morning. I don't know what he's doing out there because he's not bringing home any rabbits or pheasants, and sometimes he even goes there without his gun. He's off his food too which is very unlike him. Ever since I was a tiny kid he's drilled it into me how an army marches on its stomach and about the evils of wasting food. Now, he just pushes whatever I put in front of him round the plate. It's like he's given up but I have no idea why.

The voices are back too or at least it seems that way. Last night I found him kneeling in the hallway with his hands clasped over his ears. He was making the most horrible squealing noise, like the chickens when we wring their necks. I stood in the kitchen doorway watching him, wondering if I should say something, though I know full well that you don't get in his way while he's like that. Once when I was about five I heard him screaming his head off in the garden one night and I ran out to see what was going on. I remember I came up behind him and shouted 'Daddy', and it must have been the shock because he would never harm a hair on my head, but he swung round and hit me, knocking me clean off my feet. The next day he had no memory of it, or at least I think he hadn't as he never said a word about it and I knew not to bring it up. But last night it was different. He sounded like he was in agony and he was crying out, 'Leave me, leave me. You've tortured me enough.' It was hell to see him like that but I knew as I closed the kitchen door and tip-toed down to my room that it was best to leave it alone. The voices always go away when the morning comes anyway.

At breakfast this morning he seemed more in control. He walked into the kitchen with a basket of eggs and set them down on the table. While I was cooking them he asked me a bit more about what the vicar had said to me and I told him that he just wanted me to go and join in a church service. When I said this Sarge clenched his fists so hard his knuckles went white. He said that I was to keep focused, that the vicar and his kind are the enemy – 'You see, religion is like a worm that gets inside your head and feeds off you.' He jabbed his fingers at his temples and then his voice got louder and louder. He said religion saps your consciousness until you become nothing more than a zombie. And that's how they want you. They want you 'malleable and submissive' so they can mould you into 'an android with no free will, no independent thought'. His mouth was frothing as he spoke. It was like he couldn't get the words out fast enough. I nodded my head while I dished up the eggs, tried to reassure him that I wasn't going to go to any church. Then he grabbed my wrist and said, 'I might not have been able to give you much, but I saved you from that lot. You do know that, don't you?'

His hand started shaking then and he let go of my wrist. I told him that I did know and that I was grateful. This seemed to calm him. He ate his breakfast while I went outside and sat on the wall. I wanted to get away from him and his words. I wanted to hear my own thoughts. He talks about the vicar wanting to control me but Sarge can be just as bad. As I sat there I thought about Isobel, her pale face and her smile, such a kind smile it was and she'd directed it at me. No one's ever looked at me that way before. I made a little wish then to the dead mother in the desert that Isobel would come here again, that Sarge hadn't scared her off with his ranting at her father. Then I jumped down off the wall and went inside to find Sarge standing at the front door with a hammer and a bag of nails.

Three new bolts had appeared on the door. One at the top, one in the middle and another at the bottom. As Sarge stood back to admire his handiwork I asked why we needed new locks when we had a perfectly decent key lock. He nodded his head then and did this funny expression, like he was half excited, half disgusted. 'It's to keep them out,' he said. And he pointed at the door with the hammer. 'Now they've made their intentions clear, we have to be vigilant. They can get to us when we least expect it but we'll be ready for them.'

I didn't know who he was talking about. Surely not the vicar. I tried to imagine that posh, skinny fella breaking into our house and the thought made me giggle. Then I heard Sarge yell.

'What's so funny?'

I realized, too late, that I'd laughed out loud.

'Nothing, Sarge,' I said, straightening my face. 'Nothing at all.'

'You think our security is a laughing matter?' he said, coming at me with bulging eyes. 'Do you?'

I shook my head and stepped backwards. My mouth was dry with fear.

'Do you know what happened to soldiers who didn't watch their backs in Iraq?' he said, clenching the hammer in his fists. 'They ended up being fed to the fucking goats.'

He stared at me without blinking and I stared back. I didn't want to show him that I was scared. After a couple of minutes he dropped the hammer on to the floor with a clatter then turned and walked away. I could hear him muttering as he went.

I stood for a moment to gather myself then I felt a weird pain in my stomach. It felt like someone was twisting my insides. I ran to the bog and sat there for a while thinking that my bowels must need to empty but nothing happened so I stood up. But when I went to pull up my knickers I got the shock of my life. There were bloodstains all over them, deep-red blotches.

I quickly pulled up my trousers then ran to my room and lay on my bed, wondering how the hell I came to be bleeding.

That was five hours ago and I'm still here. The pain in my stomach has got worse and I feel hot and heavy, like there's a big stone wedged inside me. Sarge came in earlier and said he'd made some scran but I said I was feeling ill and couldn't face it. He muttered something about it being a waste of food but I think he could tell from the look of me that I was telling the truth.

Now it's dark and I'm lying here thinking. This is how it begins. Maybe this is how the dead mother in the desert went. I think back to what Sarge said about the war. 'There was all this blood. It was everywhere.'

As I write this the pain is getting worse and I imagine the blood getting heavier and heavier until it fills the bed, the room, even the lake. I need to sleep now, need to stop writing, stop thinking, because it's making me feel even more scared.

I hope you're listening to me, dead mother, and that you can hear my voice. If you could just look after me for one more night. Make the bleeding stop. And don't let me die.

15

Lisa

Warm air drifts through the room as I lie curled up with Joe beneath clean blankets. My hair smells of orange blossom, my teeth are clean, my breath is fresh. It feels like I'm dreaming but the weight of Joe in my arms proves otherwise.

We've both had warm baths. Our bellies are full. These are things most people take for granted and yet just a few hours ago I was panicking that I wouldn't be able to feed Joe. I watch him sleeping, his soft skin pink from the warm bathwater. If Isobel hadn't turned up this afternoon he would have gone to bed cold and hungry. I don't know what I would have done without her.

After locating the tin bath in the old outhouse we spent the next half an hour or so heating up kettle after kettle of lake water to fill the bath.

While we were doing that, Joe sat at the kitchen table with his head in his hands. Every time I tried to talk to him he would bang his fist on the table and demand that I take him back to Daddy. Isobel didn't say anything as we scurried back and forth between the stove and the tin bath that we'd set up in the front room but she must have wondered what was going on. She didn't ask any questions though, which I was thankful for.

After I'd spent the best part of forty minutes wrestling a kicking and screaming Joe into the bathtub Isobel was waiting in the kitchen for me with a cup of tea. While I drank it, she showed me how to use the stove, preparing the wood carefully so it catches and doesn't burn out quickly. Then she went out to the car and came back with clean blankets from her house and a cardboard box full of groceries.

'It's nothing,' she said when I protested that I couldn't possibly accept the groceries after all she'd done. 'It's just some leftovers from the church raffle.'

The sight of the box seemed to perk Joe up and he jumped down from the table to investigate.

'Presents!' he squealed, darting past me. 'Daddy left presents.'

Isobel looked worried but again she didn't say anything.

'No, these are from me, Joe,' she said, crouching down to face him. 'There's some wine gums in there too. If you're allowed them.'

She looked up at me and I nodded my head.

'Just a few though,' I said as Joe grabbed the bag of sweets from the box. 'We don't want to spoil your dinner.'

I'd already spotted some tinned baked beans in the box. Now the stove was working we could have them for dinner. There was also a box of candles, a loaf of bread, a bottle of sherry and some dried packet soups. It wasn't much but I was thankful for it.

After Isobel left I warmed up the baked beans and sat at the table with Joe to eat. At first he just continued to sit with his head in his hands but once he smelt the food he sat up and had a few mouthfuls. After two days of crisps, sweets and pre-packed sausage rolls it was a relief to see him eat something hot. For a few moments I let myself imagine that this was our home, our new reality: me and Joe, finally safe and free of Mark. But when he'd finished his mouthful of food, he threw the spoon down on the floor and started to scream. 'I hate you. Want Daddy. Don't want you.'

I went to speak, to offer words of comfort to him, to coax him, tell him that Daddy would be coming soon, but then something inside me disconnected. I couldn't do it any more. I couldn't carry on making excuses and dancing around Joe's moods like a boxer in the ring. I was tired, crazy tired, and I had no energy left for pleading and negotiating with a child who didn't want to listen. So I took his bowl, picked up the spoon from the floor and took them to the wooden tub that Isobel had found for washing-up. Taking the jug of lake water we'd collected earlier, I scrubbed the pots and tried to cancel out the noise of Joe screaming behind me.

Finally he exhausted himself and I carried him off to bed where I've been lying awake for the last hour. Despite the warmth and the full stomach, sleep just won't come. Every time I close my eyes I'm back in London, standing in the bedroom looking into the mirror as Mark comes up behind me. There's no escape from him, nowhere to truly hide.

I turn over and face the room. A sliver of moonlight through the curtainless window casts the room in a sickly bluish glow. Behind me Joe wriggles and mutters to himself.

'Shh,' I whisper. 'Go back to sleep.'

And then something odd happens. He stops wriggling and starts to laugh. It's a strange laugh, low and guttural, like it's coming from a man, not a child. I turn round to face him. His eyes are open.

'What is it, Joe? Why are you laughing?'

'It's Daddy,' he says, pointing past my head to the window. 'Daddy pulling faces at the window.'

I stare at him, my body rigid with fear.

'Don't be silly, baby,' I say, my mouth drying up. 'Daddy's not there.'

'He is,' he cries, his voice still light with laughter. 'Daddy at the window.'

I want to grab Joe and make a run for it but my body is frozen. I have my back to the window. If it is Mark out there he will be able to see me.

'Bye bye,' says Joe, waving his hands. 'Daddy gone now.'

Then he turns over and within minutes he's asleep. I lie next to him, my eyes wide open, my fists curled into balls, my brain repeating the same thing over and over again.

Mark is here.

I need to know. I need to see for myself. With a racing heart I get out of bed and make my way to the window. Moonlight exposes the garden. I see the empty cages, the broken plant pots, the remnants of a stone path. And then, just as I'm about to step away and dismiss the whole thing as a figment of Joe's imagination, I'm sure I hear the faint sound of a car engine starting up.

Could Joe have been right? Had there been somebody out there? But if it was Mark, where has he gone?

16

Soldier Number 1

Rowan Isle House, 27 August 2004 – 4 p.m.

Something good to report. After three days of stuffing newspaper down my knickers and scrubbing sheets at five in the morning the bleeding finally stopped last night. It disappeared as swiftly as it began.

So far I've managed to keep it from Sarge, though he did look a bit puzzled when he saw me wringing out my sheets for the third day in a row. I told him it was the August heat, that I'd been sweating in the night and wanted to freshen up the sheets. I don't know whether he believed me but he didn't say anything. That was good because the last thing I want to do is worry Sarge at the moment. He's in a bad way, that much is clear. His eyes are all black and bloodshot and his skin looks pale and clammy. I heard him talking to himself yesterday morning when I got up to wash the sheets. When I passed his room he was shouting out, 'Leave him be. Can't you see he's had it? Just leave the man be.'

I wanted to knock on his door and ask him if he was all right but I knew he'd just go mental so I walked away and left him to his monsters.

So the pain has gone, which is a good thing. But what's worrying me now is that whatever caused the bleeding must still be there inside my body, though

I have no idea what it might be. I had a look through Sarge's medical books but the sections on bleeding were all about battle injuries. And there was no mention of bleeding from down there. In fact, there was no mention of women at all. It seems that when it comes to war only men bleed.

6.45 p.m.

Everything is okay. I'm not dying.

I'M NOT DYING.

I needed to write that in capitals to make it real. I really thought I was heading for my grave, that something silent and invisible was killing me from the inside.

But then this evening when I was setting up the stall, Isobel arrived. My Isobel. She must have walked from the village because there was no sign of her dad or the car. I got a weird feeling in my chest when I saw her, a fluttery feeling like I was going to pass out. My hands started shaking too and I thought I was going to drop the eggs.

She wasn't wearing her school uniform this time. She was wearing a dress. White, with red poppies on it which for a moment reminded me of my bloody sheets. She said hello in that gentle voice of hers then asked if she could buy a dozen eggs. While I was putting the eggs into the box she asked me if I was okay. No one had asked me that question for such a long time and, after days of bleeding and worrying about Sarge, to hear someone ask that almost brought me to tears. I looked up at her, right into her eyes, and those eyes told me that this was a person I could trust.

And so I told her. I told her everything, about the pain and the blood and the sheets and how scared I was and how I thought I was going to die, and all the while I kept looking at those red flowers on her dress until they blurred in front of my eyes and I realized I was crying.

'It's okay.'

That's what she said to me. *It's okay.* And it felt like a warm blanket wrapped round your legs on the coldest day of the year. She put her arm on my shoulder and then she explained that what I'd experienced was something called menstruation and that it happens to all women once a month. She started hers two years ago when she was thirteen. 'Quite late really,' she said. I asked her why it happened and she said it's to do with the body getting ready to have babies. When she said this I panicked and said that I didn't want babies but she said the blood was a sign there were no babies there, and for that to happen I'd need to have sex, and then she kind of giggled and said, 'And I don't think you'll be doing that until you're a bit older.'

I nodded and said no I wouldn't be, though I didn't really know what she was talking about. Then she said that I had to make sure I was prepared next time. I'd need to go to the shop in the village and buy some sanitary towels and I said I didn't know what they were, and anyway, Sarge didn't like me going to the village and even if I did I had no money to get any of those things.

She smiled then and handed me four pound coins for the eggs, double what they cost. 'Take that,' she said. 'And put the change away for next month. You can use it to buy what you need from the shop.'

I knew I'd be disobeying Sarge if I went to the village but then I thought about the bloody sheets and my knickers stuffed with newspaper and I knew I had no choice. So I put half the coins in the money tin and half in my pocket then handed her the eggs.

'Thanks,' she said, putting the eggs into her bag.

It was a nice bag, a pretty drawstring one with flowers embroidered round the edges. I was about to compliment her on it when something amazing happened.

'Look, if you ever need to talk to someone,' she said, her voice all warm and gentle, 'come and say hello. Dad's out at the church most of the time and . . . there aren't many people my age around here. It would be nice to . . . hang out or something. You must get quite lonely living here.'

She wanted to be friends. This perfect girl actually wanted to be friends with me. I didn't know what to say. Then I heard Sarge call my name. I turned round and he was standing there in the doorway, his face all twisted.

'Can I help you?' he said, looking at Isobel.

'No, it's all right,' she said, her voice bright and happy. 'I was just paying for the eggs. My father says they're the best he's eaten. So well done, both of you. And the chickens, of course.'

She laughed then and I willed Sarge to smile too, to just be nice for once. But he carried on glaring at her, his eyes dark and brooding.

Isobel's smile disappeared then and she said goodbye. Sarge came over to the stall and we both watched her walk away, her pale hair glinting in the sun. As I stood there I felt free and happy, like the world had suddenly opened up. It was a strange feeling because it didn't have anything to do with being a soldier or following Sarge's instructions. In fact, ever since the bleeding I've felt different, like I've changed in some way that I can't quite identify. Maybe Sarge saw this change too because once Isobel had gone he looked at me and I saw something in his face that I'd never seen before.

Fear.

17

Lisa

11 December 2018

I turn over in bed and watch as the sky outside the window changes from charcoal to violet to a pale, sickly blue. I spent the night lying in one position, curled up round Joe's warm body, my head tucked next to his. Now my legs feel numb and stiff, and my eyes sting from lack of sleep. Mark. The name churns round my stomach like a piece of undigested food. Could it have been him at the window last night? I think about what I heard. I'm sure it was a car engine. But if it *had* been Mark at the window and he'd seen Joe then surely he would have tried to get in?

Without thinking, I reach down and grab my phone from my bag on the floor, forgetting that the battery is dead. I look at the black screen and realize the futility of the phone. What use is it, fully charged or not? I have no one to call, no one to help me.

Beside me, Joe stirs then sits bolt upright in the bed. His hair is matted with sweat. I gently rub his head, glad that he is waking, that I'm no longer alone with my dark thoughts.

'Good morning, angel,' I whisper, kissing his forehead. 'Did you sleep well?'

He looks at me and his face darkens.

'You go away,' he snaps, his voice croaky with sleep. 'I want my daddy.'

He pushes the heavy blankets back, jumps down from the bed and heads for the door.

'Where are you going?' I cry, stumbling after him. My legs feel like lead.

'Want Daddy,' he calls out from the darkness of the passageway.

'Daddy's not there,' I say, lowering my voice as I reach the hallway, half expecting someone to jump out at me.

Then I hear a noise, a low, persistent thud. I look up and see him. He's standing at the front door, smacking his head against the frame.

'Joe, don't do that,' I say, rushing to him. 'You'll hurt yourself.'

I try to prise him from the door but he elbows me away.

'Joe, please stop it, darling,' I say, terrified that he's going to seriously injure himself.

'Want Daddy,' he says as he stops abruptly and slumps on the floor. He looks worn out, defeated somehow.

I crouch down next to him on the floor and stroke his cheek. His skin is soft and warm, just like it was the day he was born. I will never forget the heat that emanated from him as they placed him on my chest. It burned through my skin and in doing so brought back to life something that had been slumbering inside me for so many years. Happiness. Pure, unconditional happiness. The kind I'd had as a child, when I'd sneak into my parents' bed and curl up behind my mother's sleeping form. There was no safer or warmer place, as far as I was concerned. I knew that happiness had stayed inside me, waiting to be reclaimed, and as I held my newborn son in my arms that morning I could feel it flooding through my body, nourishing it from within. The rest of that day is a blur to me now, though I vaguely remember Mark telling me to 'be careful with the baby's head' and his bullish mother warning me that I might find breastfeeding an awful bind so 'it might be best to ask for a couple of bottles of formula just to be safe'. Neither of them trusted me to make my own decisions. But I was so exhausted I didn't care. And, anyway, I knew I wouldn't need their advice. Joe was my baby. I knew instinctively what to do. Feed him, change him, comfort him, love him. Now, looking at him with his angry face and folded arms, I feel so removed from him he might as well be a stranger. How has it come to this, that my child, my flesh and blood, is pushing me away?

'Joe, listen,' I say, edging closer to him. 'We're definitely going to see Daddy soon but first we have to enjoy our lovely holiday.'

'Not holiday,' he cries, his eyes widening. 'There's no sand.'

I smile as I remember that trip to southern Spain. Joe dipping his toes into the sea for the first time, giggling as the waves came in.

'No,' I say. 'There's no sand here but there's a lovely lake and lots of . . .'

I stop myself. Here I am trying to reassure my little boy about this place when all I can think about is Mark standing at the window.

'Joe, do you remember what happened last night?' I say, trying to keep my voice light. 'Before we went to sleep.'

He shakes his head.

'You said you saw Daddy at the window,' I say, a shiver rippling down my spine as I say those words.

'Daddy?' he exclaims, his face lighting up. 'Daddy's here?'

'No, he's not here now,' I say, peering behind me into the dark corridor. 'But last night you woke up and said that you could see Daddy outside the window. He was making you giggle. Do you remember?'

'No,' says Joe, wrinkling his nose. 'Don't 'member. Will you get my breakfast now?'

'Of course,' I say, getting to my feet and taking him by the hand. 'Let's go see what we can find.'

It was a dream, I tell myself as we head to the kitchen. Joe was talking in his sleep. I used to do that all the time when I was young and it would scare the life out of my parents. My mum told me how she'd once come into my bedroom to say goodnight and found me sitting up in the bed with a demonic look on my face. When she asked if I was all right I asked her, in a very low, frightening voice, if she wouldn't mind opening the wall with the secret key. Mum said I looked like I'd been possessed but apparently I continued to do this for years right up until my teens. When she looked into it she found that some people suffer from waking nightmares, where they look awake but are still asleep and carrying on the dream as if in real time.

That must have been what happened with Joe last night, I tell myself as I fill the kettle with the last bit of lake water from the jug. He was dreaming. Mark wasn't at the window. Of course he wasn't. Yet the more I tell myself this, the more I think about the footsteps and the car engine, and the less I believe it.

'Now, Mr Joe,' I say as I light the stove and put the kettle on to boil. 'How do you fancy a lovely bowl of porridge?'

I turn round. He's not at the table.

'Joe,' I call, running into the hallway. 'Where are you, Joe?'

He's not in the living room. Maybe he's gone back to bed. I try to stem the fear that is rising up inside me as I walk back down the corridor, past the dark staircase, towards the bedroom.

'Joe,' I call. 'Come on, baby, don't scare Mummy like this. Where are you?'

The bedroom door is closed. I push it open. The bed is just as I left it, the blankets tossed aside as I ran to stop Joe from hitting his head, my redundant phone lying on the floor. But there is no sign of Joe. I go to the window and look out at the overgrown garden. The door of one of the filthy cages is blowing open and shut in the breeze. And then I see something: a shadow flitting across the garden. Joe.

I run out of the bedroom and back into the kitchen, throwing open the back door. It's freezing out here and he's only in his pyjamas.

'Joe,' I cry, stepping out of the door, my bare feet prickling with cold. 'Joe, where are you? Come on, baby, it's time for breakfast.'

I run through the long grass, past the cages and down towards the drystone wall that divides the garden from the hills.

'Joe!' I'm shouting at the top of my voice now. 'Please come back. Please.'

And then a chill courses through my body.

The lake.

I run round the side of the house, the sharp stones cutting into my feet. It starts to rain as I reach the lake and it bounces off the surface like bullets as I stagger with bleeding feet towards the edge.

'Joe!'

My voice is carried back to me. I look at the water, at the old broken boat bobbing listlessly from side to side. He can't be in there. He can't be. I only turned my back for a few seconds. I hear Mark's voice in my head. 'That's all it takes, Lisa, a couple of seconds. You fucking idiot. You stupid fucking idiot.'

The water blurs in front of my eyes as I stand frozen to the spot, tears clouding my vision.

What have I done?

Then I hear something. A scream. I turn on my heels but I can't see anything. Then I hear it again. It's coming from the side of the house.

'Joe,' I shout, running towards the sound, my shoulders lightening with relief as I realize he isn't in the lake. 'It's okay. Mummy's coming.'

There's no sign of him as I reach the side of the house but he must be here somewhere. I can hear his footsteps. When I get to the garden I call his name again, frantically now.

'Joe, this isn't funny. Come out now and stop playing.'

Up ahead, the kitchen door is still open. I hobble towards it, wincing with pain from my bleeding feet.

When I get inside I smell burning. I rush into the kitchen and grab the kettle from the hob. The water has almost boiled dry. Then I hear something rustling behind me. I turn to see Joe sitting at the table, just as he had been when I'd filled the kettle.

'Oh, Joe,' I cry, running to him. 'Where were you? I was so worried. You mustn't run off like that again. Do you hear me?'

Joe looks at me with a bewildered expression.

'Didn't,' he says, his eyes filling with tears. 'Was here.'

'Come on now, don't tell fibs,' I say. 'I'm not cross with you. I was just worried. You must never run away. Not here.'

'Didn't run 'way,' he shouts, the tears running down his face now. 'You said Mummy making porridge. Didn't run 'way. You did.'

18

Soldier Number 1

Rowan Isle House, 20 September 2004

I'm shaking as I write this because I have no idea what is
going to happen to me. Sarge has lost it completely and
it's all my fault.

The day started like a dream, a good dream that you
never want to end. I got up at seven and, as always, I went
over to the window to see if the world had changed while
I'd been asleep. Sarge says that life can turn on a heartbeat,
that you can be alive one minute, dead the next, and this
makes me nervous. That's why, ever since I was a kid, I
make sure to look out the window and check that nothing
bad's happened overnight. Then I can get on with my day.

All was as it should be when I looked out this morning.
The sun was shining on the lake and for a minute I thought
I saw the little figures dancing on the surface, the ones I
used to see when I was a kid. I've never known whether
they are real or whether I see them because I want to. I've
never told Sarge about them though. Like the vixen and
the image of the dead mother in the desert that I keep in
my head, those figures are my secret, something to hold
in my heart and treasure. Because that's the thing with
Sarge. He likes to get inside your head, control what's
going on. And I've let him do that all my life. But the
heart is different. 'Never say you know the last word about

any human heart.' Henry James said that in his book, *Louisa Pallant*. I borrowed that and *The Turn of the Screw* from the mobile library and though I found the story a bit complicated, and not as interesting as *The Turn of the Screw*, I loved that line so much that I just read it again and again until I'd memorized it. There was something about the sentence that felt like Henry James was talking directly to me and only me. I understand what he was trying to say because it's true, no one knows what goes on in my heart and they never will. I make sure of that.

Sarge likes to think he knows me better than I know myself but that's rubbish. He doesn't know the last word about my heart, he doesn't even know the first, which is probably why he did what he did today.

Where was I? I'm getting so muddled because I'm scared of what's to come and that makes it harder to think straight. Oh yeah, the figures. Well, I was standing by the window looking at them dancing and twisting when I heard someone whistle. I blinked because the sun had made white dots appear in front of my eyes, and then I saw her standing by the gate. Isobel.

She was wearing a white T-shirt, a blue pleated skirt and white sandals. Her hair was tied back so I could see her face properly. It's a lovely face. Her skin is so clear and light. Unlike mine. Mine's dark and oily and I've been getting horrible spots on my forehead recently. I can't imagine Isobel ever having spots or tangled hair or anything like that.

Anyway, I'm talking round things again. It's my nerves. I can hear Sarge banging about in the room next door. He's hammering something into the wall. If I just keep scribbling and thinking about Isobel then maybe I can block it out.

I stayed standing by the window watching her for a few moments. Then she waved her hand at me like she was beckoning me to come outside. I was a bit embarrassed because I wasn't dressed yet. I had a pair of Sarge's old army fatigues on and a grubby T-shirt that hadn't been washed for days. I didn't want Isobel to see me like this but I didn't want her to go away either. So I pulled my fingers through my hair and straightened my clothes as best I could then tiptoed past Sarge's room – he'd been out in the woods all night so would be asleep for another few hours – and went out to see Isobel.

She smiled so brightly when she saw me. I've never had anyone smile at me like that. It warmed me right through, like the sun on my face when I stand at the top of Harrowby Crag. Then she hugged me and that felt really weird. Nice weird but weird all the same. She asked me if I'd had another period and at first I had no idea what she was on about but then she said, 'You know, the bleeding.' The truth was I'd forgotten all about it but then I remembered her saying it happens every month and I realized that it was almost that time again.

She asked if I'd been to the village to get supplies and I told her I hadn't had a chance. That was true. Sarge has had me working hard in the house these last few weeks. She said that she thought that would be the case so she'd brought me some. Then she opened the bag she was holding and pulled out a blue box. 'You can have these,' she said. 'I've got loads of them.' She handed me the box and I read the word 'tampons' then 'light to medium flow'.

I had no idea what that meant. As far as I'm concerned flow is something a river does. I didn't show Isobel my confusion though. Instead I shook the box and held it to my ear. It sounded pretty hollow. Isobel looked at me funny when I did that so I stopped and tucked the box under my arm like it was the most normal thing in the world.

Then she asked me if I knew how to use them and I said I'd probably just do what I did with the newspaper and she said it wasn't quite that simple. I asked her what she meant and she smiled. Then she pulled me close to her and whispered something in my ear. I couldn't believe what she was telling me. I had to stick whatever it was in that box up my privates. I must have pulled a face then because she started to giggle and she looked so funny that I started giggling too and any worry I was feeling about the bleeding or Sarge's moods or whatever just disappeared into the air.

Even now the thought of Isobel laughing is helping me block him out. He's still hammering. What the hell can he be doing in there? I can't let myself think about it. I'll think about Isobel instead.

Well, after a minute or so she stopped laughing and she put her head to the side and looked out on to the lake. 'Do you ever go swimming in there?' she asked. The truth was I hadn't been able to bring myself to even look at the water after what Sarge did to me that day with the boat. I've been having nightmares, horrible vivid ones where I'm being held under the water and it's all black and I wake up gasping for breath. But I didn't tell Isobel this because she'd think I was a weirdo so I just said that I wasn't a very good swimmer. She smiled then and said that it was such a shame to have a beautiful lake right on the doorstep and not be able to use it, so how about we just have a little bathe. My heart sank when she said this because the last thing I wanted to do was get into that water, but she looked so happy and she'd been so kind bringing me the thingamabobs that I didn't want to let her down so I said, yes, I'd love to.

Isobel clapped her hands then and made a little whooping noise which I think meant that she was pleased. Then she started undressing. I stood there like a spare part trying not to look but I couldn't help noticing that she was wearing matching underwear: a pretty white lace bra and pants. And she had round breasts that filled her bra, not like mine that just sat there on my chest doing nothing. When she was ready she stood with her hands on her hips and told me to come on. What she meant was 'take your clothes off too' but I was mortified. My manky T-shirt and Sarge's old combats were bad enough but my underwear – if you can even call it that – was even worse. I tried not to catch Isobel's eye as I slowly pulled down my combats and yanked off my T-shirt to reveal a pair of baggy shorts and a vest.

I expected her to say something, ask me why, at my age, I wasn't wearing a bra, but she just smiled again, held out her hand and led me down to the lake.

When we got to the edge Isobel bounded straight in. She reminded me of the golden Labrador that got loose from its lead a few years back and jumped into the water. I remember Sarge and I looked out and saw a pair of red-socked ramblers running past our window, calling for the dog to stop. I'd run out too to see if I could help but when I saw the dog I stopped because it just looked like it was having fun. It didn't want to be on a lead following the usual path, it wanted to be free. That's what Isobel wanted too by the looks of her. I watched as she lay on her back with her eyes closed and let the water lap at her face. It was all so peaceful and so different to what had happened to me last time I went in that lake.

That's all I could think of when I stood at the edge of the water, those terrible few moments when Sarge held me under. I could taste the silt in my mouth, feel the panic and thudding in my chest, making my heart seem like it would burst. The water had been my punishment – now here was Isobel telling me that I should come and join her like it was a treat. None of it made any sense. In the end I think she realized that I was going to need a little more persuading and she came wading towards me, all heavy with water, and put out her hands.

'Come on,' she said. 'It's so lovely in here. Hold on to me. I won't let go. I promise you.'

And, unlike Sarge, she kept her promise. For ten minutes or so I held her hand as we floated across the surface of the water and I realized that I had become one of the figures, those magical beings that had visited me since I was a kid, who had put on little shows for me, dancing and twisting across the water. Those creatures weren't in my head but nor were they real – they were me. They had always been me. But not the me that traipses up the crag with Sarge or the me that stands peeling veg for hours on end, but the other me, the me that could maybe exist in the future or in some parallel world. The happy me.

It was the happy me that let the water cover my face and not get scared, that allowed Isobel to lead me to the deepest part of the lake and lie on our backs and float. And the happiness came about because I was with someone I trusted, someone I knew would never let me go under.

And then. I find the next bit hard to write so I'll do it quickly. Isobel and I were having so much fun that at first we didn't hear the shouting. I was lying on my back looking up at the perfect blue sky when I felt Isobel's body jerk upwards. I lifted my head and saw that she was looking across to the edge of the lake. I followed her gaze and that's when I saw him. He was standing by the old boat, his hands on his hips, and he was shouting my name so furiously I knew I had no choice but to swim back towards him.

I heard Isobel whisper something behind me, something like, 'It's okay. We were just swimming. It's not a crime.' But I knew when I saw him that I'd done something really bad. He looked terrible. His hair was all over the place and his eyes were red and puffy. He was still wearing his big army coat and his boots. But it wasn't his appearance that made me feel like I was about to face my judgement. It was the fact that he was holding his gun. And it wasn't his shotgun, it was his pistol, the one he told me he kept for protection, the one he only brought out when matters were deadly serious.

'What the hell are you doing in there?' he said, ignoring me and pointing the gun at Isobel, who was staggering out of the water behind me.

She was so scared she couldn't speak so I said that she was just cooling down, that it was such a hot day. But before I could finish my sentence he bent down and started picking Isobel's clothes off the ground.

'I don't want people like you corrupting my daughter, you hear me?' he said, glaring at Isobel.

Isobel had gone so pale I thought she was going to faint so I took her arm to steady her. When I did this Sarge went mental and threw the clothes at Isobel's head. Then he told her to cover herself up and get the hell off his land. She was shaking as she bent to pick them up and it was terrible to see. She'd been so kind to me. I wanted to tell her I was sorry, that I didn't mean for it to happen, that the few minutes I'd spent with her in the lake were the happiest I'd ever known, but Sarge was watching me and I knew if I said anything he'd start again with his raving and yelling. So instead I just stood there and looked at the ground while she pulled on her clothes.

She must have finished because I heard her whisper 'Bye', so I looked up. Her face was so sad. I wanted to hug her, to beg her to stay, but instead I just watched as she walked down the path towards the gate. There are loads of potholes on the path, Sarge is always saying he's going to fill them but never does, and as Isobel hurried away she stumbled on the uneven ground and fell over. Her body made a horrible thumping noise as she landed and I winced, feeling every bit of her pain. I wanted to go and help her, make sure she wasn't hurt, but as I made to go I felt Sarge's arm on mine. 'Leave her,' he muttered.

I turned to look at him. His face was all red and bloated, like some dead sea creature. I hated him at that moment, for how he had treated Isobel, for what he had done to me.

'Get in the house,' he said, keeping his eyes on the gate.

And I was so angry and full of hate that I did what I had never done before. I shook my head.

'I said get in the fucking house,' he said, turning to me, his voice a whisper.

His face was so close to mine that bits of beer-scented spit hit me in my eye. I wiped it with the back of my hand then told him that he had no right to tell me what to do, that Isobel was my friend and we'd just been having fun and, remembering Isobel's words, that it wasn't a crime.

He glared at me and started to sway on his feet and for a moment I thought I'd got through to him, that for the first time he'd been able to see that, yes, I may be an elite soldier in training but I am also just a kid, a kid who wants to have friends and go swimming in a cool lake on a warm day.

But I was wrong. I was very wrong. The next thing I knew I had a pistol held to my head. I could hear the blood bubbling inside me as he pressed it deeper into my temple. He didn't say anything, he didn't have to. I was terrified. I could feel the warmth of piss streaming down my legs.

'Please,' I whispered to him. 'Please don't kill me. I'm sorry. I swear I am.'

But he didn't move. He kept that gun to my head.

I closed my eyes, waited for the explosion, the pain, the darkness. My heart was racing and my throat felt like it was closing up. I didn't want to die.

Then, after what seemed like a lifetime, the pressure of the gun disappeared.

'Get the fuck inside and clean yourself up.'

I did as he asked then went to my room to wait for him. When he came in he still had the gun in his hands. I didn't want to look at him so I turned away and fixed my eyes on a black stain on the wall. It's just above where I sleep and it's been there since I was five years old when Sarge was teaching me to clean my boots with black polish. I remember I dipped my finger in the gooey mixture and tried to eat it. Sarge shook his head and told me that it wasn't meant for eating, it was made for polishing. I was a bit of a naughty kid back then so instead of going and washing my hand in the lake I just wiped it on the wall. When I did that Sarge didn't shout, he just told me to go and get a cloth and wipe it off. But I didn't do a very good job of it and it left a smudge. I remember Sarge saying that he would leave it there to remind me not to be insubordinate.

I was thinking about the old Sarge as I stood there waiting for him to speak, remembering how calm he used to be, still strict but fair. This new Sarge was dangerous and unpredictable and I didn't know how to deal with him.

He was quiet for a minute or so then he put his face up to my face and I expected him to yell. But instead he spoke in this really weird, low voice. 'From this moment on,' he said, 'you are no longer to be referred to as Soldier Number One. You have lost your rank and your liberty.' I nodded my head but because his face was so close to mine my nose rubbed against his. I remembered him doing that when I was little. I remember how he used to laugh and call me his 'funny girl'. My eyes started to well up as I thought about that but I quickly blinked the tears away before he noticed. 'You have committed a serious breach,' he went on, still in that weird voice. 'A breach that compromised the safety and security of your fellow officer and that of the barracks. Do you understand?' I should have said yes but I wanted him to know that Isobel meant no harm, so I said that he'd got the wrong end of the stick, that Isobel wasn't a threat to our safety, she was just a really sweet girl. He went quiet and I thought he must be coming round but then he stood back, lifted his gun and pointed it at my head again.

'I said,' he yelled, jabbing the gun into my forehead, 'DO. YOU. UNDERSTAND?'

I nodded my head and said yes, yes I did.

'You're to wait in this room until I come and collect you, is that clear?' he said.

I nodded again.

He stayed with the gun pointed at my head for a moment or two longer then he lowered it, turned on his heel and walked to the door. But as he went to open it he stopped and looked back at me.

'I suggest you spend this time thinking about what you've done,' he said coldly. 'Because tonight you're going to face your greatest test.'

He shut the door behind him and I carried on looking at the smudge on the wall for a couple more moments, trying to sponge his words and their meaning from my head. I tried to think of other things, happy things. I thought about Isobel but then that made me think about the look on her face when she was walking away from the lake, the horror and fear. Thinking about that was making me feel worse and I knew that the only way I could really calm myself was if I wrote it all down, so I went and sat on my doss bag and took this journal out from underneath it.

I should stop writing now but I find that using my hands stops them from shaking, though I know that what I'm writing is probably a load of nonsense and that nobody would be able to understand it if they picked it up and read it. But that's not the point. This book is for me, not for anyone else, so I'll carry on writing even though I can hear his footsteps coming down the corridor. I don't . . .

19
Lisa

It feels like something evil is in this house, some strange presence playing with my head and setting traps for me. It's impossible that I could have missed Joe sitting at the table unless he'd ducked underneath it as I turned, but that's unlikely as I would have sensed him being there. I swear there was just an empty space. He was gone. And what about the shadow in the garden? And last night when Joe thought he saw someone at the window. Though he had no recollection of that this morning. So is it me? Am I losing my mind?

I don't know what to think any more. All I know is that, after what happened this morning, I had to get out of that house for a while. So now Joe and I are in the car, parked up by the National Trust sign on the outskirts of the village. I've put *Where the Wild Things Are* on for Joe and he's chattering along merrily to the story. He seems happier now we're out of the house, less angry and agitated.

I grip the steering wheel and try to gather my thoughts. If only I had somewhere else to go besides that house, somewhere safe where Mark couldn't find us. But with limited funds even a basic hotel would only be possible for a few days and even then we'd run the risk of prying eyes, people asking questions. The house is our only option but I feel so vulnerable there. If only I could get my phone charged. I'm not going to call anybody but what if there's an emergency? Having the phone charged would make me feel safer.

Then I remember Isobel. She said she lived in the village, at the vicarage. Maybe she'd let me charge my phone at her house. At least then I'd have some peace of mind. And besides, I could do with some company. The events of the morning have left me shaken and Isobel was so helpful yesterday. I feel like I can trust her. I start up the engine and type the address into the satnav. She'd given me it as she left, telling me to pop in for a cup of tea if I was ever in the vicinity.

I crawl at a snail's pace through the village, noticing things now that I hadn't the last time I was here, like the tiny play park on the left-hand side opposite the pub. I spot a wooden climbing frame and a brightly coloured slide. The sight of it makes me feel desperately sad. Joe loves the slide at his nursery school. He should be back there now having fun and playing with his friends. Instead he's stuck with me, hiding out in some creepy house, terrified of every little sound.

The audiobook finishes as we reach the church. According to the satnav, Isobel's house is just behind the graveyard.

'Again,' cries Joe from the seat behind me. 'Play again.'

'We just need to go see the nice lady first,' I say as I stop the car outside a large Victorian house. 'Then we can listen to it again on the way h—'

I'm about to say 'home' then stop myself. Nothing about that house is remotely like a home. In fact, it's beginning to feel more like a prison.

'Right, mister, let's go,' I say, trying to keep my voice bright as I get out of the car and open the passenger door.

'Why we going see lady?' he says as I unclip his seat belt and lift him out.

'I just need to fix my phone,' I say, holding up the blank screen so he can see. 'Lady's going to help me.'

If Mark were here now he'd tell me off for speaking to Joe like this. He hated any kind of baby language, said it was detrimental to Joe in the long run. I hear his voice in my head all the time, like a running commentary, casting doubt and judgement on everything I do.

I take Joe's hand and try to put all thoughts of Mark to the back of my mind as I make my way towards Isobel's house. It's a very grand building with immaculate wrought-iron gates outside and bay trees on either side of the front door. I feel grubby as I open the gate, the stale smell of lake water clinging to my clothes like a second skin. I look down at Joe. There's a clump of jam from this morning's breakfast stuck to the front of his jumper. I bend down and try to scrape it off with my fingers but I end up smearing it even more.

'Oh, Joe,' I say as I stand up. 'Why can't you be a bit more careful?'

Joe scowls at me and I realize that is exactly what Mark would have said. Mark with his order and neatness and insistence that everything be in its correct place. Sod it, I think to myself. It's a bit of jam which, in the grand scheme of things, isn't the end of the world.

'Never mind, baby,' I say, stroking his soft face. 'Let's go and see the nice lady, shall we?'

He flinches at my touch and gives me a look that is so reminiscent of Mark it chills me. How can he have brainwashed my son so much? How twisted can one man be?

When we reach the door I run my fingers through my hair then ring the bell. The noise of it fills the air. It's an old-fashioned sound that reverberates like church bells. After a few moments I hear the key turning in the lock. When the door opens I gasp.

It's not Isobel standing there but a bent old man with bluish paper-thin skin. He's dressed all in black except for a white scarf wrapped round his neck. As I look closer I realize that I've seen him somewhere before. It's the vicar. I saw him standing outside the church when we drove into the village that first day.

'Yes?' he says suspiciously, probably in disgust at my messy appearance. 'Can I help you?'

'Erm, I was –' I say, my voice catching. The vicar is making me feel like Mark used to do, like an incompetent child. 'I was hoping to speak to Isobel if she's here.'

He looks stricken suddenly, the colour draining from his face.

'What do you want with Isobel?' he says, half closing the door.

'Oh, it's nothing serious,' I say, trying to calm him down. His agitated behaviour makes me think he might have some sort of dementia. 'My phone's gone dead and I've got no way of charging it in the place I'm staying so I wondered if I could charge it here.'

I hold my dead phone up and he looks at it with wide eyes as though it's an unexploded bomb.

'Isobel can't help you,' he says briskly. 'She's not here.'

'Do you know when she'll be –?' I begin, flinching as Joe kicks me in the back of my calf.

'Don't want to see lady,' he says, his voice hardening as it always does when he's about to have a tantrum.

'Shh, Joe,' I say, grabbing his hand and pulling him to my side.

'Sorry about that,' I say to the vicar whose face is now shadowed by the half-closed door. 'He can be a little monkey sometimes. I was just going to ask if you knew when she'd be back. Isobel.'

'No,' he says, his eyes bulging. 'No, I do not. She's not here and that's an end to it.'

He slams the door in my face and I stand for a moment trying to work out what just happened.

'Dementia,' I think to myself as I walk back down the path. 'Poor man.'

But as we make our way along the street towards the pub I see Isobel coming towards me. She's wearing a white dress with large red flowers printed across the top. It looks a few sizes too small and clings tightly to her hips. Her hair is loose around her shoulders and her eyes are ringed with smudged mascara, like she's been crying or asleep. She looks like a different person.

'Lisa,' she says, seemingly unperturbed by her appearance. 'Where are you off to?'

Her dishevelled state has thrown me so much that for a moment I don't know what to say so I just stand there looking at her.

'Lisa,' she says, raising her eyebrows. 'Are you okay?'

'Er, yes,' I say, taking Joe's hand. 'I just . . . I just went to your house because I wondered if I could be cheeky and ask if I could charge my phone. There's no electricity at the house, see, and I just thought –'

'That's no problem,' she says, placing her hand on my arm to stop me gabbling. 'I was just on my way back there.'

She pulls at my arm but I stay where I am.

'What is it, Lisa?'

'Well, it's just your dad answered the door,' I say, remembering the hostile look on his face. 'And he was a bit off with me. I don't think he wanted visitors.'

Her smile fades and she nods her head.

'Oh, poor Dad,' she says, looking over my shoulder in the direction of the house. 'He's not himself these days. He gets nervous over the slightest little thing.'

She leans towards me and a scent of cinnamon and clove floats across the air. It's a Christmassy scent that propels me back to my childhood kitchen in Highgate where my dad would spend the autumn months religiously adding more ingredients to his legendary Christmas cake.

'I'm attempting to make a Christmas pudding,' she says, lifting up the carrier bag she is holding. 'And I had to dash to town to get supplies. Though I think I've left it too late this year what with one thing and another. Still, you can never have too many cloves at Christmas, can you?'

'They smell lovely,' I say, rubbing my arms to warm myself up.

'Oh, you're freezing,' she says with a frown. 'Come on, let's go up to the house and charge that phone for you. Dad will be having his nap now.'

I reluctantly follow her back to the house, hoping that she's right and the old man is safely tucked up in bed. I can't face another encounter with him.

'It's this way,' says Isobel, unlocking a gate at the side of the house.

I follow her round to the back garden. I see a set of French doors up ahead. They remind me of the ones Mark had fitted in the kitchen. As we approach them an image blindsides me. A flash of glass, screams then sirens. I blink the memory away as Isobel slides the door open and we step into a very formal living room.

There are two green Chesterfield sofas on either side of an oblong oak coffee table. The walls are covered in framed prints of pastoral scenes but the room is dominated by a huge open fire. It crackles and spits as Joe and I stand staring at it in wonder.

'Sit yourselves down,' says Isobel. 'And I'll go get us some drinks. You can charge your phone over there.'

She points to a rather grand-looking desk. There's a plug socket on the wall above it.

'Thanks, Isobel,' I say, but when I turn to look she has already disappeared into the hall.

After I've plugged my phone in I lift Joe on to the sofa then take a look around. I feel uneasy in this house. There's a feeling of dust and decay about it despite its immaculate facade, as though it's been frozen in time. I try to repress a shiver as Isobel comes back into the room holding a blue-and-white-striped jar.

'Now, who would like a biscuit?' she says, holding the jar towards Joe. 'I've got Jammy Dodgers or choc chip cookies.'

Joe's face lights up as he delves his little hand into the jar and pulls out a Jammy Dodger. I look at Isobel and smile, though inside I feel wretched. How is a complete stranger able to deal with my own child so effortlessly when everything I do is wrong?

'Now if you take your biscuit in there,' she says, pointing to a door leading off from the living room, 'you'll find some books and toys from when I was a little girl. If you promise to be careful you can play with them. Would you like that?'

Joe nods his head and trots off happily, leaving me wondering if his bad behaviour is down to me.

'Right, let's get a drink for Mummy,' says Isobel. 'What would you like? Tea or coffee?'

'A coffee would be great,' I say wearily. 'I didn't get much sleep last night.'

I close my eyes as she goes to get the drinks. In my mind's eye I see snow, thick snow getting higher and higher. It's creeping under the doors and windows, filling the room, trapping me. I wake with a start as Isobel comes back into the room.

'Here we are,' she says, placing the coffee pot and assorted cups and jugs on the coffee table. 'Help yourself to milk and sugar.'

She sits down on the opposite sofa and pours a cup of coffee for us both. I try not to stare at her eyes as I take the cup from her. The strange thing is that she seems completely unaware of what she looks like. Part of me wants to tell her that her mascara is smudged but I feel I don't know her well enough to do that so instead I sip my coffee and pretend not to notice.

'You've got a beautiful house, Isobel,' I say, gesturing to the room. 'It must take some looking after.'

'It *is* a beautiful house but it's not mine,' says Isobel. 'It's my father's place. Though I've lived here all my life. My mother died when I was young and . . . well, Dad's quite frail and he needs me.'

'Oh,' I say. I try to focus on what she's saying but I can't stop looking at her face. It's so pale she's almost translucent.

She goes to speak but is interrupted by a sharp voice calling her name.

'Isobel. Is that you, Isobel?'

It's the vicar. I jump from my seat.

'I have to go,' I say, unplugging my phone and throwing it into my bag.

'Don't be silly. You can't dash off yet. Your phone's not fully charged,' she says, getting up slowly from the sofa. 'I'll just go and check on him.'

'Honestly, Isobel, I should go,' I say, feeling nervous now. 'He told me he didn't want me here.'

'It's fine,' she says, her face serene. 'Listen, how about we go for a proper drink at the Golden Lion?'

Every part of me knows I should say no, that going to the pub is a bad idea. But the thought of returning to the house with just Joe for company makes me feel ill. I need some adult company, some light-hearted conversation.

'Okay,' I say, smiling. 'That would be lovely.'

'Excellent,' she says. 'I'll just see if Dad's okay. I won't be a minute.'

She walks out and I stand up and head into the playroom where I'm met with a scene from every child's dream. There are floor-to-ceiling bookshelves stacked with books of all shapes and sizes, teddy bears and wooden building blocks scattered around the floor, and in the corner, in pride of place, stands the most beautiful doll's house I have ever seen. It has a pointed red roof and perfectly symmetrical windows; a shiny black door with ivy creeping round the top. And then I realize. It's a re-creation of this house, the vicarage. It must have been a present for Isobel when she was a child. What an amazing thing to be given. Your own house in miniature, your own life in doll form.

Then I hear chattering. I look round the back of the house and see Joe lying on his front. The back is opened up and there are a series of exquisitely decorated rooms. I recognize the living room, with its Chesterfield sofas and oak table. The bedrooms all have four-poster beds with embroidered silk curtains in blues and greens and pinks. I look down at Joe. He's holding a dark-haired doll in his hands.

'Now, dolly, find your friend,' he says, taking the doll and leading her up a flight of wooden steps. 'Dolly's sad.'

He pushes the doll through an arched doorway and into a tiny bedroom where a blonde-haired doll in a long white dress is sitting on a wooden chair.

'There,' says Joe, grabbing both dolls. 'Dollies have cuddles now.'

'Ah, you've found it.'

I turn round and see Isobel standing at the door. She's reapplied her make-up and is wearing a more casual outfit of jeans and a black woollen sweater.

'Do you want to help me tuck the girls up in bed, Joe?' she says.

Joe nods his head as Isobel comes towards him.

'This dolly go to bed,' he says, handing her the dark-haired doll. 'She tired.'

'Okay,' says Isobel, taking the doll and putting her in the bed with the blue curtains. 'That's it, Grace. You go to sleep now.'

She closes the back of the doll's house and looks up at me.

'Right. Let's go to the pub, eh?'

20

Soldier Number 1

Rowan Isle House, 23 September 2004

I've never felt so scared as I have these last few days. Even now it's over and I'm back in my bedroom with my journal my hands still shake when I think of it.

I remember waking up in a dark room, as dark as I imagine the bottom of the lake to be; a place where nothing can live or grow, where no light can get in. And it was hot, so hot that I was wet all over with sweat. The darkness and heat made me feel dizzy, like I was spinning in the air above myself. After a few minutes I started to feel a terrible ache in the back of my head. When I put my hand to it I had felt a lump, the size of an egg, though I had no idea what happened. Maybe I'd fallen. That must have been it. When Sarge came into my room while I was writing I must have got such a shock that I fell over, hit my head on the ground and knocked myself out. That's the only explanation because he can't have hurt me. Not Sarge. Anyway, keep writing. Keep writing it down. That's what I need to do. It might not make any sense but just feeling the pen scratching at the paper is making me feel better.

So where was I? Woke up. Lump the size of an egg. That was it, I woke up with a terrible pain in my head and saw that I was lying in the middle of the floor in this strange room. After a while the darkness lifted and sunlight came pouring in. It seemed to be coming from above me, though when I looked up I couldn't see a window. The ceiling was very high and there was a thick ledge running all the way round the top of the walls. The window must have been hidden behind the ledge. That's what I reckoned.

I thought I was alone cos it was so quiet but then, as I came to, I saw Sarge. He was sitting on the floor in the corner of the room with his knees pulled up to his chest. I noticed he had his army uniform on, his proper one, the one he keeps in a special bag hanging up in his cupboard. I'd never seen him wearing it before. I wanted to ask him why he had it on but before I got the chance he stood up and came towards me.

'You know why you're here, don't you, girl?' he said. He put his hands on his hips and kind of spat out the word 'girl' like it was a dirty word, which in a way it was because only a few hours earlier I'd been Number 1, a soldier, one of the elite. Now I was nothing but a girl.

At that point I had no idea why he'd brought me here so I shook my head in answer to his question. When I did that he laughed but it wasn't a funny laugh because his eyes were cold.

'You have been brought here because you have committed a serious transgression,' he said. 'What do you have to say for yourself?'

I realized that he was talking about Isobel again and I knew that I should apologize for swimming in the lake with her, tell him what he wanted to hear, but I just couldn't do it. I couldn't betray Isobel like that, say that she wasn't important to me, because she was. She is. So I just sat there and said nothing.

Then Sarge put his head down and made this weird humming noise that went on for several minutes. It got louder and louder then he stopped and looked up at me. 'Well, your silence speaks volumes,' he said. 'So I'm afraid you've left me no choice.'

He stared at me for a few moments then his eyes softened and he looked sad, sadder than I'd ever seen him before. He carried on staring at me, like he was willing me to speak. But I couldn't. My throat was so dry and tight that even if I'd wanted to I wouldn't have been able to get the words out.

Then, keeping his eyes on me, he stood up and said: 'Interview terminated at sixteen hundred hours. You fool. You stupid little fool. You have no idea what you've just done.'

He whispered the last bit and shook his head. Then he turned and walked towards the door. When he got to it he looked up at the ceiling and muttered, 'Forgive me.'

I don't think he was talking to me because he never looked back at me and I wondered if he was hearing the voices, whether they had got inside his head again. I didn't know and I couldn't ask him because after that he opened the door, stepped outside and locked it behind him.

21

Lisa

The pub is empty when we arrive save for a couple of elderly men standing at the bar nursing pints of the local ale and grimacing at the Christmas hits medley playing in the background. It feels strange to be in a pub, to be anywhere halfway normal, anywhere that isn't the house. I've been there barely two days and already I feel like it's the only world that exists. I can smell it on me as Isobel leads us to a table by the window; a mix of dead animal, damp and something else, something bad. I try not to think about it as we take our seats but the smell remains lodged in my nose.

'Right, what will you have to drink?' asks Isobel, clapping her hands together. The noise makes Joe look up. When he sees it's Isobel making it, he smiles.

''Gain,' he says, clapping his own hands together. 'Do it 'gain.'

Isobel does as he asks once, twice, three times, then gives up and tells him she'll die of thirst if she goes on clapping. This makes Joe laugh even more. He's taken a real shine to her. I should be happy that Joe is finally relaxing but why can't it be me who makes him smile instead of this stranger?

'So, what are we having?' says Isobel, standing up and pushing her blonde hair behind her ears.

'I'll just have a Diet Coke,' I say. 'And Joe will have an orange juice, please.'

'Can I not tempt you with something a little stronger?' says Isobel, wrinkling her nose. 'It is Christmas after all. Or at least it will be soon.'

'Okay,' I say, relaxing a little. 'I'll have a white wine. A small one.'

'Great,' she says with a smile. 'And would Mr Joe like some crisps?'

'Cripps,' cries Joes, clapping his hands together again, all memory of Mark and his rigid dietary rules evaporating. 'Cheesnunion.'

'Cheesnunion, good choice,' says Isobel. 'They're my favourites too. Right, won't be a sec.'

I watch her as she walks over to the bar. She looks elegant, even in just casual jeans and sweater. Strange to think that less than an hour or so ago she was standing in the street in an ill-fitting dress and smudged make-up. But then she hadn't been expecting us and, anyway, I'm not really in a position to talk. I look down at my creased clothes, the smell of damp rising off them, and try to imagine what Mark would say if he saw me. 'Jesus, Lisa. Ever heard of an iron?'

I feel his eyes on me as I sit in this unfamiliar place, judging me, waiting for me to slip up. I look at Joe as the opening bars of 'Merry Christmas Everybody' strike up and I remember Mark's face bearing down on me as I desperately tried to untangle the fairy lights to put on to the Christmas tree, remember what I'm running from. A bit of damp and a weird house is a small price to pay for freedom, surely?

'Do you like this song?' I say, tapping my fingers on the table and singing along with Noddy Holder. Joe scowls at me. I obviously don't have Isobel's touch.

'Nice rendition.'

I look up. The man we met in the shop the other day is standing holding a tray with our drinks on. There's no sign of Isobel.

'I don't think we've been formally introduced,' he says, setting the tray down on the table and handing Joe his crisps. 'I'm Jimmy. I run this place.'

'Oh,' I say, just wanting him to go away. 'Nice to meet you properly. It's a lovely pub you've got here.'

'Don't lie,' he says, his top lip curling into a smirk. 'It's a bog-standard Yorkshire boozer. Bet you're used to more classy affairs where you come from. Where did you say that was again?'

'She didn't,' says Isobel, squeezing past him to get to her seat. 'Now, Jimmy, what did I tell you about badgering newbies? Lisa's just come out for a quiet drink.'

'Sorry, I'm being nosy,' he says, his eyes still firmly on me. 'But you'd tell me if you minded, wouldn't you?'

I take a sip of my drink, ignoring his question.

'Isobel tells me you're staying up at Rowan Isle,' he says, leaning forward so that I can smell the peppermint on his breath.

'That's right,' I say, gulping down my words.

'For a holiday?' he says, his voice incredulous.

'Er, yes,' I say, my voice trembling.

I feel like I'm back with Mark, being tested and found wanting.

'Strange time of year to take a holiday,' he says. 'Especially with a little'un. You staying for Christmas, I take it?'

'I . . . well, I'm not sure,' I say, my chest tightening. 'I haven't really . . . we'll have to see.'

'Come on, Jimmy,' says Isobel, noticing my shaking hands. 'That's enough questioning, eh?'

'Forgive me,' he says, holding his hands in the air. 'Like I said, I'm a nosy beggar. But I must say, I don't blame you for being on edge. I'd be the same if I had to stay in that house after everything that went on there.'

'What do you mean?' I say, putting my drink down.

'Jimmy,' says Isobel sternly. 'Enough, eh?'

She gestures to Joe, who is sitting on the banquette next to me, munching his crisps.

'Hey, Joe,' she says, holding out her hand towards him. 'Would you like to meet Big Tom?'

Joe shakes his head and Isobel pulls a face of mock horror.

'You don't want to meet Big Tom?' she says, her eyes widening. 'The lovely marmalade cat? He's just over there by the fire keeping warm but I know he would love to have a cuddle from you.'

'Pusscat,' says Joe, jumping up from his seat and sending the crisps flying. 'Go see pusscat.'

'Okay, darling,' I say. I go to stand but Isobel has already swooped him up.

'I'll take him,' she says. 'You stay there and enjoy the peace.'

I smile, hearing Joe's excited chattering as they walk towards the fire.

'Not a big drinker, eh?' says Jimmy, gesturing to the glass of wine I've barely touched.

'Not really, no,' I say.

I glance across at the fire where Joe is sitting on a stool with a fat ginger tom perched on his knee. Isobel leans forward to tickle the cat's chin and Joe lets out a squeal of contented laughter.

'Well, that's certainly a rarity around here,' says Jimmy with a smile. 'Not that I'm complaining cos if this lot didn't like their drink I'd be out of a job.' He gestures to the room. It's got busier since we arrived and the young barmaid is looking frazzled as a group of elderly men bark their drinks orders at her.

'So, where were we?' says Jimmy, seemingly oblivious to the chaos ensuing behind him.

'You were telling me about the house,' I say. 'About something that happened there.'

'Oh yeah,' he says, folding his arms and leaning forward. 'Well, I don't like to alarm you but Rowan Isle House has a dark history. So dark that it's known locally as the House of Horrors.'

I look at him, try to read his face for a sign that he is joking, but his expression is deadly serious.

'What happened?' I say, shivering as the door opens and a gust of freezing air drifts in along with a middle-aged couple in puffa jackets and hiking boots. I keep my head lowered, glad we're tucked away in a corner.

'A bloke got murdered,' he says, lowering his voice.

My mouth goes dry as he tells me how this man, an ex-soldier, had moved to Rowan Isle House with his young daughter in the early nineties.

'He'd fought in the first Gulf War,' he says, drumming his fingers on the table. 'High ranking, so they say, maybe even SAS. But he'd lost his mind. Isobel says how he was known locally as a madman on account of him wandering into the village and waving his gun around. Nowadays I guess he'd be diagnosed with PTSD but back then he was just the local nut job.'

I look down at the table, memories of that room and her gentle voice swirling round my head. Then I recall the name the others had for her: the nut job. But she was my friend. Why had she not told me about this? About her past?

'The girl was troubled,' he says, raising his eyebrows to emphasize the point. 'Feral even, some might say. The father had kept her holed up in that house, wouldn't let her mix with other kids. She was basically a prisoner.'

The word slices into my spine as thoughts of a darkened room and a feral girl lying on a bare bed, shouting expletives to the ceiling, creep unbidden into my head. Stop, Lisa, I tell myself, don't let them in, whatever you do, don't let those thoughts in.

'Anyway, one night, just before Christmas, the girl snapped,' says Jimmy. He clicks his fingers and the noise makes me jump.

'Snapped?' I say, trying my very best to remain calm. 'What do you mean?'

'She killed him,' says Jimmy, his voice deadpan. 'Guess she must have had enough of it all. Apparently, the police found her shut up in a room in the house, muttering away to herself about how she'd shot him. His body was never recovered but police found his blood soaked into the snow in the woods and it was all over her clothes too. People say when they brought her out of that house she didn't look human. She looked like some kind of rabid animal.'

'What . . . what happened to her?' I ask, though I already know the answer.

'The girl?' says Jimmy, drumming his fingers on the table again. 'She confessed to killing her father and ended up in some place for young offenders. After they took her away, they shut up that house and no one ever set foot in it again until you turned up a few days ago. Mind, some of the kids from the village go up there for a dare on Halloween to scare themselves shitless. And there've been "sightings" of the madman over the years too. Some say he haunts the crag above the house, others say they've seen his shadow in the window of the house. It's all nonsense though, daft small-village banter designed to put the frighteners on people. Nothing for you to worry about.'

He looks at me as though expecting me to respond but I'm distracted by the sound of a woman screaming. I jump, staring wildly around the room, but nobody else seems to be hearing it. It's then I realize that the screaming is coming from inside my head. I've returned to that room, that dark place. Beside me, Jimmy starts to tell me about the party he's planning for New Year's Eve but his voice is drowned out by hers and I'm back there, lying on the bed, hearing her scream over and over again.

'I'm sorry, I have to go,' I say, getting up from my seat. 'It's past Joe's bedtime.'

'Are you okay, Lisa?' says Jimmy. 'What is it?'

I ignore him and weave my way round the table, almost knocking it over in my haste to escape.

'Joe,' I call over the mush of Christmas songs that seems to have got steadily louder. 'Come on, baby, time to go home.'

I see his blond head on the other side of the room. He's still sitting by the fire with Isobel beside him. I call his name again as I approach and they both turn to face me. I know I'm drawing attention to myself but I can't help it.

'Playing with Tom,' he says with a frown. 'Don't want to go.'

He gestures to the large ginger cat that is reclined on his lap. Its yellow eyes are half closed and I can hear it purring. The purring seems to grow louder as I approach until it becomes unbearable, like an attack of tinnitus.

'Joe, we have to say bye to Tom now,' I say, my eyes strangely drawn to the fire. 'It's way past your bedtime.'

Isobel gets to her feet but as she does I see a glimmer of flame behind her, hear the crackle of the logs as the fire consumes them, and suddenly I see myself, two years earlier, lying in that strange room while the woman I thought was my friend tells me about the house by the lake, the safe place that is mine if I need it.

My body starts to tremble. I hear Isobel asking me if I'm all right, if I want a glass of water, but I don't answer. Instead I grab Joe from the stool, upending the sleeping cat, who cries with contempt as it hits the ground.

'Pusscat,' yells Joe, thumping me in the chest as I march towards the door. 'You hurt pusscat!'

Ignoring his ranting, I yank the door open and head out into the freezing night, cursing myself for leaving the car parked outside Isobel's house, for letting her persuade me to go to the pub.

'Want see pusscat,' yells Joe as I run with him towards the vicarage, its pointed roof a black silhouette against the purple night sky. 'You hurt him. He was my friend.'

'Tom will be fine,' I say, grappling to locate my keys in the deep folds of my coat pocket. 'Cats always fall on their feet.'

Joe mutters something at me as I place him on the pavement and point the keys, which have got twisted up in my pocket, at the car. As the lock releases I hear footsteps coming from the direction of the church.

'Come on, Joe,' I say, opening the back door. 'Let's get out of the cold.'

'Bye bye.'

I turn on my heels. Joe is standing with his back to me, waving his hand.

'Joe?' I say, spinning him round. 'Who are you talking to?'

'Saying bye bye,' he says, rubbing his tired eyes with the back of his hand. 'To the man.'

I look up, my stomach twisting with fear, just in time to see a figure, small and hunched, disappear into the darkness.

22

Soldier Number 1

'Open your eyes!'

The shock of his voice made me jump. I turned and tried to salute but my legs wobbled and I almost fell over.

Sarge was still dressed in his best uniform and he'd had a haircut. It was like we'd switched roles: he was now the elite soldier and I was the straggly-haired mess.

'Turn round,' he commanded.

At first I was confused. I didn't know which direction he meant so I turned to face the wall. Then I felt his hands on my shoulders and he spun me round and pushed me towards the other wall, where, I noticed for the first time, a mirror was hanging.

'What do you see?'

'I see me, Sarge.'

'You?' he said, a weird sneer creeping across his face. 'And who might you be?'

I told him that I was his daughter, Soldier Number 1.

When I said this he grabbed my shoulders with both hands and pushed me closer to the mirror so that my face was touching the glass.

'Really?' he said, with spit spraying from his mouth. 'That's what you are? Is that right?'

I nodded my head. I didn't know what he was talking about. Who else would I be?

'See, I always thought that's what you were,' he said, holding the back of my hair in his fist. 'And that's what you'd always be, but yesterday you showed me you were something else. That you weren't a good soldier any more.'

I told him that I was a good soldier, that I'd always done as he asked, that it was just a swim, an innocent swim, that I was still a good soldier.

When I said this he pulled me back by my hair so I was about half a metre away from the mirror. I could see myself clearly. My face was red from where he'd dragged my hair back and my eyes were swollen from crying.

'Now listen to me,' he said, pressing his mouth to my ear. 'I put this mirror in here so you could have a good look at yourself, ask why you succumbed to temptation, why you let the enemy get inside your head. Does that look like a good soldier, eh?'

He jabbed his finger at the side of my head as he said this.

'Well, does it?'

I shook my head.

'No,' he said, letting go of my hair. 'No, it doesn't. Now I want you to sit there and take a long, long look at yourself and see if you can see the mark of the enemy on you.'

He gave me a shove and I slumped to the ground. Then he came up behind me and pulled me to my feet. He said that what he was doing was fair, and that any good soldier needs to take their punishment graciously. I had no idea what he was on about but then I saw he had a line of rope wrapped round his arm. He slowly unloosened it and then, grabbing both my hands, he tied the rope round them tightly. I asked him why he was tying me up, said that I wasn't going anywhere, but he just ignored me. The mirror was directly in front of me, and as I twisted my arms and begged for release Sarge kept telling me to look at that mirror, to see if I could find the good soldier.

All the while I cried out, begged him to stop. I had no idea why he was doing it. What had I done wrong? He'd never been like this before. Even when I'd played up as a kid, the worst I'd got was a slap round the ear, never this. Never this.

After a while my arms started to go numb and this scared me. I begged him to untie the rope but he just ignored me and walked to the other side of the room. After a few minutes he started talking but he didn't sound like Sarge. His voice had changed. It was like some demon had got inside him.

He told me that the world as I knew it had changed. Out there, out in the village and beyond, across the country, everything had gone to dust. It was just him and me. We were the only ones left.

What he said seemed to come in and out, like waves, his voice loud then soft, muffled then clear, so I just caught certain words. Twenty-four hours. All gone. Despots. Time of reckoning. Illegal war. He said that bit over and over. Though I didn't know which war he was talking about: the war in the desert or a new war, one that had just begun out there, that had turned everything to dust. It certainly sounded illegal. But then he said other things.

Sweeping it clean. 'I'm sweeping it clean', that was it. Then he said her name. Isobel. Said she'd gone too. And her criminal dad. I wanted to know where she'd gone but I didn't dare ask. Then he started talking about religion and he got all agitated. 'Death to the zealots,' he cried. 'Death to the lot of them.'

By this point my arms had gone so numb it felt like they'd disconnected from my body. I tried to focus on Sarge's voice cos it was the only solid thing. And then, all of a sudden, it stopped. He stopped. I heard his footsteps on the stone floor and then he began to untie me. My arms were like jelly and flopped by my side. Sarge just stood there, looking at me. His face was completely blank. It was like he was looking at a stranger. I wanted him back. I wanted my dad back.

'Sarge,' I said, my voice trembling with nerves. 'Can we . . . can we stop now? I've learned my lesson. I promise you I'll never do it again.'

I was saying what he wanted to hear, not what I believed because I didn't know what lesson I'd needed to learn or what I'd done wrong. But I didn't want to stay in that room. I wanted to get out and see what had happened outside, see if Isobel was all right.

Maybe he read my mind because instead of letting me out he just shook his head and said I had to carry on looking in that mirror to remember who I was and what I could become. 'What are you?' he cried. 'A good soldier or a sheep? It's your choice.'

He left me then and I lay curled up on my side staring at myself in that bloody mirror. As the hours passed I memorized every little bit of my face: the dark eyes swollen with tears, the long nose with the bump at the bridge, same as Sarge's, the lips chapped from lack of water. But though I stared and stared as hard as I could, what I saw wasn't a good soldier or a sheep. I saw me, a scared little kid, crying for her daddy to come and set her free.

In the end he did come. He brought with him a plate of bread and dripping and a mug of tepid water. I was so famished I wolfed it down within seconds, almost choking as I stuffed it into my mouth. When I'd finished I told him once again that I'd learned my lesson. I even lied and said that I'd seen a good soldier in that mirror, seen the person I had been and the person I still could be. I told him that I was ready to leave this place, ready to get back to normal, but he just shrugged his shoulders, picked up the empty plate and cup, and headed for the door.

I screamed then, begged him to let me out, but it was hopeless. I knew that by the expression on his face when he got to the door and turned to look at me.

'I'm sorry,' he said, his voice all husky and quiet. 'But I'm afraid I can't let you out. You see, this is just the beginning. And believe me, girl, you're going to wish that you'd never been born.'

23

Lisa

12 December

When I wake up I see a circle of light on the ceiling. It flutters from side to side, hovering but never settling on any one spot. My head aches. I check the time on my phone. It's 1 p.m. We've slept in.

I lie there for a while, watching the room turn pink with the winter sun, but then Joe wriggles beside me.

'Too hot,' he says, kicking the covers off. 'Can have drink?'

I'm just about to answer when there's a knock at the front door.

'I get it,' cries Joe, and before I can stop him he's out of the bed and running out of the room.

'Joe,' I shout, leaping from the bed on to the freezing stone floor. 'Joe. Wait for me.'

I walk down the corridor, the events of the previous evening flashing in front of my eyes like images on a projection screen: Isobel's strange father cowering behind the door, the fat ginger cat purring before the fire, Jimmy, the screaming and those words I've tried to block out ever since hearing them: 'She killed him.'

I hear voices as I reach the hallway. Who can it be?

'Lisa?'

I look up. Isobel is standing at the front door. She's wearing a black woollen winter coat and a thick baby-pink scarf. In her hands she holds a box of eggs.

'Oh, hello,' I say, looking behind me to see where Joe has got to. 'I'm sorry, I was just . . . Did Joe let you in?'

'Yes,' says Isobel, smiling. 'He's gone to have a play in my car.'

I step to the door and look out. Joe is sitting at the wheel of the car, making an almighty noise sounding the horn.

'I should bring him in,' I say, my head beginning to throb.

'Oh, he's having fun,' says Isobel. 'Look at his little face.'

She's right. He's beaming with happiness. After being cooped up in this house these last few days, anything would seem like fun, even a boring old car horn.

'I just popped over to see how you were,' says Isobel, cradling the box of eggs to her chest. 'I was a bit worried about you last night, the way you rushed off from the pub like that.'

'Rushed off?' I repeat, my voice competing with the blaring noise of the horn.

'I thought Jimmy might have scared you with his silly talk,' she says, rolling her eyes. 'Honestly, he can be a bit much at times.'

I think back to the previous evening and the woman Jimmy says is a killer. My friend. A murderer. I still can't make sense of it. Then I remember leaving the pub, trying to get Joe into the car and hearing him say 'bye bye' in that strange voice.

'There was someone . . .' I begin, recalling the dark figure I saw disappearing up the street. 'Someone watching . . . I –'

'Lisa, you don't look well. Why don't you come inside and sit down?' says Isobel, guiding me back into the house. 'I'll make you a cup of tea.'

I feel disorientated as I walk into the kitchen and sit down at the table, like I've been floating above everything and am only now coming down to land. I watch as Isobel takes a box of matches from the shelf under the window.

'This will take a few minutes to get going,' she says as she lights the stove. 'Gosh, it's like an ice box in here.'

I look down at my palms. They are hot and clammy. My head feels wet with sweat. How can that be when it's mid-December and I've spent the night in an unheated house?

'I was worried when I saw Joe at the door,' she says, smiling nervously. 'The fact that he'd opened it meant it was unlocked. It was a relief to see that you were okay.'

My cheeks redden with shame. How could I have been so stupid as to leave the door unbolted? I shudder as I think about what could have happened. What if it hadn't been Isobel at the door? Christ, Joe could have been taken or he could have wandered off. What a fuck-up I am, what a complete and utter fuck-up.

'Anyway, let's get you that cup of tea,' she says, turning back to the stove.

I watch as she makes the tea, wondering what she must think of me. A frazzled mother who leaves the door open? Isobel can only be a few years older than me but I feel like an incompetent child next to her. That's certainly what

Mark thinks. And I've tried to prove him wrong but I just keep slipping up. Again and again and again.

'I'm sorry,' I say, my eyes filling with tears. 'I'm so sorry.'

'Hey,' says Isobel, putting the kettle down. 'Don't be silly. You've nothing to be sorry for. God, if forgetting to lock the door were a crime then I'd have been banged up a long time ago.'

She smiles then sits down at the table next to me.

'I'm just so ashamed,' I say, putting my head in my hands. 'I really am. You must think I'm a complete idiot.'

'No, I don't,' says Isobel, placing her hand on mine. 'What I think you are is a mum. A mum who's trying to look after a boisterous little lad all on her own and who would rather die than ask for help. Am I right?'

'Yes,' I whisper, tears welling in my eyes. 'It's just been so . . . so . . .'

'You don't have to say anything,' says Isobel. 'We've all been there. Divorce, separation, whatever, they take their toll, mentally and physically. It's why my dad, bless him, counsels young couples for months before they get married. He wants them to be sure they're making the right decision because, if not, it's a hell of a battle getting out of it once you've tied the knot. I've seen women lose their mind over it. Throw in a little one and the stress alone is enough to kill you.'

She looks at me intently for a moment and I avert my eyes. No matter how kind Isobel is, I can't risk telling her why I'm really here. It's too dangerous.

'I should go check on Joe,' I say eventually, getting up from the table. 'The car horn's stopped.'

'I've locked the doors,' says Isobel, putting her hand into her pocket and pulling out her car keys. 'Here, catch.'

She throws the keys. I reach out to catch them but they drop on to the stone floor with a clatter.

'Oops,' says Isobel as I stoop to pick them up. 'I don't know about tea, we need to get some coffee into you.'

I smile but inside I feel unsettled. I want to be alone so I can clear my head. If only I could get my strength back then I could think about what to do next.

I hear Isobel pour the tea as I go out into the hallway and open the front door. My head throbs as I step on to the uneven tarmac and I feel heavy and lethargic, the result of too much sleep. A shaft of sharp winter sun falls on to the car window. I squint as I approach, temporarily blinded by the light. It's eerily quiet. No murmur from Joe as I point the key fob at the car and push the button. It unlocks with a click. I'm right next to the door but as I go to open it an old memory returns to me.

I'm putting Joe into his car seat in the back of the car. It's a freezing-cold day and he's wearing his snowsuit, which is so thick I'm finding it hard to secure the seat belt properly. When I finally get it closed I hear Mark's voice behind me. 'Are you sure you should be taking him to the pool in this weather, Lisa?' I remember turning round and seeing his face, that familiar look of mistrust cast across it. I'd told him that the pool was heated, that it would be good for Joe to have a swim, though actually it was me who needed to get out of the house and lose myself in the water. 'Are you sure you haven't forgotten anything?' he'd said with a strange smile on his face. 'Anything at all?' I'd shaken my head, impatient with him

166

now. I just wanted to get to the pool. Then he'd laughed and pulled my purse out of his pocket. 'Wouldn't get very far without this, would you? Honestly, Lisa, you'd forget your head if it wasn't screwed on, wouldn't you?' He'd held my wrist then and I'd pulled away, grabbing my purse and putting it into my bag where I was sure it had been when I left the house. It seems in my haste to get away I must have left it behind. As I'd closed the door I could sense Mark putting another black mark next to my name, another reason why I needed him to keep me right.

A sharp noise interrupts my thoughts. Joe is pressing the car horn again. I try to shake off the memory but, as I open the car door, the twisted feeling in my stomach, the one I always get when I think about Mark, remains.

'Hello, beautiful boy,' I say to Joe, who is resting his head on the steering wheel. 'Shall we go inside and get a nice hot drink?'

He turns to look at me and his face darkens.

'You go away,' he yells, pressing his fist on the car horn.

'Joe, stop being naughty,' I say, leaning in to prise his fist from the horn. 'That's not a nice way to talk to Mummy.'

'You're not Mummy,' he says, his face turning pink. 'You're bad person.'

At these words something inside me snaps. Almost four years' worth of pain and sadness, anger and grief come spilling forth and I grab him by both arms and haul him out of the car. He screams and yells, kicking his legs into my stomach and headbutting my chest. It takes every bit of strength to keep him in my arms as I stagger towards the house.

'Is everything all right? What's happened?'

I look up and see Isobel coming out of the door, her face stricken.

'Let go me . . . horble person,' screams Joe.

He launches one mighty kick that catches me in the abdomen. I lose my grip on him and we both tumble to the ground.

'My God,' shrieks Isobel.

I'm completely winded and a sharp pain slices into my leg where I hit the tarmac. I stumble to my feet. Joe, apparently unscathed, has run to Isobel and is cuddling into her.

'Are you all right, Lisa?' she says. 'That was a nasty fall.'

'I'm fine,' I say, brushing myself down.

Joe stares at me as I approach and as I look into his eyes I remember why I'd been so intent on getting to the pool that day. I imagine myself floating in deep water, all the pain in my body drifting away, and I know what I need to do.

'Can I ask a favour?' I say as Isobel stands looking at me, Joe's hand in hers.

'Of course,' she says. 'But I think you should come inside and clean up that knee. It's likely grazed.'

'It's fine, honestly,' I say, trying not to wince as the pain in my knee intensifies. 'Listen, Isobel, would you mind looking after Joe for half an hour? I've got a bit of a headache and . . . a walk might clear it.'

'Yes, of course,' says Isobel, her eyes narrowing. 'I've got some painkillers in my bag if you want some.'

'No thanks,' I say. 'The fresh air should help.'

'Are you sure?'

'Yep,' I say. 'Absolutely.'

'Okay,' she says, looking at me warily. 'Now, Joe. Shall we go and see if we can find some biscuits?'

Joe nods his head excitedly and I watch as they make their way back into the house, my shoulders lightening. Then I turn and start to walk.

24

Rowan Isle House, 27 September 2004

I have passed the test, that's what he just told me. I've passed the bloody test. And he thinks that matters. He thinks the fact I'm still here in body means I've come out of it okay but he's wrong. He's so wrong it's scary.

Because the truth is, something broke inside me while I was in that room, some vital part that can never be brought back and never be mended. My fingernails are still bleeding from where I scraped them on the rope, desperately trying to untie my wrists. My eyes are red and sore from lack of sleep. There was no chance of sleep in there because every time I closed my eyes I saw his face, not the face I'd grown up knowing, but the other one, the new one. It was a stranger's face. An evil face.

But I don't want to talk about that now. I never want to think about it again.

Before he let me out he put a blindfold on me and lifted me into his arms. I was so tired I fell asleep and when I woke up I was back in my own room, tucked up in my doss bag.

I say 'he' because that is what I'm going to call him from now on. That's what he is to me: a thing, a being; not a person and certainly not a sergeant. A sergeant has to earn the respect of his soldiers and I lost any respect for him when he put me in that room. I screamed and cried and begged to be let out but he just left me there like a rotten animal. So he will never be Sarge to me again. He is nothing to me. In fact, he may as well be dead.

Tonight, he came to my room and told me to come down to the kitchen as he had a surprise for me. I didn't want to go to the kitchen but I didn't want to risk another punishment so I got out of bed and went with him. When I stepped into the kitchen I saw he'd laid the table with proper plates and knives and forks and brought out a rib of beef from a cow he'd shot, presumably while I'd been in that room. I sat down and watched as he lifted it out of the oven and put it down on the table, the blood oozing out of it as he stuck the knife in, and I felt sick.

'You must be starving,' he said, piling up my plate with bleeding meat. 'Go on, get stuck in.'

And he smiled. He smiled like this was all normal. Like I hadn't just been imprisoned for days, like we were some kind of ordinary family like the people in the village, sitting down to have Sunday lunch and talking about the weather.

I tried to eat the beef but it stuck in my throat. I started to cough and he passed me a cup of water. I went to drink it then hesitated. I looked at him looking at me and for the first time in my life I felt afraid. What if the food and the water were poisoned? What if the meal was a trick and he was planning on putting me back in that room?

After that I told him I was tired and came in here to hide inside my doss bag and write in this book. I can hear him out back. He's fixing up the chicken coop. Seems like he's back to normal. All the crazy behaviour, talking to himself and staying up all night, that's all stopped now. And the scary thing is that it's stopped since he trapped me in that room. It's like whatever demons were drilling into his head have been destroyed and I was the sacrifice. For days he transferred those demons to me, planted monsters in my head, made me believe I was going mad, that the world outside had ceased to be, had been destroyed by evil forces, and that only the two of us remained.

But he was lying. The world hasn't been destroyed, it has carried on as normal. This morning, after breakfast, I went and stood by the lake and looked out towards the village. There must have been a dozen cars went past, a few lorries and a couple of delivery trucks. Life was still going on. Beautiful, ordinary life. The trees and the hills weren't battle-scarred and scorched like he told me, they were just as green and lush as they'd always been. In fact, they were more lush, more lovely than I have ever seen them. Because once you've been denied light and air and basic human needs, like I was in that room, you start to switch off, bit by bit. In that room there was no colour, no sunshine, no laughter, no animals, no weather, no smells. But most importantly there was no warmth, no comfort, no love.

That is what I craved more than anything while I was in there. Love. The feeling that someone cares. A kind word, a cup of tea set next to your doss bag, kind eyes, a gentle voice asking how was your day. And I realize that in these last few months there's been one person who made me feel loved, one person who, according to him, needs to be destroyed. Well, I won't let him. Isobel is the only friend I've got, the only kind person in this dark world, and I intend to fight for her with every breath in my body.

For so many years, he tried to tell me that I wasn't a person or a girl, that I was a soldier, a number. But he did that to stop me asking questions, to keep me under his control, to stop me being me. I know that now. So, today I become myself again and it starts by bringing back the name my mother gave me, a name that means decency.

I like the way it sounds when I say it aloud, the way it echoes softly like a whisper. From now on, dear friend, or whoever is reading this old journal of mine, you are in the company of a girl, an ordinary thirteen-year-old girl who likes reading and cooking and talking to her friend, Isobel. So, without further ado, I would like to introduce you to Grace.

25

Lisa

I stand at the edge of the lake looking out over the water. It's freezing but I'm thankful to be away, from the house and its ghosts, from Mark's voice that has lodged itself inside my head these last few days and, though I hate to admit it, from Joe and his constant tantrums.

As I stand watching the water ripple in the breeze I see my father's face, just above the surface of the lake, his hands outstretched.

'Come on, Lisa,' he cries. 'You're almost there.'

I recall the Saturday mornings we would spend together at Hampstead Lido, my dad and me. Mum had always been terrified of water, due to a near-drowning incident in the Thames at Windsor when she was six, but my dad had been determined that her fear would not be passed on to me so he took it upon himself to teach me how to swim. 'You never know when you'll need to save yourself, Lisa,' he used to say to me as we strolled through Hampstead village to the Lido. 'And, besides, swimming is good for the soul. That's what I've always thought.' I see his soft brown eyes twinkling. I close mine and let myself be calmed by the memory of him.

He was so patient, even when I got frustrated and jumped out of the pool. Dad never lost his cool, he just gently coaxed me back, told me that once I could swim a length the sense of pride would be immeasurable. And because he had faith in me, I didn't want to let him down. I wanted to be proud but I also wanted him to be proud of me too when I swam that length, so I stuck at it and within a few weeks I had achieved the goal. I remember Dad took me to the park cafe to celebrate with a slice of apple pie and a cup of steaming hot chocolate. I hear his lilting north London accent in my head now as I open my eyes and look out at the soothing water again. 'You did it, Lisa. I always knew you could. Now, whatever are you going to do next?'

That was the wonderful thing about my dad. No matter what I did, he never gave up on me, never stopped cheering me on and believing that I could become the best I could be. He believed in me right up to the end, with never a moment's doubt. Why the hell couldn't I have lived up to that? Why did I have to mess up so spectacularly?

The pale sun is beginning to dip in the sky now and I feel my spirits fade along with the light. Anxiety nips at my chest as I think of Joe alone in that house with a woman I've only just met. I can imagine what Mark would say about that. 'There you go again, Lisa, shirking your responsibilities.'

The thought of Mark makes me want to jump into the lake and spend a blissful few moments swimming away my anxiety, though I know I would freeze in this weather. Mark hated me going swimming. He said it made me go strange for hours afterwards. 'Like you've left a crucial part of your brain behind at the pool.' He was being spiteful but in a way he was right, I did feel altered after swimming. I felt balanced and calm but also protected somehow, like the water had formed a barrier between me and the world, a kind of armour. Dad had been right, learning to swim had saved me, though just not in the way he imagined.

The light is fading faster now, turning the water a murky grey. It's time I went back to the house.

'Lisa? Are you all right?'

I look up. Isobel is standing at the door, her face almost translucent in the fading winter light.

'Yes, I'm feeling much better,' I say as I reach the house. 'Just needed some air, that's all.'

'I understand,' she says, smiling. 'Though you must be freezing.'

She puts her hand on my arm and guides me back into the house which, in my absence, has been transformed. Warm, woody air envelops me as I step inside and my skin tingles. The fire has been lit in the living-room grate and Joe is lying on his belly in front of it, playing with the toy animals I hurriedly packed into my bag when we left London. I stand in the doorway, still shivering but unable to take my eyes off my little boy. He looks so contented and settled. Isobel has combed his hair and his face is pink and scrubbed clean. As I stand there listening to him making lion roars, lost in his play, the dark feeling returns, the sense that I have let my child down in the worst possible way; that being a mother, no matter how much I want it, will always be beyond me, just out of reach.

'I should have combed your hair,' I whisper.

At this, Joe looks up and sees me standing there. He gathers his animals into his arms, as though worried I'm going to take them away, then he scowls and turns his back on me. A tear escapes from my eye but I swiftly wipe it away. Joe mustn't see me crying.

'I found these in the kitchen.'

I turn to see Isobel standing behind me. She's holding a pile of clothes.

'Old jumpers,' she says briskly. 'They don't look that stylish but they're warm at least. Why don't you get changed and I'll keep an eye on Joe.'

I take the jumpers, like an obedient schoolgirl, and make my way down the passageway to the bedroom. Isobel has been busy making the bed and folding Joe's clothes into neat piles. As I peel off my thin cotton top, deep sadness permeates my bones. Why can't I be a good mother? Why am I always messing up?

When I get back to the living room I find Isobel sitting on the rug with Joe. He's waving a toy lion at her and she screams in mock terror. 'Save me, save me, Joe! Don't let him eat me.'

Joe giggles and does it again. His laughter is so natural, so innocent, it physically hurts to hear. Standing in the doorway, I clear my throat and they look up at me.

'Here's Mummy,' says Isobel, getting to her feet. 'Hey, I bet that feels warmer. Tell you what, if you give me your other clothes I'll take them back and give them a wash in my machine.'

'You've done more than enough, Isobel,' I say. 'Looking after Joe all this time. I can sort out the clothes. It's fine, really.'

She regards me for a moment, her expression a mixture of confusion and pity.

'I'm sorry,' she says, taking her coat from the back of the armchair. 'I have a tendency to over-fuss, I know. It's just I've never had kids and – well . . . I always thought I'd have a brood of them by now.'

She's a young woman yet she acts so much older than her years. It's curious. The sadness in her eyes makes me think that she's been hurt in the past.

'You're very good with Joe,' I say as we walk to the door. 'It seems to come so naturally to you, unlike me.'

'Children make me happy,' she says, her eyes suddenly glistening with tears. 'Though I've reconciled myself to not being a mum now. My father says it's God's will but it's still quite tough to take.'

'Oh, Isobel, I didn't realize,' I say. 'I shouldn't have –'

'No, please,' she says, wiping her face briskly. 'I'm fine. I've had a long time to get used to it.'

She smiles and I see something of myself in her expression, a fragility I hadn't noticed before.

'Anyway, it was a pleasure,' she says as I open the door. 'You've got a lovely boy there. A right little sweetheart.'

'Yes,' I say, though I suddenly feel anxious at the thought of Isobel leaving. Joe is calm when she's here. If only he could be like that with me.

She smiles then pats my shoulder reassuringly as if reading my mind.

'It will get better,' she says. 'I promise you.'

I nod my head briskly, trying to keep the tears that are gathering at bay.

'Oh, and if you're peckish later,' she says, stepping out into the dark December evening, 'I've popped a couple of jacket potatoes in the oven. They'll be perfect with a can of beans warmed up on top. Give them another forty-five minutes and they'll be nice and crispy.'

'Isobel, you shouldn't have,' I say. 'You've done so much for us already.'

'It's nothing,' she says, wrapping her scarf round her shoulders. 'Just a couple of spuds I had going spare. Poor Dad's got no appetite these days and I'm trying to avoid carbs. Better that you and Joe enjoy them than they go to waste. Oh, and I also left you a newspaper. One of the parishioners left it behind after the service this morning. I'm not much of a newspaper person but I thought you might like a read.'

'Thanks, Isobel,' I say. 'For everything. I really do appreciate it.'

'Not a problem,' she says. 'And, listen, if you need anything, anything at all, you've got my number. Okay?'

I nod my head.

'You get inside,' she calls. 'It's freezing out here and I think you've had enough fresh air for one day.'

'A girl can never have enough fresh air,' I say, remembering her words. 'That's what she always used to say.'

'Who?'

'Oh, no one,' I say, checking myself. 'It doesn't matter. Listen, thanks again, Isobel. You've been such a help. I'd better go and check on Joe now.'

I say goodbye and head back into the house. As I close the door I hear Isobel's boots crunching on the gravel then the sound of the car engine starting up. In the living room I find Joe still playing with the animals, his head on the floor, eye level with the lions, tigers and elephants. I go over and sit down next to him.

179

'Can I play too?' I say, picking up a lion and attempting a feeble roar.

He shakes his head then grabs the lion from my hands.

'Okay,' I sigh. 'Well, how about I make us some dinner. Isobel's left us some lovely baked potatoes. You like them, don't you?'

He ignores me and returns to his game. I sit for a few moments longer looking at the back of his head before eventually admitting defeat and heading into the kitchen.

The potatoes will take another forty minutes, according to Isobel, and with Joe playing happily next door I sit down at the table and pick up the bulky copy of the *Sunday Times*. Ripping off the cellophane cover, I skim over the latest Brexit developments, but as I turn the page I come face to face with a headline that makes my blood turn to ice.

HUNT CONTINUES FOR MISSING MOTHER AND SON

PART TWO

26

Grace

23 November 2004

Today I found out what real life feels like and it was magical, like some exciting new kingdom I've just been given the keys to. I want to hold on to this feeling for ever, the feeling of being a normal girl doing normal things. It all began this morning, when he had gone out to the woods. As soon as he was out of sight I sneaked out and went up to the village. I knew that he would go mental once he came back and saw I'd gone but I didn't care. He gave up all rights over me when he did what he did in that room.

I will admit that it felt weird to be away from the house though and every few minutes, as I walked along the road that leads to the village, I stopped and looked behind me just to check it was still there. I saw the lake and the wooden boat he made for me when I was four years old. I saw the tarpaulin roof of the house wobbling in the wind. And those sights reassured me. Even with everything that's happened I still can't imagine any other home. So, yes, I could go to the village and defy him but I was always going to go back, not for him but for the house and all the things I loved.

It was easy to find her place. All I had to do was look for the church steeple. As I walked through the village

I could see it sticking out above the tops of the little cottages like a big rocket. I kept my eyes fixed on that steeple because I could feel people staring at me and I wanted to block them out. I know what the people in this village think of me and him: the freak and his brown-skinned daughter, living in a broken-down old house, shooting animals and wearing strange clothes. I know that because I'd heard them when I was a kid. It was in the pub, the one I'm walking past now.

He had taken me there with him one day to try and sell the landlord some cuts of meat. He must have been really low on funds to do something like that because he mostly avoided the village at all costs. I was happy though, because it felt like a nice trip out and the pub was all warm and cosy and full of lovely cooking smells. Anyway, while he was at the bar talking to the landlord I sat down at one of the tables. It was a Sunday and there was a load of people in there eating dinner. I could feel them staring at me. Staring at my army gear, my unbrushed hair, my muddy boots. Then one of the women said something I've never forgotten. She was an old woman with rolls of fat on her neck and arms, and bulging eyes, and she had a big plate full of Yorkshire pudding and gravy in front of her. She looked over at me then nudged the man beside her and said in a loud whisper: 'Poor kid. Do you think she knows she's a dirty raghead?'

I had no idea what raghead meant so, when we got out of the pub, I stopped and asked him. And then I wished I hadn't cos he just went crazy and ran back inside waving the cash the landlord had given him for the meat. He stood in the middle of the pub, ripped the notes into pieces and threw them on the floor, yelling, 'That's what you can do with your money, you ignorant bastards!'

Afterwards, once we were safely back at the house, he told me that it didn't matter, that I wasn't to worry about the opinions of small-minded people and that we would be fine as long as we trusted each other and stuck together. But despite his reassurances I couldn't stop thinking about that woman's words and what they meant.

For the first time in my life I realized that I was different from everyone else. From the people in the village, from the characters in the books I read, from the rosy-cheeked ramblers with their red socks and rucksacks, who liked to hike up on the crag. No one was like me. I didn't belong. And I carried that feeling with me down the years and did as he asked. We stuck together like the two outcasts we were and shut out the world. And I thought that was the only life that existed, the only one I needed. Until the day he locked me in that room.

When Isobel saw me on the doorstep her eyes lit up and she said it was lovely to see me. No one has ever said those words to me before. But she meant them. I know she did.

When I stepped inside the house I felt like I'd been transported into one of my library books. It was the most perfect house I'd ever seen, a proper Green Gables. The walls were covered in pretty floral wallpaper and there were framed pictures of ladies in crinoline dresses and houses with white fences. The living room was very grand, with leather sofas and a big wooden desk. I reckoned that must be where Isobel's dad, the vicar, sat to write his sermons.

Isobel told me that her dad was at the church all day and wouldn't be back till late. I don't know why she felt she had to say that. Would it have been different if he'd been there? Would he have welcomed me into his house as warmly as Isobel had? I certainly looked out of place in my grubby army fatigues and hob-nailed boots, like I'd been blown out of the desert and landed in the middle of an English fairy tale.

She took me into the kitchen, which was so clean it made my eyes hurt, and made us both big cups of hot chocolate with tiny sweets on top which I'd never seen before. Isobel told me they were called marshmallows and that they melted into the hot chocolate and made it taste delicious. She was right. It was the sweetest, most lovely thing I've ever had, nothing like the stuff he makes, which is just a spoonful of cocoa with hot water. This was creamy and gooey and made me feel like I was floating on the ceiling with happiness.

After we'd had our drinks Isobel said she'd show me her room. It was just as pretty as I'd imagined, with pale-yellow curtains tied back with ribbon and a huge bed with fluffy pillows and frilly sheets and curtains all round it. Isobel told me it was called a four-poster. The walls were covered with pictures of men in baggy trousers and vests, who, Isobel told me, were a band, but I'd never heard of them because the only bands he ever mentions are the marching bands he knew when he was in the army and I didn't like to ask Isobel if she liked them because she'd probably think I was weird so I just stayed quiet and looked around. The one thing I noticed most about the room was just how much stuff Isobel had. Books and clothes and pretty little trinkets seemed to cover every surface. How was it possible to have so much? Her dad must be a very rich man, I figured. But the best thing in there, the thing I was most envious of, was the big doll's house in the corner of the room. It was the most beautiful thing I have ever seen. And what made it so magical was that it was a miniature version of the vicarage itself. It had the same exterior, sandy-coloured brick with a dark-red door, the same pointy roof and tall chimneys, and inside the same décor, right down to the yellow curtains in Isobel's room. She told me that her mother had put the doll's house together before she died. She'd wanted something for Isobel to remember her by. When she said this I felt like hugging Isobel and never letting go. She had lost her mum like I had. She'd grown up with just her dad in a big house and she must have had questions that her dad didn't want to hear, just like I did. I wanted to tell Isobel that I understood, that we were the same, but before I got the chance she took my arm and told me to sit down on the bed next to her while she showed me her make-up case.

'Do you like this?' she said, pulling out a gold tube. 'It's dusky rose, my favourite shade.'

She took the top of the tube and wound it up to reveal what looked like a big red crayon.

'Is that what you paint with?' I said as she passed it to me to take a closer look.

'My face, yes,' she said, giggling. 'Do you ever wear make-up?'

'No,' I said, handing back the lipstick. I didn't really know what she was talking about, to be honest.

'That's a shame,' she said, pulling out a tub with glittery powder inside. 'You'd look lovely with a bit of mascara and blusher. Hey, why don't I give you a makeover?'

I had no idea what a makeover was, but I liked being with Isobel and I didn't want the time to end so I agreed. When I said yes, she clapped her hands together and looked so excited, like she'd just won the biggest prize in the world. Then she brought a chair over to the bed and sat down in front of me.

'I'm going to start with moisturizer,' she said, squeezing a line of white cream out of a silvery tube. 'Then we'll have a good base for the make-up.'

While she applied the make-up, which made my face tickle and my nose go sneezy, she told me more about herself. She goes to school in Threshfield, which is about five miles away. It's a big school, she said, and kids go there from all over Yorkshire, some coming in from as far as Leeds. She said she liked Art and History best and was thinking of studying one of them at university. I had no idea what she was talking about but it sounded lovely. I wanted to tell her about the stories I'd read in the books from the mobile library – about *Anne of Green Gables* and *Great Expectations* (my two favourites), about the poem in Sarge's book about love being like water and the photo of the dead mother in the desert, and how all those things made me feel. But every time I tried to get the words out, my brain froze. I felt like my world would seem so small and silly to Isobel so I kept it all in my head and listened to her while she told me about things I'd never heard of like netball, revision timetables and gel nails.

The way she talked about those things, with that serious look on her face, made me think they must be very important so I nodded my head and said 'hmm' a lot, though to be honest it was all a bit boring. But then, when she was putting some weird black stuff on my eyes that smelt like creosote, she started to giggle. I asked her what was up and she said that I was funny. I asked her why and she said it was a good thing, that I wasn't like the other girls. I was sweet. Sweet wasn't a word I would use to describe myself but Isobel seemed to think I was and that made me happy. She continued with the make-up then, but while she was doing it she asked if I'd ever had a boyfriend and I just went quiet because I didn't really know what she meant. I hadn't had any friends, boy or girl. Isobel smiled then and said that she had a boyfriend. She said he was older than her and lived away from the village but he was really 'hot' and they met up lots to do stuff. I asked what kind of stuff and she started giggling again and said that they did a lot of kissing and were going to do much more once they could find the right place.

I felt very confused but I didn't show it cos I didn't want her to think I was stupid so I just sat there while she talked and put more stuff on my face. When she'd finished she went over to the window and grabbed a mirror. 'Are you ready to see the new you?' she said, holding the mirror behind her back. I said yes and she pulled out the mirror and shoved it in front of my face.

The shock of what I saw nearly threw me off the bed. I couldn't believe it. I had disappeared and in my place, staring back at me with those familiar dark, shapely eyebrows and black-lined eyes, was the dead mother in the desert. I didn't say anything to Isobel, though she kept asking if I liked it. I said I did and then she started talking about her boyfriend again, but I wasn't listening. All I could think of was what I had just seen in the mirror. After a few minutes I told Isobel that I had to go. She pulled a sad face and asked me if I wanted to stay for dinner. I couldn't think what to say so I followed her down the stairs, letting her think I was going to join her in the kitchen, then I opened the front door and ran all the way home.

Thankfully he was still out when I got back so I got the chance to pull myself together. I can hear him now though. He's making scran in the kitchen as I sit here writing this on the bed. I can smell the usual scent of animal carcasses boiling up. I'm used to that smell, it's the smell of home, but it doesn't comfort me any more. Not after today when I saw what a real home should be. I just wish I hadn't run away from Isobel like that. She must think I'm mad. I have to go back and see her, say sorry for running off, tell her that I want to be her friend, want to spend time in her pretty bedroom with the books and the doll's house and the smell of flowers in the air. I've had a taste of normal life now and it's not the scary thing he's always said it is. It's real and comforting and solid, just like Isobel. I want to be a normal girl and do normal things, and I know I'll only be that way if I stick with Isobel. She's the only person I trust now, my only ally.

27

Lisa

Outside the window, a light snow begins to fall. It brushes against the glass like small feathers.

I read the headline again.

Below it is a mugshot of me, pale-faced and wild-haired, while next to that is a photo of Mark sitting at a table alongside two police officers, one male, one female. He looks broken. His eyes are swollen and red, his face unshaven, his hair matted and unkempt. It looks like he has given a press conference as underneath the photo, in quotation marks, is written: 'Please, just bring my boy home.'

There's a lengthy transcript of the press conference, five columns long, accompanying it, which I read with trembling hands.

At one point the reporter asks Mark if he believes Joe is in danger. 'I hope not, but then Lisa is so unpredictable, I can't rule that out,' Mark replies. At the end of the report there's a summary of the case, of what had gone before and of the story I have spent the last few days trying to rewrite.

> In January 2018, Lisa Ward was released from prison where she had served twelve months for assaulting her

husband. Mr Ward was left with life-changing injuries to his face and torso after being attacked with a broken glass. He was granted full custody of their child, 3-year-old Joe, but had recently allowed Mrs Ward supervised visits. It was during one of those visits, on 9 December, that Mrs Ward abducted Joe. Police have advised the public not to approach Mrs Ward who they describe as a volatile and dangerous woman.

I stay sitting at the table, unable to move. Mark's stricken face looks back at me from the newspaper, his words now imprinted on my brain: *Please, just bring my boy home.*

I hear Joe playing merrily in the room next door but his high-pitched lion roars set me on edge. I need to be with him now, I tell myself, as I close the newspaper and get up from the table. Now more than ever. The passageway is dark and I shiver as I think of the stories attached to this house, the mad father and the girl. Grace.

Arriving at the prison was one of the most terrifying experiences of my life. The invasive body searches, so intimate and yet detached, as though the guards were dealing with a piece of meat, the screams and shouts from the other cells as I was walked to mine, flanked by two sombre-faced guards, the smell of bleach and excrement in the air, the panic as the cell door closed behind me. I felt like I had arrived at the gates of hell and that the only way I could possibly get through it was by shutting down. So for the first few weeks I did just that. I didn't speak, barely ate, just lay on my bed with my eyes closed thinking about Joe's lovely face.

I was so spaced out that I barely noticed the woman in the bunk above me until sometime in the third week, when I was crying myself to sleep yet again.

'You got to toughen up.'

The voice was gruff, northern, and in my agitated state I thought for a moment that it was coming from inside my head.

'If you want to survive in here you got to stop crying or they'll 'ave you.'

It was then I realized the voice was coming from above me. I didn't answer her but I did stop crying and after that something changed. The woman, who introduced herself the following day as Grace, became my confidante, a friend of sorts. Thinking about it now, I can't imagine I would have survived prison if I hadn't been put in her cell. Though we couldn't have been more different, Grace got me through those first few weeks, she toughened me up, made me see that life was worth living and that I had to be strong for the sake of my child. I never found out what crime Grace had committed as she never told me much about herself or her background, though I could see that the other women were wary of her, this strange, straggly-haired woman with fierce eyes. They used to call her 'Mad Grace' or 'the wild woman', though never, I noticed, to her face. Nobody dared challenge her, that was clear. At the time, I was so focused on my own survival, on getting through the prison ordeal one day at a time, that I gave little thought to the crime that had brought Grace there. She was kind to me and, in my terrified state, that was all that mattered.

The living room is illuminated by candlelight when I enter and the fire Isobel lit is still going strong. Joe is lying on his back holding a lion in the air.

I sit down on the armchair in the corner of the room, folding my arms across my chest to stop them from shaking. The yellow net curtain on the far window shivers as cold air blows in through the rotten frames. This place is the stuff of nightmares but I have no other choice now. I have made the news in one of the biggest national papers; most likely my face will have been splashed across the television and the internet too. If this place had Wi-Fi I could scroll through my phone, see what else is out there, but I figure that is a mercy. This way I can hide away, pretend it isn't happening.

My thoughts turn once again to Grace. Now, sitting here in the house she shared with her father, watching my little boy playing on the rug, oblivious to it all, I think back to Jimmy's words – but I can't reconcile those descriptions with the woman I knew. Yes, Grace was eccentric and clearly troubled, but she wasn't a killer, I'm sure of it. We shared that cell twenty-two hours a day for twelve months and during that time I'd opened up to her in ways in which I'd never done with anyone else before. Grace was my friend and she was good, I know that in my heart, and that goodness was reinforced by the gesture she made on the day I was released from prison.

When I left the prison gates there was nobody there to meet me, no familiar faces, no hugs, no reassuring voice telling me that everything was going to be all right. But why should there have been? Mark was still furious at what I'd done and had refused to bring Joe for visits the whole time I was inside. The idea that he would be standing outside the prison gates with open arms was absurd. My friends had disappeared, no doubt appalled at the story of this violent, dangerous woman and the frenzied attack on her poor, defenceless husband. And I didn't hear from Beth and Harry at all. Beth, my oldest friend, with the watchful eyes, the one who had warned me about Mark and his controlling ways – even she had stepped away. As for family, well, there was no one left. My father had died and my mother had been so grief-stricken in the years that followed, she pretty much left me, a child, to fend for myself. My abiding memory of those years is of sitting by the fire in the living room of the Highgate flat eating cold rice pudding from a tin. That was my small link to my dad. He loved tinned rice pudding and we would often share one warmed up and spooned into two dessert bowls with a splodge of strawberry jam on top, on cold winter afternoons after school. After his death I couldn't bring myself to perform the ceremony of the bowls and jam but eating the rice brought me closer to him and helped me block out the pain. As for my mother, she finally booked herself into therapy to deal with her overwhelming grief a few years later when I was about to start university. She seemed to respond well and for a few months it felt like I finally had my mother back, but then she met a new man, a property developer named Tony, and they embarked on a new life together in Portugal. I heard from her sporadically but it was clear she had new priorities and that her distant daughter wasn't one of them. The gulf widened when I met Mark because I decided he was the only family I needed. After a while I stopped all communication with my mother and tried to put her and my old life behind me.

So as I stood outside the prison gate that cold January afternoon I knew that I was all alone in the world and I faced the daunting task of having to rebuild my life from scratch. My future was bleak and uncertain – and it didn't feature Joe. Joe. My beautiful baby boy, the child whose birth was supposed to have heralded the beginning of an exciting new future, a family, a life. But I had ripped all that apart in one moment of madness. At that point, standing outside the prison, there was very little hope. I was forbidden from seeing Joe until I could reassure the social worker I could secure work and a roof over my head. I also had to take anger management classes to control what the judge had described as my 'volatile temper'.

My situation couldn't have been more hopeless but then I put my hand in my pocket and found the crumpled piece of paper Grace had thrust at me as I left the cell. It was a rough drawing showing a map with the name of a village scribbled across, Harrowby, and a picture of a house, the words 'Rowan Isle House' printed in capital letters below. At the top of the map, Grace had written: *If you ever need a place to stay, it's yours. You won't need keys, just give the door a good push. And remember, Lisa, you're stronger than you realize.*

I'd thought it was a sweet gesture then put it to the back of my mind, though later, when I had found a job working on reception at an estate agency in Clapham, I'd googled Harrowby on the office computer and found that it was in a remote part of the Yorkshire Dales. At that time, the idea of upping sticks and tramping off to Yorkshire didn't even cross my mind. For one thing, I was just finding my feet after coming out of prison – as well as the new job, I'd also managed to secure a house-share in Balham, on the other side of the river from Joe and Mark. And for another, well, I was a London girl who had little clue about the north of England, let alone some obscure Yorkshire village in the middle of nowhere.

But the reality of being apart from Joe was so painful I found it difficult to cope. I could deal with it in prison because it was an alien environment, somewhere Joe had never been part of, but going to visit him in our old neighbourhood, walking past the places I had taken him to as a baby – the park, the little cafe on the high street where they gave him boxes of cloth books to play with, the library where I got him his first library card, aged nine months – and the fact that my visits to him had to be supervised by Mark, was too much to bear. Every time I said goodbye to him at the door of the house that was once my family home and trundled back on the Tube to the attic room in a house full of strangers, I felt like my heart was being ripped apart. The pain was physical and more acute than anything I had ever felt before. Once December came around and Christmas songs started to be played on the radio I felt like I could quite easily die from heartache. The thought of spending Christmas holed up in a room in some strange house while my little boy was celebrating with his dad and family was inconceivable. So I formulated a plan.

I arrived at Mark's for the supervised visit at the usual time of 9 a.m., with Grace's map safely tucked inside my jacket and a beanie hat pulled down over my newly short, dyed hair. Mark was in a flustered state as he had a work deadline. He looked exhausted, like he hadn't slept for days. I made him a coffee and told him I'd take Joe out to the garden to play in the Wendy house to give Mark a chance to get some work done. He'd hesitated for a moment but then the idea of clearing a few hours' work seemed to outweigh any suspicions he might have had of me and he disappeared upstairs to his study. After that I acted swiftly, grabbing my large bag that was still in the understairs cupboard where I'd left it before I went to prison and filling it with some of Joe's clothes and his favourite plastic animals. Then, wrapping Joe in his warm winter coat, I'd taken his hand, left the house and dashed to my car, which I'd deliberately parked in the next street. Joe had clocked that something was up before we'd even left London and the rest of the journey consisted of him alternating between crying, screaming and calling out for Mark. It was hell, but as I sit here looking at him playing so happily on the rug in front of me I have no doubt that I made the right decision. I'm his mummy. Without him I don't make sense. I had to be with him this Christmas.

'Come on, Joe,' I say, getting up from the chair and blowing out the candles. 'It's getting late now. How about we cuddle in and have a story?'

He looks up. His eyes are tired.

'Can I bring lions?' he says, holding up a fistful of the plastic toys.

'Of course you can,' I say. 'I'm sure they'd like to hear the story too.'

He raises his arms for me to lift him but as I bend down to pick him up there's a loud pounding on the front door.

'Door,' says Joe, snuggling into my chest. 'Let's go see.'

But I can't move. My feet are frozen to the spot. The pounding starts again, more urgent this time, then I hear a voice – a man's voice – calling my name and my stomach twists inside.

28

Grace

25 November 2004

I'm writing this in the woods, sitting in my doss bag under a big old oak tree. It all started two nights ago when I shut this journal and went to get some scran. I'd forgotten all about the make-up Isobel had put on me and when I walked into the kitchen he was just taking a pan of potatoes off the hob. Well, he took one look at me and dropped the whole lot, boiling water and all, on to the floor. Then he went so pale I thought he was going to faint. He gripped the table with both hands and sort of bared his teeth at me. He looked like a wolf.

Then he just started muttering something under his breath.

'What is it?' I said. 'What are you saying?'

But then I heard it. He was saying her name, over and over. *Noora Noora Noora.*

Then he took my hand, gripped it tightly and said, 'Do you forgive me, Noora? Tell me you forgive me?'

His eyes were all wild and flashing, just like they had been when he'd trapped me in the room, and I got scared then. I knew this was only going to get worse and that I might even end up back in that room.

Then he fell to his knees and clasped his hands together, like he was praying or something.

'You . . .' he said, shaking his head from side to side. 'Where did you come from? How did you find me?'

I opened my mouth to tell him it was just me and then I remembered the make-up and my reflection in the mirror. He wasn't seeing me, he was seeing her. The dead mother. And you know what? I liked the fact that he was scared so I just stood there and let him think that I was her. Let him feel scared like I'd felt when he'd locked me in that room.

'I'm sorry,' he said. His hands were still gripping the table but his face had softened. 'I didn't mean to do it. I really didn't. Do you forgive me, Noora? Do you forgive me?'

Noora. It's funny the effect a name can have on you. I remember the pride I felt when he'd started calling me Number 1 after my hunting success. Even though Grace was my name, Number 1 was the name I'd earned. It said so much. Like he was never 'Dad' but Sarge because that's what he'd always been to me, a rank, a superior, a soldier. Never a dad. But Noora. Well, that name has the same effect on me as Isobel's name. It's a warm hand on my back. Beautiful and comforting. And hearing it, thinking about her lovely face smiling up at me from the photo, filled me with a burst of strength.

'Please, I beg you,' he cried, still on his knees. 'Answer me. Do you forgive me? Tell me you forgive me?'

I stood looking at him. His eyes were pleading with me just as I'd pleaded with him to let me out of that room. Now he wanted my forgiveness. After the terrible way he treated me, the coldness he showed me day after day.

'No, I don't,' I said, staring back at him with Noora's eyes. 'I will never forgive you.'

Then I turned and walked out of the kitchen. I could hear him wailing behind me but I didn't go back. Instead I went to my room and grabbed my doss bag and some clothes. As I walked past his bedroom on my way out I saw a book lying on his bed. It was the one with the squiggly writing in it that he kept by his bed at all times, the one with her photograph in it. I remember him catching me with it that time, when I first saw her face, and how mad he was. In fact, every time I saw him with it he looked crazed. It had that effect on him. So I decided to do him a favour, a kind of farewell gift. I went into his room, grabbed the book and stuffed it into my bag. Maybe without this he'd stop the madness.

When I passed the kitchen I could hear him wailing still. He was ranting about the wolves and the monsters. 'There are monsters in my mind, Noora,' he cried. 'Controlling. Eating me alive. They did it, not me. They did it. Believe me. Please . . . believe me.'

I couldn't bear to listen any more so I stepped away and walked out of the front door. I walked and I walked until I wore myself out and slumped in this little clearing on the far edge of the woods. I feel safe here now, though he's been out looking for me. I heard him coming that first night and I scarpered into the trees, taking the bag with me, and watched him from my hiding place. He was frantic. Calling my name, not hers, over and over again like a crazed person. But then that's what he is. Crazed. I realize that now. And if you spend enough time around crazy people, it rubs off. I don't want to be like him. I want to be normal. I want to be free.

And yet as I write this I can't help feeling sad for the man he used to be, the loving dad who cherished me for the first ten years of my life. The days before the military training began, the days of *The Wind in the Willows*, him taking on the voices of Ratty, Mole, Badger and Toad, me telling him not to stop but to do those voices again and again and again. Life felt safe then. We were living inside a story, so it seemed, a perfect world where nothing bad happened and everything was arranged in neat chapters. But then I turned eleven and it all fell apart.

I can see the book I took from his bedroom. It's lying on the ground beside me, unopened. I know he'll be frantic when he sees it's missing cos there's not a day gone by when he hasn't read that book, clutched it in his hands, spoken to it, shouted at it. Once, I even saw him throw it against a wall. It was like the book had a spirit of its own and I could never be sure if that spirit was good or evil. But I knew that it brought out the worst in him. We could have had the most ordinary day, when we'd have gone hunting, say, or baked a batch of bread or cleaned out the chickens, a day when not a cross word passed between us, but as soon as evening came and he picked up that book, everything would change. His face would contort and all the happiness would drain from him like water down a plughole.

So even though I want to see what's inside, there is a part of me that's scared to. What if it has the same effect on me as it had on him? What if opening it releases things that can never be put back, like that woman in the story with the box? But if I don't then he will always be a mystery to me and I don't want that. I want to find out why he did what he did, why he locked me in that room and tortured me. And I know, deep inside, that the answers lie somewhere in that book.

So my plan is this. I'll open it and if anything bad happens I'll take it to the top of Harrowby Tarn and burn it. That's what you're supposed to do with evil things, with things that have become possessed. I read that in a book I borrowed from the mobile library called *Great Mysteries of Northern England*. I might even ask Isobel to get her dad to help me burn it. That's another thing I read, that priests and vicars and religious folk can get rid of evil spirits by reciting words and chucking holy water about.

Yes, that's what I'll do if the worst comes to the worst. But, after all, it's just a book, just a story. And nothing truly bad ever came from reading a story.

29
Lisa

With Joe in my arms, I walk trance-like to the front door. It seems to swell and expand before me like a giant shadow. As I draw closer the banging starts again and I almost drop Joe.

'Lisa? Are you in there? It's just me, Jimmy.'

Jimmy. The landlord from the pub. My body sags with relief. It isn't Mark or the police. We're still safe. For now.

'Is it Daddy?' says Joe. His eyes are sleepy and he rests his head on my shoulder as I fumble with the stiff door handle.

'No, darling,' I say. 'It's just the man from the pub. We'll see what he wants then tuck you into bed. You're tired out.'

I give the door one final yank and almost tumble out on to the step.

'Steady,' says Jimmy, stepping forward and grabbing my arm.

'Hi,' I say as I regain my balance. 'Sorry I took so long to answer. I . . . I was just getting Joe down.'

'Oh God, did I wake him?' says Jimmy apologetically. 'I'm really sorry. I was just a bit worried after the other night, you running off like you did. I thought I'd scared you with all that talk about the mad fella. To be honest,

I was in a bit of a daft mood and I guess my bantering went a bit too far. I'm sorry.'

'It's fine,' I say, slightly bemused at him turning up like this, though grateful to see a friendly face.

'Anyway, I brought you this,' he says, holding up a bottle of white wine. 'Isobel thinks I scared you with my stories too. I don't always judge situations very well.'

'I guess it did spook me out a little,' I say, shivering in the cold draught. 'Listen, why don't you come in?'

'If you're sure,' says Jimmy, looking rather sheepish suddenly. 'I wouldn't want to impose or anything.'

'You're not,' I say, pulling Joe closer to my chest. 'It's nice to see you.'

He smiles then follows me into the house.

'Want Daddy,' whispers Joe sleepily, his head tucked under my chin. 'He tell me bedtime story.'

'Missing his dad, eh?' says Jimmy. 'Is he going to be coming up to join you?'

I search his face for any sign that he knows. That headline must have made its way on to the kitchen tables of several homes around here, the pub included. Yet it doesn't seem like Jimmy has seen it.

'No,' I say, more firmly than intended. 'Er, no, we're not together any more, his dad and me.'

I feel Joe's head grow heavier on my chest.

'I'd better get him to bed now,' I say. 'Why don't you make yourself comfortable in the living room and I'll be with you in just a sec.'

As I walk away I hear his footsteps on the stone kitchen floor. I should be peeved that he's snooping but this isn't my house and the only thing he's likely to come across is an old tin of powdered milk. But when I get to the bedroom I remember the newspaper on the kitchen table, my name and face splashed across the inside, and my legs buckle. Joe is fast asleep in my arms now. I lay him down gently on the bed, tuck the thick woollen blankets tightly round him, then quickly make my way back to the kitchen.

'Christ, this place is like a museum,' says Jimmy as I enter.

He's standing by the stove, looking up at the dusty shelves. 'I was looking for some glasses,' he says, turning to me, smiling. 'But it seems these are the nearest thing.'

He takes down a couple of wooden beakers from the shelf, wiping the rims with his sleeve.

'Thank God for screw tops, eh?' he says, gesturing to the bottle of wine that stands opened on the table. 'A man could die of thirst. And how come there's no taps?'

'I have to collect the water from the lake,' I say, swiping the newspaper from the table and tucking it under my arm. 'There's no water in the house, no electricity, no gas.'

'Fucking hell,' he exclaims, his eyes widening as he pulls out a chair and sits down. 'How the hell do you manage? And you say you came here for a holiday? You must be made of stern stuff.'

'It's been . . . an experience,' I say, sitting down opposite him and placing the newspaper on my lap. 'But then it's also been quite refreshing. You know, getting away from it all.'

'I suppose,' he says, pouring me a beaker of wine. 'But I can't imagine it's that relaxing being here. I'd be scared shitless, to be honest.'

He leans across and passes me the beaker.

'That too,' I say, smiling. 'Particularly after hearing your stories the other night.'

'Yeah, I shouldn't have gone on like that,' he says, taking a sip of wine. 'Anyway, now I'm here, it's the last thing I want to think of. Let's just hope that mad woman's safely away in jail, not prowling around here somewhere.' He shudders. 'So how did you find it?' he says, moving his chair forward a little. 'This place? Was it on a website or something?'

I drink some wine, try to gather my story.

'Er, no,' I say, the alcohol stinging my gullet. 'It was a . . . a friend who recommended it.'

'A friend?' he says, his eyes burning into me. 'From round here?'

I shake my head.

'Then how did they know about it?' he says, frowning. 'Thing about Harrowby is that when it comes to the leisure and tourism websites, there are basically three things featured: my pub, the woodland, which has just been bought by the National Trust, and Ken's pie shop up by the park – and that's only been mentioned recently cos some magazine editor got lost on her way to the Lakes and popped in for directions. Ken managed to flog her half-a-dozen steak and ales and she ended up writing a feature on them, saying they'd give Duchy Originals a run for their money.'

He pauses to drink, then continues.

'Anyway, what I'm saying is that this place is so small we get to know everything, and I mean everything.'

He stares and I look down at the table.

'And being in the hospitality industry, I keep an eye on all those websites,' he says, his face softening. 'Your Trip Advisors, your Last Minute, all that. And I have never come across this place advertised as a holiday home. I mean, look at it. It's falling apart. Who the hell would rent it out like this?' He throws his hands in the air and laughs. I smile at him, while in my head scrambling around for some way of changing the subject.

'So you grew up here then?' I say. 'In the village?'

'Nah,' he says, shaking his head vigorously. 'I've lived here for six years now but I'm a city boy, born and bred in Leeds. Though the pub trade is in my blood. My folks ran a bar in the centre.'

'So how did you end up here?'

'Hmm, long story,' he says, rolling his eyes. 'But let's just say that after a pretty messy break-up I was looking for a change of scene. I'd worked as a bar manager in Headingley for a couple of years after leaving school and, well, it didn't help that my ex continued to drink in there with her new man. I wanted a fresh start, really. And I'd always fancied running a country pub. When I saw the leasehold for my place advertised online I thought, bugger it, what have I got to lose, so I went for it.'

'It must have been a shock to the system, moving from the city to somewhere as remote as this.'

'Oh yeah, big time,' he says, scratching the top of his head. 'And you'd know that, coming here from London. But then I'm a chatty sod, always have been. I'll talk to anyone so after a few weeks I'd made friends, settled in, and what with the locals and the ramblers I do a decent trade so I can't complain. Not that it was ever my life's dream to live in Harrowby I hasten to add, but it's all right for now. And it's done me good, after all that shit with the ex. No one gives a toss about you in the city, you may as well be a speck of dirt on the bottom of their shoe. It's different here. People look out for you. They watch your back.'

He stops and looks at me a little too intently for comfort, and I worry that maybe he did see the newspaper after all and has put two and two together. But then he picks up the bottle of wine and refills my beaker.

'How about you?' he says, taking another sip of his drink. 'Have you always lived in London?'

'Yes,' I reply, the wine warming my body. 'I grew up in Highgate just next to the cemetery.'

'I think I've heard of that,' he says, his eyes widening. 'Is it near to Arsenal?'

'Not far,' I say, smiling. 'Though I'm not much of a football fan.'

'Neither am I,' he says with a laugh. 'I mean, whatever Leeds United are playing at the moment, it's certainly not football.'

'Are they your team?'

'For my sins,' he says, rolling his eyes. 'Anyway, enough of football. I'm probably boring you to tears.'

'No, you're not,' I say, draining my wine. 'It's nice.'

Jimmy fills my beaker again and soon the bottle is empty. My eyes feel tired, though it feels good to be sitting here with someone. Even the football talk is a light relief from the relentless anxiety I've been experiencing. For the first time in years I feel relaxed and at ease. Jimmy tells me some more about his childhood growing up in pubs and the close relationship he had with his parents. I like his honesty, the fact that he doesn't feel he has to be anything but himself. It's refreshing.

'Oh God, sorry,' he says, looking at his watch as I drain the last of my wine from the beaker. 'I didn't mean to stay this late.'

He stands up and as I watch him put his jacket on I feel an overwhelming sense of loneliness. I don't want him to go. I want to extend this feeling of happiness, of normality, for a few more hours. I want to be held.

'Don't go just yet,' I say, standing up from the chair a little too quickly so that white spots dance in front of my eyes. 'It's . . . it's nice to have you here.'

He looks confused for a moment then his expression softens.

I touch his hand and pull him towards me.

'You're lovely,' he whispers, placing a soft kiss on my cheek.

He smells of peppermint and firewood.

I turn my head and his mouth meets mine. His kiss is soft and butterfly light, so different from Mark's wet, sloppy lips. I ease forward, letting his tongue explore my mouth, my lips, my teeth, and as I do so everything falls away. There is no reality other than this one, no anxiety, no fear, just pure pleasure.

'Are you sure?' he whispers, running his tongue down the side of my neck.

'Yes,' I reply, warmth fluttering through my body.

He pulls back then gets up from the table and holds out his hand. Taking it in mine, I let him lead me into the living room, where the dying embers of the fire are crackling softly in the grate. And as he lays me down, a velvet darkness seems to envelop me. There is no Joe, no Mark, no Grace, no screams, no prison cells, no nightmares. There is nothing but the rise and fall of his chest as he lies on top of me, the gentle beating of a stranger's heart as he holds me close and, for just a few hours, takes away the pain.

30

Grace

Hours must have passed since I read Sarge's book but I have no idea what time it is or what day. I'm not even sure who I am. I only know I'm alive because I can feel my lungs rising and falling and I can keep this pen moving, keep it translating my thoughts from my head to the page.

If anyone finds this they will see blood splattered on the pages. Don't let that scare you. It's not my blood. I've just been doing what he taught me to do. Killing. As soon as I read his book and found out the truth I had to take out my anger on something, something that couldn't fight back. I had my paring knife with me in case of emergencies and I took it out of my bag and went looking. It was easy, so easy I wish, in a warped way, that he had been here to see me do it. What would you say to that, mister, eh? Would you say I passed the test? Would you give me a badge, a medal? Or would you lock me in a room and try to turn me mad?

It wasn't a good kill. I knew that the moment I set eyes on her. She was lying under an old oak tree, one leg jutting out at an odd angle: a young deer with large, frightened eyes. She saw me as I approached, made to run off, but her leg was so mangled she couldn't move. She was trapped. I should have put her out of her misery. Made a quick cut, not let her suffer. But I was in such pain myself, a deep pain right down in my heart like I had never felt before.

When the deer stopped struggling I sat up and wiped my eyes. The sun disappeared behind a cloud and the light faded but I knew, despite the horror of what I'd done, that something had changed. Something fundamental. And I realized that I hadn't just killed the deer, I had killed Grace too.

I know, as I write this now with the blood of the deer staining my hands, that if Grace is dead then everything she was is dead too. The soldier, the skivvy, the prisoner, the person he could control. It's over. The nightmare is over and I am free.

I feel like the person I've always been: a girl. And that's what terrified him, that's what he could never let me be. If I had been allowed to be a girl then I would have done what girls do. I would have used my brain. I would have grown strong, questioned things. I would have made friends and laughed and loved. I would have painted my face with make-up if I'd wanted to, worn nice clothes if I'd wanted to, and then I might have discovered that all that was a bit daft so I'd bin them and try something new. But that wouldn't matter because it would all have been part of growing, naturally, into whoever I was meant to be. He tried to stop that. He tried to interfere with nature. And that is something I can never forgive because I've lost so many years of being who I am, being a girl.

The one person who could have helped, who could have understood, was ripped away from me. He did that because he knew how much she would have loved me and how much I would have needed her. He feared that more than any bullet, more than any bomb. Because that love was stronger than the greatest enemy. He always told me: 'Know your enemy and do everything in your power to destroy them.' And, after reading that book, it's clear that he did just that.

I want my mother. I want her so badly it hurts right here in my stomach. I want her to hold me in her arms, stroke my head gently and tell me that everything is going to be all right, that I'm safe and loved and protected. I want to close my eyes and know that she's looking after me while I sleep and that when I wake up there'll be blue skies and sunshine and no more pain. I want my mother.

31

Lisa

I'm huddled under a huge fir tree, its needles tickling my cheek. The smell of it reminds me of Christmas with Mum and Dad. Then I look up and see that I'm back there, in the living room of the Highgate flat where I grew up. It's very early in the morning, the sun not yet up, but Mum and Dad are here in their dressing gowns, watching as I unwrap my presents. Mum is perched on the arm of the sofa, Dad is crouched by my side.

'What do you think it is, Lisa?' he says, his eyes twinkling as he passes me a large silver parcel.

I take the present in my hands and look at it for a moment. My eyes are still sleepy and, with the curtains closed and the Christmas tree lights glowing, the room takes on a vague, fractured quality. There is a sense of unreality, of time suspended. The outside world doesn't exist, only we do: my mum, my dad and me, safe and happy in our fairy-lit house.

'Go on, darling,' says my dad, giving me a gentle nudge. 'You can open it.'

I look down at the present again. Something about it is bothering me. Something isn't quite right.

'Lisa?'

I hear my mother's voice as I rip open the paper.

'Lisa, what is it?'

My hand still grips the opened present while the discarded paper, red and blood-soaked, is scattered across the floor.

'Take it.'

Suddenly my parents are gone and Mark is standing in front of me.

'I said take it. It's yours.'

He grabs the present and thrusts it into my face. I see the glass tumbler at the very last moment, see the dried blood coated round its rim, then I feel it slice into my cheek. I put my hand to my mouth, the taste of blood on my tongue and in my nostrils.

'Lisa!'

I open my eyes. I'm lying on my back, the smell of blood and pine trees lingering around me.

'Lisa, are you okay?'

I turn over and see a man lying next to me on the sofa. He has short chestnut hair and almond-shaped brown eyes. He is completely naked.

Startled, I jump to my feet.

'Lisa, what is it?' he says, pushing the covers away. 'You were screaming in your sleep. Was it a nightmare?'

As I stand looking at him the dream slowly peels away and the events of the previous evening return to me. The bottle of wine, the kiss. We must have . . .

'You have to go,' I say, collecting my clothes, which are lying in a tangled heap by the sofa. 'Joe will be awake soon. He can't see this.'

'It's okay,' he says gently, holding his hands up. 'Everything's okay.'

He's talking to me like I'm an idiot, a child who has no control over herself. Mark used to do the same thing. From the moment we met at university he infantilized me, told me what I should wear, how I should revise, which friends I should see, what I should eat in restaurants. When we got married he booked the church and the honeymoon, he chose the rings and drew up the guest list. Once we were married I didn't have to think for myself at all. Every bill was organized on a spreadsheet that he kept on his computer, the grocery shopping was done – by him – online, he even laid out my clothes each morning. 'I just don't want you to worry about anything, Lisa,' he would say when I protested. 'You've been through enough.'

And he was right, I told myself, I had been through enough. When I met Mark I was still grieving for my father, though it had been seven years since his death. I had blocked out the world after Dad died, numbed my feelings to such an extent that the idea of having someone take me under their wing and make decisions about the ordinary day-to-day things that, back then, seemed so overwhelming, was an appealing one. My mother had been so distraught after my dad died that she had pretty much left me to my own devices so I arrived at university with no practical skills whatsoever. I couldn't cook or clean or even change a light bulb. I was useless. And then, suddenly, here was Mark, this intelligent, good-looking man, who appeared to adore me and who wanted to help me navigate the confusion that was life.

But in my numb state I had confused adoration with obsession, competence with control, and as time went on, Mark's behaviour became more and more cloying. Joe's birth had left me physically and mentally drained. In those early months I felt anxious all the time, my nerves were frayed and I was living in a constant state of fear. Everyone around me was a potential threat, that's how I saw it. Beth realized that I was struggling and told me to go and see the GP, thought maybe I was suffering from postnatal depression. Her sister had suffered with it and she recognized the signs. But when I raised this with Mark he told me that Beth was overreacting, that I was just tired and needed to rest. So he drew up a timetable where I was made to go to bed at 6 p.m. and stay there until morning. He wouldn't let me come down to see Joe or to eat together. I was forced to stay up there while he brought me trays of 'calming' meals: mashed potato with butter, mugs of warm milk, chicken soup. It was like I'd regressed, become the child he'd always wanted me to be. After weeks of this I couldn't take any more and a few nights later I fought back. I will regret that decision for the rest of my life as that was the night I lost everything. But I only regret the violence, not the fighting back. What I should have done was get out of that bed and calmly tell Mark that it was over, that he couldn't control me any more. But I was weak then and my head was full of rage and fear. It's different now. I'm different. I'm stronger and no man is going to tell me what to do any more.

'I said I'd like you to leave,' I repeat, my voice firm and clear. 'Now.'

He gets to his feet and picks his clothes up from the floor.

'Lisa, I don't understand,' he says, pulling his trousers on. 'Last night? You were . . . it was . . . it was so lovely, I –'

'Please, Jimmy,' I say, getting frustrated. 'Can we just leave it?'

'Leave it?' he exclaims, grabbing his jumper and pulling it over his head. 'After what happened last night?'

I have no idea what he means. My memory of the previous evening is sketchy to say the least.

'Look, I just need to see to Joe now,' I say, glancing towards the open door that leads out to the hallway.

'I understand,' he says softly. 'You've got a child. It's complicated. And you've been through so much.'

He comes towards me and places his hand on my shoulder.

'Get off me,' I cry, grabbing his arms. I push him away from me. He staggers and almost loses his footing.

'Lisa, what is this?' he exclaims. 'What's wrong with you?'

'Just leave me alone,' I shout. 'Do you hear me? Get out!'

The ferocity of my voice seems to shock him. He nods his head, grabs his coat from the back of the sofa and walks out of the room.

32

Grace

26 November 2004

I can't trust people. People let you down. Hurt you. I know that now.

I'd decided to go and see Isobel this morning because, after what happened with the book and the deer, I just wanted to see something pure, and she is the purest person I know. Or at least I thought she was.

I set off early, around 7.30, because I knew the vicar would have left for church by then. As I walked through the village I planned out the day in my head. First we'd have a bit of breakfast, maybe with some of that delicious hot chocolate she made me last time, then I thought I'd ask her if I could look at some of the books she had on the shelf in her bedroom. I could see the two of us sitting in the living room, me in one armchair, her in the other, both of us reading while the open fire crackled in the grate. That was as far as I managed to plan as by then I'd reached the vicarage, but the thought of that cosy scene made me feel all warm inside so I was in a happy mood when I knocked on the door.

I waited for a couple of minutes but there was no answer so I went round the back of the house. There was a pretty garden, nice and neat, with potted plants and a tall wooden bird table. All the things he used to say were 'signs of a civilization in freefall' but that I thought actually looked quite nice. At that point I thought maybe Isobel and I could come out here later and watch the birds feeding on the bird table. But I was about to find out there would be no reading, no nice times.

As I got close to the house I saw there was a big window at the back which had doors built into it. The doors were open, which I thought was a bit weird considering the time of year, and for a moment I got worried, thought someone had broken in. What was it he used to always say? There are thieves everywhere in these parts, Grace, folk that would slit your throat soon as look at you, that would slice their own granny for a couple of quid. I heard his words in my head as I made my way towards the doors, gripping the handle of the paring knife I'd slipped into my pocket that morning. If there was a battle to be fought then I'd come prepared. But then I came to the doors and . . . I came to the doors and . . . well, I can't quite put into words what happened next. It was so terrible. Worse than anything I'd ever seen before. But I suppose I need to try to describe it because if I write it down then it will be out of my head, that image, and I will never have to see it again.

Okay. Here goes.

I got to the doors and saw movement in the room. At first I thought it was the vicar but then I looked closer and saw a big hairy man standing by the fireplace. He had his arms round Isobel's neck. She was making gasping noises like she couldn't get her breath. Her face was all red. It was a horrifying sight. He was killing her. Right in front of my eyes. I had to do something. I had to save her.

Within seconds I was in there, hauling him off her. He was a big man but I'm strong and, unlike most girls my age, I've been taught soldiering skills. I felt like I had him subdued but then Isobel screamed and shouted, 'Grace, no.' She looked shocked because she's only ever seen me as the young girl who sells the eggs, she has no idea that I've been trained to be an elite soldier. Anyway, I was in battle mode and, much as I wanted to reassure her, I ignored her screams and got him in a chokehold just like I'd been taught, and then, when he was completely still, I put the knife to his throat. I told Isobel to run, to get out of there as fast as she could and that I would deal with this bastard, but she just stood there shaking her head.

'Grace, stop it,' she said. 'Let him go.'

I couldn't understand it. This monster was attacking her and she wanted me to let him go. I told her this. Told her that if she made a run for it I'd deal with him, finish him off nice and cleanly. No need for police or anything like that. And when I said this she looked at me like *I* was the scumbag, like *I* was the most disgusting thing she'd ever laid eyes on. Then she took a deep breath and told me if I didn't let him go she would call the police. She said that Steve was her boyfriend and he wasn't harming her, they were just kissing. When she said this I felt sick with shame. I'd made a complete idiot of myself. This man wasn't attacking Isobel. She wanted him to do what he was doing. Slowly, I loosened my grip.

When he was free he staggered to the sofa with his hand on his neck. 'Fucking nutter,' he said. 'You nearly killed me.'

I looked at Isobel then, hoping she would say something comforting to me, ask me to stay, tell him she'd made a big mistake and that he'd have to go. I wanted her to be like she was the first time I came here, all lovely and sweet and smiling. I wanted to go see her doll's house and listen to her talk about art.

But instead she just went running over to him and put her arms round him. 'Oh my God, my baby, are you okay?' Baby. That's what she called him. How can a grown man be a baby? Her baby. I just stood there watching them, the knife still clasped in my hands. She looked up at me then and told me to get out. She said it so coldly I was taken aback. It was like, in the space of a few minutes, I'd become a stranger to her. A dangerous stranger.

'Just go, Grace.'

That's what she said. Three words. But each one was a bullet to my chest. I could imagine how those people in Iraq felt, the ones *he* had to kill. Standing in the street while shots come at you so quickly you don't even realize it until you're hit and you die.

But when I got back here, when I saw the blood on the ground and on my journal, I saw what Isobel had seen this morning. I wasn't like her or any other normal girl and I'd been fooling myself in thinking I ever could be. Because no matter how hard I try to be like them, to see life as they do, to react to situations like they do, to be calm and controlled and respectable, it's no use. It might not have been like that at the beginning, and had the dead mother in the desert raised me instead of him then maybe things would have been different. But she didn't.

He did. He made me this way and in doing so condemned me to hell.

I can smell the doe's blood as I write this. It stinks of soil and metal and death. He told me about the smell of death when I was a bairn, told me how once you've had it in your nostrils it never goes away. And now I know what he means.

33
Lisa

'Mummy?'

I look up and see Joe standing in front of me. He has dressed himself in yesterday's clothes and is holding a toy lion in his hands.

'Why you in bed?' he says, looking at me quizzically. 'You tired?'

The simplicity of the question melts me. Yes, Joe, I am tired. I'm tired of running like this, tired of messing up again and again. But something about the way he is looking at me, his eyes full of trust and innocence, makes me get out of the bed.

'I was just having a little rest, baby,' I say, sweeping him up into my arms. 'But I feel better now. Wow, haven't you been a good boy, getting yourself dressed.'

He nods his head and looks down at his crumpled sweatshirt and joggers as if to inspect them.

'Now, we need to get some breakfast and brush our teeth,' I say as I carry him into the kitchen. 'And then we can . . .'

My phone is lying on the table. I pick it up and look at the time: 11.57. It was early morning when I threw Jimmy out, the sun hadn't even come up. How long had I been asleep? I look at Joe and shudder as I think of him wandering around this place by himself all morning. Anything could have happened.

'Pull yourself together, Lisa,' I mutter to myself as I head to the scullery to find the bucket Isobel used for collecting water. 'Right, Mr Joe,' I say, putting him down on the floor. 'We need to take this big bucket and go get some water from the lake. Will you help me?'

He nods his head.

'Good boy,' I say, hooking the bucket handle over my wrist. 'But first we need to get our coats. It'll be cold out there.'

There are two bread rolls and some tangerines on the kitchen counter. I take a roll and hand it to Joe.

'Here, baby. You eat this while I go and get our coats.'

I pull a chair out and lift him on to it.

'Mummy have some,' he says, breaking off a piece of bread and handing it to me. 'Make Mummy better.'

My eyes fill with tears but I blink them away as I take the morsel of bread. I can't let Joe see me crying.

'Mmm,' I say as I eat it. 'That is delicious. Thank you. Now you enjoy the rest of it and I'll just grab our coats.'

He nods his head but as I walk away the familiar guilty feeling returns, gnawing at my stomach. He shouldn't be here. He should be at home in the warmth with all his familiar things around him. But then I think of that newspaper article, the police, the look in Mark's eyes, and I know that if I cave in now I will lose Joe for ever. I grab the coats from the hook by the door and rush back into the kitchen, fearful that Joe might have disappeared into thin air in the seconds since I left him, but he's still there, happily munching away on his bread roll. I stand for a moment looking at the back of his head, his curly hair matted from sleep and sticking out at all angles, and I feel my heart will burst. How is it possible to love someone as deeply as this? To feel like you will die without them yet would happily die for them? As I look at him I whisper, under my breath, that things are going to get better, that I will stay strong now, with no distractions, no doubts.

'Right,' I say briskly, heading across to him. 'Let's get your coat on.'

He looks up at me, breadcrumbs scattered across his front, and holds up his arms. I lift him down from the chair, put his coat on, then mine, and as we head outside to the lake, I feel something resembling peace.

The air is cold but the sun is out and it casts a horizontal light across the surface of the water as we approach the lake. There is something pure and clean about the day, the sharpness of the air, the pale-grey luminosity of the sky, that makes it seem like the world has been swept clean overnight; that we can start again.

Joe trots off ahead of me, pausing by the edge of the lake to pick something up off the ground. I walk faster to catch up and when I reach him he looks at me and hands me a pebble.

'Present,' he says, his blue eyes reflecting the winter light. 'For you.'

'Thank you, baby,' I say, turning the pebble over in my palm. 'It's beautiful. And look, there are more.'

I crouch beside him and pick up a handful of the mossy, damp stones.

'Watch this,' I say as I skim one across the lake. 'Look at the ripples.'

'I do it,' says Joe, bending down to pick up another pebble. 'I try.'

He spins the pebble into the lake. It doesn't carry very far and plops into the water just inches from our feet. It doesn't matter though. He's loving the game.

'Good shot, Joe,' I say, rubbing his head. 'Now, my turn.'

We stand like that for a good ten minutes, skimming pebbles and watching them flutter across the lake. When I throw one particularly large pebble it makes a great splashing noise as it hits the water.

'Ooh, that was like a big fish,' I say, putting my hand across my eyes to shade them from the sharp sunlight. 'Hey, Joe, shall we be fishermen?'

There's a load of old bracken gathered in a pile by the gate. I walk across and find a long, thin branch then bring it back to the lake.

'Look, here's my fishing rod,' I say as I lower the branch into the lake. 'Now, let's see if we can find a fish.'

'Fish,' whispers Joe, his eyes fixed firmly on the water.

'Oooh,' I cry, yanking at the branch. 'I think I caught something. Wait . . . ooh . . . it's a heavy one.'

I haul the branch out, then pull a face at Joe.

'Oh no, missed it,' I say, clicking my tongue. 'That silly old fish was just too big.'

Joe giggles and claps his hands excitedly.

'Again,' he cries. 'Get fish again.'

'Again?' I say, putting my hands on my hips. 'You want me to try again? Oh, I don't know. Do you think I've enough puff left?'

'Yes, yes, again,' he cries. 'Want to see the big fish.'

'Okay,' I say, lifting up the branch. 'Let's see if we can catch him this time.'

I swing the branch towards the water and repeat the charade of trying to haul out the big fish. Beside me, Joe shrieks with laughter.

'Again. Again.'

I do as he says and we're laughing so much I don't notice the car pulling up.

'Wow, that looks like fun.'

The voice makes me jump. I drop the branch and turn to see Isobel walking towards us. She's dressed for the weather in her long black coat and furry hat.

'Did you catch anything, Joe?' she says, crouching down next to him, the edge of her coat trailing in the water.

'Big fish,' he cries, pointing towards the lake. 'In there.'

'A big fish?' she repeats, her eyes wide. 'Big enough for my dinner?'

Joe laughs and my heart sinks. Though it's nice to see Isobel, part of me wishes she would just go away. Joe and I were making a breakthrough there and for the first time in God knows how long he had called me 'Mummy'. Now Isobel is here and he only has eyes for her.

'Right,' she says, getting to her feet. 'How do you two fancy coming to hear some Christmas carols? There's a children's concert on at the church. I organize it for Dad every year and it's lots of fun. The children get to see the baby Jesus in the crib and sing some carols, then it's back to the church hall for a little party with Father Christmas.'

At those words Joe squeals with delight.

'Father Christmas! Want to see Father Christmas.'

He jumps into Isobel's arms, his face beaming with happiness.

'Ooh,' cries Isobel, pretending to fall backwards. 'I think that's my answer. Let's get going then. It starts in twenty minutes.'

I smile politely as I follow Isobel to the car but inside I feel nervous. What if someone recognizes me from the article? If it made the *Sunday Times* then the story must be all over the news, TV as well as the papers. I reassure myself with the thought that the photo shows a woman with long blonde hair and now mine's short and dark. But as I get into the passenger seat I feel a lump of panic settle into my stomach. Please let it be dark in there, I think to myself as Isobel starts the car and we head off towards the village.

Five minutes later we're at the church and as we step inside I forget my nerves for a few moments. It looks so beautiful. The pews have been decorated with evergreens and holly berries, candles flicker all around, and up on the altar, gathered round the crib of the baby Jesus, are about a dozen children aged between three and five.

'Where's Father Christmas?' says Joe, his voice echoing around the tiny space.

'He's coming later,' whispers Isobel, taking his hand. 'But first I'm going to take you to see baby Jesus. Would you like that?'

Joe nods his head and Isobel gestures to me to sit in the front pew.

'I'll take him up,' she says, smiling. 'You can get a good view from there.'

I hesitate. Might it be better to sit at the back, so I can't be seen? But then most of the people in here are parents whose attention is solely on their kids up on the altar. Still, I make sure not to make eye contact with any of them as I slip into the pew and watch Joe and Isobel take their places alongside the crib. Isobel raises her hand to someone at the back of the church and the opening bars of 'Once in Royal David's City' strike up on the organ. It's the most beautiful sound and as I watch the children sing I'm transported back to my own childhood and the tiny All Saints Church where my parents and I would go on Christmas Eve to listen to the carols. I catch Joe's eye and wave but he looks away then nuzzles his head into Isobel's leg. Whatever closeness we'd just achieved by the lake has been ripped away and I'm back where I started. All around me sit parents with their children; families all huddled together, getting ready for Christmas. And here I am. An outcast. A failure. I look down at the carol hymn sheet but the words dissolve in front of my eyes.

'Are you all right, dear?'

I turn to see an elderly lady sitting next to me.

'You look upset,' she says, leaning closer. 'Would you like a handkerchief?'

I shake my head and stare straight ahead at the altar. I can't let her see my face.

'What's your name, love?' she whispers. 'I could have sworn I'd seen your face before.'

I go to speak but my mouth is dry. Instead I shake my head. I have to get out of here. Now. But if I make a fuss the woman will get suspicious so I stay where I am. The rest of the carols go by in a blur and as the final note plays I slip out of the pew and head outside into the fresh air.

It's quiet in the churchyard and I stand for a moment practising the breathing exercises they taught me at the counselling sessions. After a few minutes, the tightness in my chest begins to subside.

'There you are.'

I turn and see Isobel heading towards me. She's holding a plastic cup in her hands, steam rising from it.

'I was just getting some air,' I tell her as she approaches. 'Where's Joe?'

'He's with the other kids at the party,' she says. 'Father Christmas has just arrived and they're all going nuts.'

I don't like the idea of Joe being left alone with strangers. If I keep my head down I can go and get him out quickly.

'We need to be heading home now,' I say to Isobel. 'Where is the entrance to the hall?'

'It's just an annexe off the church,' says Isobel. 'But don't rush off. Stay for a bit. Joe's having such a nice time.'

'Well, maybe for another half-hour,' I say, following Isobel back into the church.

The hall rings out with the sound of children's laughter. The party is in full swing and a large Father Christmas is making his way round the room with a red sack of toys. Under different circumstances it would be perfect, but I can't relax. I scan the room to see if the old woman from my pew is here but thankfully there's no sign of her. I smile at Joe, who is sitting on the floor surrounded by wrapping paper and balloons. A little girl cuddles into him and shows him the toy train Father Christmas has given her.

'He must be missing his friends,' says Isobel, taking a sip from her cup of mulled wine. 'From nursery? He is at nursery, isn't he?'

I nod my head, uncomfortable with the sudden probing. I'll give Joe five more minutes and then we really need to go.

'Is it a good nursery?' she continues. 'I know that city ones can be a bit . . . overcrowded.'

Her voice is loud and I'm aware that people overhearing who have read the paper might put two and two together. I need to get her away from the subject of Joe and London, so I ask the first thing that comes into my head.

'Grace,' I say, more firmly than intended, 'did you know her?'

'Grace,' repeats Isobel, her smile fading. 'Which Grace?'

'The girl who lived at the house,' I say, remembering what Jimmy said about the whole village being shocked by what happened. 'Rowan Isle. You must have been about the same age as her. I just wondered whether you knew her.'

'I knew of her,' says Isobel, draining her mug. 'Though I didn't know her particularly well. It was such a sad case. The whole village was rocked by it, but Grace and her dad were strange. She was known for being wild and prone to angry outbursts, so I guess it was only a matter of time before something terrible happened.'

She shakes her head.

'Tired now. We go home.'

I look down and see Joe standing at my feet. He's holding a plastic Spider-Man figure in his hand and has jam smeared across his mouth.

'Hello, beautiful boy,' I say, stooping down and heaving him on to my waist. 'Yes, let's go back now and have a little rest. Have you had a good time?'

He nods his head then nuzzles into the crook of my neck, sleepily.

'You've exhausted yourself,' laughs Isobel. 'That's always a sign of a good party. Listen, I just need to check on something then I'll drive you home. Wait here and I'll be straight back.'

She walks out of the hall leaving Joe and me standing in the middle of the floor. A young mum standing by the buffet table smiles over at us. We're too conspicuous in here. I need to get away.

'Come on, Joe,' I say gently as we head for the exit. 'We'll wait for Isobel out here.'

I open the door and step back out into the churchyard. It's dark now and a great yellow moon looms above the trees. I see a shadow in the corner by the church and a familiar voice speaking, though distorted by anger.

'Where are you?' she hisses into the phone. 'I thought you said you'd text when you'd arrived.'

She turns then and sees me, the light of the phone screen illuminating her face.

Isobel.

'Oh, Lisa, Joe,' she says, coming towards us, her voice softening. 'There you are. Now, give me two seconds and I'll bring the car round. What a day it's been, eh? What a bloomin' day.'

34

Grace

28 November 2004

The sun has just come up and I'm sitting under the oak tree watching the wood awaken. Another night of sleeping out here. It was cold and damp and uncomfortable and, I'm not going to lie, I would have preferred to have been back at the house, in my warm room, but I can't go back there. I can't see him. Not after what I've discovered.

It's a beautiful sight, the wood at this hour. Each blade of grass glistens with the morning dew, like someone's gone through it with a bucket of soapsuds and given it a good old clean. The trees and bracken are shrouded in a light mist, like something from a fairy tale, one where the monster has been beaten and a new day is beginning. Looking at these old trees, I feel safe and protected. After all, they have stood unmoved for hundreds of years and they'll carry on long after I've gone. What harm can possibly come to me if I'm sheltered here amongst them? So I focus on the trees and the bracken and the soft sounds of the wood pigeons and I try my very best to stay calm, but my heart is jumping around my chest like a mouse caught in a cage.

For a moment my head feels fuzzy, a good kind of fuzzy, the kind that lets you forget everything, and I wonder why my chest feels so tight. And then I remember. She came to see me. She wants me to help her. And I don't know if I can.

It was early evening. I was having a kip in my spot under the oak tree as I'd been up since dawn, after a night dreaming of the doe and the dead mother in the desert. I was so shattered the next day that by teatime I was dead to the world. My doss bag was pulled up tight round my ears so at first I couldn't hear the crying, and if I had it would have sounded like the beginning of another strange dream, which in a way it was. Then I felt a weight on my arm and that woke me up. Someone was shaking me, violently. I was under attack and I had to act fast so I pulled the cover back, all set for a fight, but there was no enemy there, it was just her. Just Isobel.

She looked terrible. Her face was all red and puffy and her hair was all over the place, like she'd just got out of bed or something. I'd never seen her like this. She looked so bad that for a moment I forgot that I'd been angry with her. I just wanted to give her a cuddle. But then she opened her mouth and it all came back to me.

'First things first, you shouldn't have done what you did yesterday,' she said. 'It was so embarrassing. Poor Steve nearly had a heart attack.'

That name again. Steve. It felt like a stone in my throat. But it jolted me awake too and once I was awake I started to feel angry. I told her that if that's how she felt she could bugger off, go back to Steve and her stupid house and her stupid dad and leave me the hell alone. Then I lay down and pulled my doss bag over my head again.

I thought that would be it but she started tugging at me again. I pulled the bag tighter so it was so far over my head I could barely breathe, but she wouldn't let up. Eventually I threw the bag off and leapt to my feet with my fists clenched beside me, ready to fight, to take her on. Isobel looked terrified and stepped backwards into the bracken.

Then she put her hands out in front of her, defensively, and said that she was sorry, sorry for shouting at me. She said she hadn't come to argue or fight, she'd come to ask for my help.

Well, that surprised me all right. Help? What kind of help could this girl with her perfect life and perfect home want from someone like me?

But I was curious so I unclenched my fists and told her to sit down. She looked at the doss bag and wrinkled her face. It was covered in bloodstains and bits of mud and bracken, a world away from her immaculate bed with its crisp cotton sheets, but, give her her dues, she sat down all the same.

I asked her how she knew I was here and she said she'd seen me earlier when I was up on the crag. She'd been up there looking for Steve as that's where they usually meet but he hadn't turned up. 'Then I saw you and I knew it was a sign,' she said. 'That you were the one person who could help me.' She said she'd followed me down the crag and through the woods, thinking that I'd be heading for Rowan Isle House, but then saw me settling down under the tree. 'You looked exhausted,' she said. 'So I thought I'd wait a bit, but now I can't wait any longer. You have to help me, Grace, please say you will.'

I told her that she'd made me feel bad the other day, that the things she'd said to me hurt more than any knife could. She repeated that she was sorry, but she said it so fast it was like she just wanted to shut me up so she could say what she wanted to say.

I was curious to know what she wanted and, if I'm honest, it felt good to have her sitting next to me. After embarrassing myself so badly the other day I thought I'd never see her again. I'd missed her.

So I told her to tell me whatever it was she wanted my help with. She went all quiet, like she'd lost her nerve. She looked down at the ground and started pulling bits of grass up. I got impatient then and told her to spit it out otherwise we'd be here all night.

She nodded her head and said, 'Okay, okay,' then she looked up at me and said that her dad had banned her from seeing Steve. He'd arrived home unexpectedly the other evening and caught them in the bedroom. I tried to imagine the look on the vicar's face, seeing his daughter in the position I'd seen her in. Had he felt like I had? Like he wanted to rip Steve's throat out? I can't imagine the vicar getting violent, but then certain things shake us up so much they bring something out in us, a weird force we didn't know was there before. I was thinking all this as Isobel continued talking. She was going on about how she hated her father and that she wished he was dead.

When she said this, I was shocked. Surely she didn't mean that? But her face had changed when she said it. She didn't look like Isobel any more. Her expression was like one I'd seen on a bull when I was little. We'd taken a wrong turn one day and ended up in some strange field. We didn't see the bull until it was too late. He'd pulled me to safety but not before I'd looked that beast straight in the eye. What I saw in its black eyes was pure brute rage. And I could see the same in Isobel's. For just a few minutes she'd turned into an animal.

She said that her dad had told her she was a wicked girl, that she had committed a grave sin and would need to pay for it. He said that she had sullied the memory of her mother, and not only that but her mother, he said, would have disowned her if she had seen what he had seen. He told her that things were going to change, that he had given her too much freedom and had paid the price for it.

When she stopped talking her expression changed and she was Isobel once more, but I felt weird. It was like I'd just seen into her soul or something and I didn't really like what was there.

She seemed to sense this because she stood up and said she had to go. I told her that she still hadn't asked me what she wanted me to help with. She looked at me and smiled then and said something that took me by surprise. She said that I was the only real friend she had in the world. I found that very hard to believe. Her only friend? I mean, what about school and history of art and all that? Surely she had loads of friends, friends who could talk to her about all that stuff? After all, she was Isobel. Girls like her always have friends. At least, they do in the books I read. In reality I know nothing about friends, only that I've never had one.

But it felt good to hear her say it and all the pain I'd felt when she shouted at me the other day fell away. I couldn't be angry with her. She was my Isobel. And she was my only friend in the world too.

I told her this and then something strange happened. She started to cry. Not just a little weep but great, breathless sobs. She said that she wanted to kill herself, that life without Steve wasn't worth living. That was hard to hear, that she loved this Steve person so much she was ready to die for him. But all the same, I knew I had to do something, because I couldn't live in a world without Isobel. I felt for her what she felt for Steve and one day she might just see sense and feel the same way about me, but for now being friends was enough and I had to do what friends do and help her.

So I put my arm round her shoulders and told her that everything was going to be all right, that she just had to tell me how I could help.

She looked up at me. She was still sobbing and it was hard to hear her. But when I finally made out what she was saying, my heart froze. She said that she and Steve had planned to run away together. They were going to meet at the crag the following night – this evening – at 11 p.m. and head off from there. Steve had told her to take some money from the vicar's safe so they'd have enough to get going.

I was shocked when I heard this. I didn't think Isobel had it in her to be a thief. And what about the vicar? He didn't deserve that. All he was doing was looking out for his daughter. I didn't say this to Isobel though, just listened as she told me how she wanted me to come and keep a lookout while she and Steve made their escape.

'You know how to look after yourself,' she said to me, gesturing to the bloodstains on the doss bag. 'If my father follows us I'll just go to pieces, but if you're there you can threaten him.'

She stopped then and looked down at her hands. She was twisting the sleeve of her coat between her fingers.

'Threaten him?' I asked, still not sure quite why the vicar needed to be dealt with like this.

'Just keep him distracted,' she said, still twisting her sleeve. 'So Steve and I can get away.'

She stopped crying then and looked at me. Her face was so sad it made my heart hurt. But I couldn't promise her anything, so I told her I'd think about it and give her my answer tomorrow. She said she understood, then she got up, hugged me, told me I was the best friend anyone could ever wish for and that if I helped her she'd be grateful to me for ever. That was strange to hear, though it was quite nice too as it meant that she would always be my friend.

However, when she left I started to feel uneasy. I went over what she'd told me again and again in my head and the more I thought about it the more I felt that it was Steve who was making Isobel do this. He was a bad influence on her. Isobel loved her father and she loved her home. Now she was going to have to leave both and it was all down to him. I felt sorry for the vicar. He just wanted what was best for his daughter, like all fathers do. And that made me think of *him*, the man I used to call Sarge. Maybe that's why he did what he did, because he wanted the best for me. And instead of sticking around and asking him, I'd just bolted.

The sun is fully up now and I have made a decision. I'm going to try to forget about the room and the torture, the book and the mother in the desert, and go back to the house. One last time.

35

Lisa

I stand on the side of the road and watch as Isobel's car disappears over the brow of the hill. We had driven through the village in silence. Isobel kept her eyes fixed on the road ahead, her hands gripping the steering wheel tightly as though fearful the car would skid off into a ditch of its own accord.

She was polite when we left the car, smiled at Joe, said she was glad we'd enjoyed the party, though there was a frostiness that hadn't been there before, a sense that I'd offended her in some way, though I couldn't for the life of me think how.

'Right, Joe,' I say, taking Dad's torch out of my pocket. 'Hold my hand now. It's dark and we don't want to get lost.'

I feel his warm hand in mine as we walk tentatively towards the house, the thin sliver of yellow torchlight guiding our way. Beside me, Joe starts humming a tune that after a few moments I recognize as 'Jingle Bells', the song that had been playing on a loop at the party.

'That's a nice song,' I say as we reach the door. 'Did you like the party?'

'Saw Father Christmas,' he says as I push my body weight against the door. 'He gave me present.'

'Yes,' I say breathlessly as, on the third push, the door yields. 'And it was a lovely present. You'll have to introduce Spider-Man to your lions, I'm sure they – Joe, slow down.'

It is pitch black inside the house, though I can hear Joe's footsteps up ahead.

'Joe, wait for me,' I call, shining the torch along the hallway. 'We need to light some candles in the living room. Joe? Where are you?'

I point the torch ahead of me and see the outline of the kitchen door frame. Stepping slowly towards it, I cast the light across the room. The black stove looms ahead of me like some kind of crouching beast; the table is scattered with crumbs and orange peel from this morning's makeshift breakfast.

'Joe?' I say, backing away from the kitchen door and going to the living room. 'Joe, please answer me. Where are you?'

He's not in the living room, though I shine the torch behind the sofa and both chairs in case he's hiding behind them. Nothing.

'Joe, baby,' I call as I make my way down the narrow passageway towards the bedrooms. 'Joe?'

And then I see him. He's standing outside the bedroom with a blanket over his shoulders. He looks at me then lets out an ear-piercing yell.

'Joe, what are you doing?' I cry, my ears ringing with the noise.

'Being a wild thing,' he says, 'with terrible roars.'

He's smiling innocently, waiting for me to come back with the response I always make when we read the story – 'and gnashed their terrible teeth' – but I'm so shaken I can barely speak.

'Joe,' I say, lifting him into my arms. 'You . . . you must never do that again, do you hear me? Never. Mummy was so frightened.'

I pull him into my chest but he resists and jerks his body backwards.

'You horble,' he cries, his face twisting with rage. 'I want Daddy now. Daddy not tell me off. Daddy's nice.'

His eyes fill with tears.

'Shh,' I whisper, stroking his head gently. 'I didn't tell you off, Joe, I was just scared, that's all. I thought you were a monster.'

'You a monster,' he yells, pummelling his fists into my chest. 'That's what Daddy says. You a horble monster.'

He lifts his hand up and strikes me on the side of my face. The shock almost knocks me off my feet but I steady myself quickly.

'Joe,' I say as calmly as I can. 'You mustn't hit Mummy. That really hurt.'

He wriggles out of my arms then turns and runs towards the staircase, the blanket in his arms.

I go after him, but he's running so fast I can hear his footsteps on the stairs. Then I hear something: a faint humming noise which grows louder as I approach the staircase.

'Oh what fun tis to ride . . .'

'Jingle Bells'. Joe is still singing it.

'That's a lovely song,' I call out to the empty passageway. 'Now shall we go and light the fire and make some cocoa? Then we can sing some more Christmas songs. What do you say?'

I pause at the foot of the stairs and listen. There's a clatter of footsteps overhead and then he starts to giggle.

'Come on, Joe,' I call up the stairs. 'It's too dark to play hide and seek. Now come downstairs and we'll get a nice hot drink.'

The footsteps intensify, loud and heavy like he's dancing or jumping up and down.

'Joe,' I call, my voice louder and firmer. 'Please come down. Now.'

The footsteps stop. I wait for him to emerge at the top of the stairs, my heart pulsating in my chest, but there is no sign of him.

'Joe?'

I realize I will have to go up there and get him. It's dark and he could fall and injure himself. Gripping the banister with my right hand, I slowly make my way up the stairs, calling to him as I go.

'Coming ready or not,' I cry, trying to keep my voice steady as I shine the torch ahead of me. 'No more hiding, baby.'

The air smells stale and cloying as I go further up the stairs and as I reach the landing a cloud of thick dust hits me and I start to cough. Putting my hand to my mouth, I slowly make my way along the narrow passage.

There's a half-closed door ahead of me and as I shine the torch at it I see that the walls and floor inside have all been painted white. I blink to adjust my eyes but the glare of white makes me feel dizzy and disorientated.

'Joe,' I call as I step towards the door. 'Joe, where are you?'

I take hold of the door handle, my mouth dry and clammy, and then I hear it again. The song. But something about it sounds wrong. It's a distorted sound, like an old LP being played on the wrong speed. And then I realize it's not Joe's voice I can hear singing, it's something much more disturbing. The voice behind that door, growing louder and louder as I stand trembling with fear, my hand gripping the handle, is a man's voice. I need to get Joe out of there. Now.

'Joe,' I cry as I push the door open and burst into the room, shining the torch in front of me. 'Joe –'

I hear myself scream as I drop the torch and see, in ghoulish green light, the shadow of a tall figure.

I stand motionless as it comes towards me. I should get the hell out of here but my legs have turned to stone.

'No,' I cry as it bears down on me. 'Please ... don't hurt me.'

I drop to my haunches and cover my head with my hands, waiting for the blow to come, but nothing happens. I look up and see Joe standing by the door, the blanket still draped over his shoulders.

'Joe, run downstairs,' I say. 'Run. Quickly!'

Then I feel a hand on my shoulder and a low, familiar voice calls Joe's name. I turn to see Mark, his face half in shadow. He's wearing a black winter coat with the collar turned up.

'Get out of my way, Lisa,' he says, his voice thick with hatred.

'No,' I cry as he pushes past me and scoops Joe up in his arms. 'Please, Mark, no.'

'Daddy,' shrieks Joe delightedly, shrugging the blanket off his shoulders. 'Daddy come.'

'Yes, my darling,' Mark says, clutching Joe tightly to his chest. 'Daddy's come. You're safe now. I'm going to take you home.'

'Mark, please,' I say as he walks towards the door. 'Don't take him. Please. I beg you.'

I lunge for Joe but Mark pushes me away. I fall backwards and land in a heap on the floor. As I struggle to my feet I hear the door close with a thud and the sound of a bolt sliding.

'No,' I scream, running for the door. 'Please, Mark. No.'

36

Grace

It's so cold I can see my breath floating on the air in front
of me like a will-o'-the-wisp as I sit writing this. When I
was a kid he used to tell me that things lived in this wood
that were beyond explanation – sprites and goblins and
the like – and I believed him. When we came out hunting
he'd walk behind me through the trees and do this silly
voice. 'Is that you, Grace?' he'd say, all high-pitched and
squeaky. 'Have you come to see us?' And being a daft kid,
I would fall for it and answer, 'Yes, it's me. I've brought
you some scran.' Then I'd lay some bits of stale bread
down on the ground and look around me to see if they
were coming. 'Thing you gotta remember, Grace,' he'd
say, coming up behind me, 'is that they're shy, the little
people. They won't come out while we're here.' And I was
such a silly little kid, I'd just buy that rubbish. I'd walk off
with him back to the house and that night I'd lie in my
doss bag and imagine some goblin sitting on a toadstool
eating my stale bread. I did that because he told me there
were spirits in that wood, magical things beyond my
imagination, and I trusted him. He told me I had to have
faith and that just because I couldn't see something with
my own eyes didn't mean it wasn't true. So I kept faith in
him and all the things he told me. I mean, why wouldn't

I? He was my father and he would never lie to me. At least that's what I thought back then. Now I know it was all nonsense, every bit of it.

But despite the fact I knew he'd lied to me I still held those trips into the wood close to my heart and I was thinking about them when I went back to the house this morning. Thinking about being a kid and the times we'd had gave me a warm feeling inside. I had to hold on to that if I was to give him another chance, that was what I was telling myself as I made my way up the path towards the house. There had to be a reason why he'd lied about the dead mother in the desert. And there had to be a reason why he'd locked me in that room. He'd never let me down before. We'd been a good team. I'd never forget how proud he was when I made my first kill. And he could be kind too. If I was poorly he'd make soup and put cold flannels on my forehead and sing me my favourite song about old Stewball the racehorse who never drank water, but only drank wine.

I started humming that song to myself as I walked round the back of the house. He was always in the kitchen making scran at that time of the morning so that was where I was heading. I was singing that song and I was happy and I was ready to forgive him. The racehorse's bridle was silver, his mane was gold and all was right with the world. That's how it felt. The world was a good place to be. Until I turned the corner and saw her lying there on the grass.

Her beautiful eyes were wide open and facing the sky. Her right leg was bloody and mangled where the trap had got her. My vixen.

I started to scream and the noise I made was like the ram we found one day who'd got its horns caught in the briars. It was snorting and raging and scraping its hooves on the ground. It was ready to kill in order to set itself free.

I carried on screaming as I ran up the steps and pushed the kitchen door open. He wasn't in there and there was no smell of cooking. I guessed he must still be in bed but then I heard snoring coming from the parlour. I stormed in there and saw him lying slumped in my gran's old armchair, an empty tankard hanging from his hand.

And I knew in that moment what I had to do. I ran out of the house and went straight to the outbuilding and grabbed my gun. I was going to need it now. Then I slung it over my shoulder and made my way to the village. A couple of old ladies gave me funny looks as I marched past the Post Office but I didn't care. I was free now. With my vixen gone there was only one friend left and I couldn't lose her. I just couldn't.

When I got to the vicarage I banged on the door in a frenzy and when Isobel opened it I gave her just three words – 'I'll help you' – then turned and walked off down the path. But when I got to the edge of the village I heard her call my name. I looked round and saw her, all red-faced, running after me.

She asked me why I had a gun and I told her I was off hunting. I felt bad for lying but she couldn't know the truth. I had to keep her trust.

She told me to meet her at the crag tonight at eleven. I nodded my head. Her face lit up then and she hugged me and told me how grateful she was that I was helping her.

I didn't need her thanks so I didn't say anything, just nodded and headed back here and fell asleep under my doss bag until the sound of the old tawny owl woke me up an hour ago.

So Isobel thinks I'm going to help her escape with Steve. But what she doesn't realize is that I have another plan. I will not let that monster take her away from me. I love her. She is my only friend. And if I've learned anything from that liar who brought me up it's that you will do anything to be with the person you love.

You'll die for them.

Kill for them.

37

Lisa

I grip the handle and pull at it hard. It's locked fast.

'Let me out,' I cry in a raw, desperate voice. 'Please, Mark, you have to bring him back. I need him. I need my baby.'

My hands are still gripping the handle. I take them away then start pounding my fists on the door.

'Please,' I yell. 'Please let me out.'

But the silence on the other side of the door tells me that my pleas will not be answered. I turn away, my ears ringing. The darkened room seems to spin around me as I stumble about trying to find my bearings. Then my foot catches something hard. I look down and I can just make out the shape of the torch that I dropped earlier. I pick it up and point it in front of me.

The room is sparse. The walls and floor have been painted white, like some sort of sterile laboratory. The blanket Joe had been wearing when Mark grabbed him is lying where he dropped it by the door. I stoop to pick it up and hold it to my face. It smells of old dust and animal skin. I drop it back on to the floor, nausea swelling inside me.

Then as my brain starts to focus I remember Isobel. I'd put her number into my phone the other day. Patting my jeans, I feel the reassuring bulk of my phone in my pocket.

I pull it out and see that, miraculously, it has a signal, though the battery is down to the last bar. I scroll through my contacts until I reach Isobel's number.

It rings and rings.

'Please answer, Isobel,' I mutter under my breath. 'Please.'

But she doesn't answer and, after a pause, I hear an automated voice asking me to leave a message.

'Isobel, it's Lisa,' I say, trying to catch my breath. 'I'm at the house and . . . Mark was here when we got back. He's taken Joe and locked me in the room upstairs. Please come and help me . . . if you . . . when you get this message. Please.'

It cuts off and I'm left holding the phone in my hands, staring impotently at the screen as it fades from light to dark. I press the screen. It stays dark. The battery has gone.

Fuck.

I have to get out of here. There must be another way out. A window or something.

I step further into the room and shine the torch into each corner, finding nothing but dust and spider's webs. There's no light trickling into the room but that might be because the moon has gone behind a cloud. There must be a window here somewhere. The problem is that the ceiling is curved in such a way it's impossible to see clearly from this angle. I switch the torch on again then spot a wooden chair in the corner of the room.

I lift the chair and ease it closer to the wall. It wobbles as I climb on but I steady myself by putting my hand on the back of it. Once I'm up there I turn off the torch and squint to adjust my eyes. A faint silver light trickles down on to the floor from above. From this angle I can see a wide ledge running round the edge of the ceiling. I place my palms on the ledge and ease myself forward. Following the diminishing trail of light, I look up to the right and see a tiny, rectangular window just within reaching distance.

The window is thick with grime and dust and has an old-fashioned iron stay that juts out at an angle, away from the frame. Taking the stay in one hand, I push at the glass with the other. It's stiff with dirt but after a couple of tries it finally yields and I'm met with a shock of cold air.

Leaning forward, I open the window wider and poke my head out. I can see the hills in front of me and the outline of the cages in the garden. So this room is at the back of the house then. If it was at the front I could have shouted towards the road, shone the torch, hoped some motorist would notice and come to help. But out this way is just an expanse of wilderness with only the rabbits and foxes to hear my cries.

Still, I have to try. There could be someone out there, a hunter or poacher, some overenthusiastic rambler taking a midnight stroll. The window is too small to climb through but I push my body as far out as possible and scream at the top of my voice.

'HELP! CAN ANYBODY HEAR ME? PLEASE HELP. PLEASE.'

My voice comes out reedy and thin. There is no one coming to help. The only person at large, the only one who can hear me, is the person who bolted the door, the person who now has my child, and that thought makes me feel sick with terror.

'MARK! COME BACK AND LET ME OUT. YOU CAN'T DO THIS TO ME. PLEASE, MARK!'

I shout again a few more times but there is nothing. It's hopeless.

I ease myself back on to the ledge, but as I go to close the window something on the inner ledge catches my eye. I lean forward to take a closer look. It's a book of some sort. I reach out and grab it as a gust of icy wind strikes the glass and sends the pages fluttering. Holding it to my chest, I step carefully back down on to the chair.

The book is damp and yellow, bleached by the sun. I turn it over in my hands. It's leather-bound and has the remnants of some kind of gold lettering across the front. A name perhaps? It reminds me of the diaries I used to get from my parents every Christmas, the ones with a lock and a tiny key and my initials embossed on the front. I place it on my lap and open it up. The first few pages are damp and stuck together. Whatever handwriting had been there has been dissolved. The last few pages, however, are intact. I flatten the book out and point the torch closer. The handwriting is messy and smudged but I can just about make it out.

I start to read and a chill flutters right through my body as I realize that this isn't some childish diary, it's a first-hand account of a murder.

38

Grace

I want to write one last entry in this book before closing it down for good. In thirty minutes I'm due to meet Isobel at the crag and after that I'm not sure what's going to happen to me.

I am no longer an elite soldier but an assassin. It's not going to be like shooting rabbits or sheep. This is the real thing. Serious. But I tell myself not to lose my resolve, to think about the vixen and her broken body, of never seeing Isobel again. I have to go through with this.

It's just begun to snow. Light flakes for now but I can tell from the change in the air that it'll become much thicker as the night goes on. He always loved the snow. Said it reminded him of when he was a boy and his grand-dad used to take him up to the hills to build a snowman. I can't imagine him being a boy.

I remember when I was about seven years old the two of us walked up to Harrowby Crag in the middle of a snowdrift. I was quite scared because it was coming on thick but he insisted we were going to build a snowman. He always walked so fast I found it hard to keep up and the snow was so thick that I soon lost sight of him. I stopped to get my bearings and as I looked around me everything seemed wrong. When people write about snow in books it's always a magical thing, soft gentle flakes, a world turned white, but I didn't feel magical as I stood there that day. Instead I felt like I'd been transported to another planet, a cold, hostile world. I wanted to run, to get back to the house, light the stove and get warm, but back then I did whatever he told me to do and he had told me we were going to build a snowman so I started walking in the direction he had gone. In the end the snow got too thick to see and we had to turn round and go home. The next day we saw that some of the sheep in the next field had perished in the blizzard. I remember Sarge being sad that morning, said that he'd just wanted me to have fun and ended up nearly freezing us both to death. I told him that it was okay, that I liked the warm and he liked the cold, and then he smiled and said, 'That's right, pet.'

It's strange but I'd forgotten all about that night until now. Funny what you remember when you're trying to forget.

As I write this I can see the photo of the dead mother in the desert poking out of the top of his book. A few days ago I would have said it was her who made sure I didn't come to harm in the blizzard that night, that she was protecting me from above. Now I know the truth, I know it couldn't possibly have been her, but I still believe there was something watching over us that night, some all-seeing eye. He would go mad at me for saying this but I like to think it was God. That's right. God. The thing that I'm not meant to believe in, that's the root of all evil, all suffering and war. 'A bloody fairy tale with no hope of a happy ending' – that's how he used to describe religion.

But just cos he didn't believe in God it doesn't mean he or she or it or whatever doesn't exist, does it?

I think back to the day the vicar came to buy the eggs, the fear in the eyes of the man I once called Sarge. He made it seem like the vicar was a bad man when really it was the other way round. He feared the vicar because that quiet man represented everything he hated: truth, stability, God. I saw those things in the vicar that day and it didn't scare me because those were the things I craved more than anything, to have proper guidance, not as an elite soldier but as a girl, a normal girl.

When he asked me to go to the church I'd wanted to say yes because I was interested in it. I was sick of being told that it was this or that. I wanted to see for myself. I could see that the vicar was a decent man, a man I could trust, and I still feel that way now, even without going to church. The vicar wouldn't lie to me like others have, he's a good man.

Which is why I think Isobel is wrong to want to go against her father. She's got a lot of things wrong and I'm hoping I can set her straight. Because the person who needs to be punished, the person who needs to be kept away from Isobel, isn't her father, it's Steve. He's the one that needs to be dealt with. He thinks he can take Isobel away from me, but I won't let him.

The snow is coming thicker now and it's getting close to time. I have to get my doss bag packed up and put this book somewhere safe while I go carry out the mission. It's a big one, this. It's what I've been in training for my whole life yet that doesn't stop me feeling sick with nerves.

Anyway, enough with this writing. I've said everything I need to say. It's time to put away my stories and get ready. Know your enemy, that's what he always used to tell me. Know your enemy and be prepared to go down fighting. Well, Sarge, that is exactly what I intend to do.

PART THREE

39

Grace

I have to write it down. Have to write and then everything will make sense.

Surely it will make sense.

What have I done?

Write, Grace, write it down. Get it out of your head.

Easier said than done when your hands are shaking so hard you can barely hold the pen.

Okay, here goes.

This is the account of what happened in Harrowby Woods on the 28th November 2004.

The mission.

At five minutes to eleven I crossed the road from the woods and made my way towards the crag. As I approached I could see Isobel. Her blonde hair was tied back with a dark-red ribbon. It was the most lovely sight. She looked like a sprite, like the wisps he used to talk about, the ones in the woods that we had to greet as we passed.

But then as I got closer I saw him. Steve. He was sitting on an old tree stump, smoking a cigarette. From this angle I could see him clearly. He had long dark hair that fell into his eyes. Unkempt, as Sarge would have described it. He looked up when he heard me coming and jumped to his feet. That was when I got a good look at his face. He had dark eyes and a wide nose. His mouth was curled into a kind of sneer. He seemed to dislike me as much as I did him.

'Grace,' cried Isobel, noticing me. 'You made it.'

She ran towards me and then, seeing the gun, her face fell.

'What . . . what have you brought that for? I said we were –'

'Excuse me, Isobel,' I said, gently moving her aside. 'I just need to talk to Steve.'

I walked towards him and pointed the gun.

His eyes widened as I approached and he stepped backwards. I could almost smell the fear coming off him. Good. That was what I wanted.

'Now,' I said, standing so close to him I could hear his shallow breathing. 'I'm going to ask you nicely. Leave Isobel alone, do you understand?'

'Grace, what are you doing? This is crazy.'

I heard Isobel's voice behind me, but I ignored it.

'I said do you understand?'

He tried to look defiant, but I could see his hands were trembling.

'I want you to leave Isobel alone,' I repeated, moving the tip of the gun closer so it was almost touching his chest. 'Go away from here, far away, and don't come back. Do you hear me?'

He stared at me then smiled and shook his head.

'You're insane,' he said. 'Everyone knows that. Come on, Isobel. Let's get out of here.'

But before she could respond I thrust the gun into his face.

'You touch her and I'll blow your brains out,' I said, almost whispering. 'Do you understand?'

He gulped then threw a side glance at Isobel. My plan was working. He was going to leave. Isobel was safe. She was still mine.

But then I heard a voice. And it was calling my name.

As the figure emerged from the trees I instinctively backed away, placing my body between it and Isobel. I had to protect her at all costs. But then, as it drew closer, I saw who it was.

It looked like he hadn't shaved in days. Clumps of snow stuck to his thick dark beard and his eyes were wild and blazing. Isobel screamed when she saw him and went running to Steve. I stayed still and watched as he approached. That was the best course of action when it came to him: stay still and observe.

'Grace! What the hell do you think you're doing, girl?'

His voice was menacing enough to make me nervous. But I quickly made an observation: he had no gun. My pulse slowed down a bit then. Unarmed, he posed less of a threat. Though, as always with him, I would need to stay vigilant. There was no knowing what he would do next.

'That's none of your business,' I said, glancing across at Isobel, who now had her arms wrapped round Steve, her head resting on his shoulder. 'You don't have the right to order me about any more.'

'What did you say?' he muttered, staggering slowly towards me. 'You're my daughter and you're out here in the middle of the night waving a gun around. Get home now, Grace. I mean it.'

I told him it was impossible, that I couldn't go home cos I didn't trust him any more.

'Don't trust me?' he cried, throwing his hands in the air. 'What are you talking about? I'm the only person you can trust. You think this lot are to be trusted, the religious criminals?'

He gestured to Isobel and Steve. I heard Isobel give a snort. It was probably the first and only time she'd ever been called a criminal. They both looked nervous though. I was still holding the gun and Sarge was a menacing sight.

'Just come back to the house, pet,' he repeated, holding his hand out towards me. 'Please. You shouldn't be out here.'

I didn't reply, just stood there staring him down. I'd never done that before, never held his gaze like that, and it seemed to scare him because he quickly looked away.

After a few moments I found my voice. I told him that I'd taken his book and read it and that I'd discovered what he'd done all those years ago, that he'd lied to me about my mother, that she never died in the desert but had lived. That he had snatched me from her when I was just a few months old and brought me to the house on the lake. I told him that I'd seen the letters she'd written begging him to return me to her and that he had kept those letters tucked inside that book, hidden from me, with all the other secrets. And for that, I cried, I could never ever forgive him.

'Please,' he said, his eyes filling with tears. 'Please, pet. Just come home and we can talk about this. But not here, eh? Not here.'

266

'It's too late,' I said defiantly. 'You've lost me. Do you understand? You're nothing to me now. Nothing.'

I looked up at him once I'd finished my rant and his whole body seemed to crumple. He staggered backwards, his hand clutched to his chest.

'No,' he said, shaking his head. 'No, no, pet. You've got it all wrong.'

I told him that I'd read my mother's letters and that it was clear what had happened. There was no mistaking it. He had taken me from her in the summer of 1991 and removed me to Rowan Isle House where he has kept me captive ever since.

He lurched towards me when I said this, shouting that the letters were a load of nonsense, that they weren't even written by my mother but by her sister, a good-for-nothing woman who was after a pay-out.

I knew then that he was desperate, clutching at straws, because in all the letters I'd read there had been no mention of money. There had just been a searing sadness pouring out of my mother. She wanted her child back. It was as simple as that.

'She never died in the desert, did she?' I said, keeping my eyes fixed on his. 'You just took me from her. How did you manage it? Didn't she try to stop you?'

'She was sleeping,' he said, looking down at his boots. 'It was early morning. You were wide awake, lying in your crib, gurgling away. I looked in at you and you smiled up at me and I knew in that moment that I had to get you away from there. For your own sake. I found your birth certificate and some fresh clothes then took you back to the base, where I organized a flight back to the UK.'

'And they let you take a baby?' I said, shaking my head. 'Just like that?'

'They knew you were my daughter,' he said, looking up at me, his eyes watering. 'But I told them . . . I told them your mother was dead.'

A shiver went right through me when he said those words. I wanted to hit him. I wanted to hurt him the way he had hurt me. Hurt us.

'All my life I had a mother,' I cried. 'A mother who loved and wanted me, and you took me away from her and brought me to that hellhole.'

His eyes blazed then and he raised his fists at me.

'Hellhole?' he screamed. 'You think you know about hellholes? You think you know what it is to live like they were living? Snipers on every corner. Car bombs. Kidnappings. And I was meant to leave you there? My own flesh and blood. My child.'

'It was my home,' I cried, tears clouding my eyes.

'It was a fucking war zone,' he yelled. 'If I'd left you there I would have been signing your death warrant. I might as well have dug your grave myself.'

'You did that anyway,' I said, wiping my eyes with the back of my hand. 'I've never had a proper life. You made sure of that. I've lived like an animal, like the fox in that bloody trap.'

'I gave you freedom,' he said. 'I took you away from all the wretchedness, all the dangers of the world.'

'You made me scared of everything and everyone. Made me believe not only that my mother was dead but that I could never make a friend, never have a normal life, never trust anyone. And then you locked me up.'

'I made a soldier out of you,' he said, his voice low and ominous. 'A survivor. You have to break someone to build them up again and when you do they come back stronger. Look at you, girl. You're better than this.'

He gestured to Isobel and Steve, his face contorted with disgust.

'These people aren't your friends,' he said. 'They're liars and criminals.'

'You're the criminal,' I cried. 'You kidnapped me. You broke the law. Isobel would never betray me or hurt me. She'd do anything for me.'

'Is that so?' he said, shaking his head. 'Thing is, girl, you don't seem to understand what a true battle feels like. You don't seem to understand that I saved your life.'

'You destroyed it,' I cried. 'You might as well have just left me there to die. In fact, I wish you had.'

He rushed at me then with such force that I was nearly knocked off my feet.

'Do you know what it feels like to die, girl?' he yelled. 'You think it's noble or peaceful, eh? No, dying's not like that. It's noisy and dirty and it takes a long time for the end to come. I know that cos I've killed people. I've watched them writhe around in agony with their insides hanging out.'

Behind him I heard Isobel gasp and Steve telling her that everything was all right, that they would be out of here soon. I needed Sarge to stop, to shut up. He was tainting everything with his madness, he was letting Isobel think that I was a crazy person and pushing her further towards Steve. This wasn't how it was supposed

269

to be. He had ruined everything by turning up like this. And he wasn't finished.

'I watched my friends die,' he continued, his face just inches from mine. 'Blown to smithereens and for what? An illegal war started by criminals, madmen who cited the bullshit *her* old man spouts as a reason for mass slaughter.'

'I know what you went through,' I said, watching as a piece of spittle hung suspended from the corner of his mouth. 'And I know that's why you're like you are, why you hear the voices.'

'You don't know anything,' he cried. 'You're a child.'

'She's not a child.'

Isobel's voice pierced the air then I heard Steve telling her to be quiet, that she should leave it alone.

'Listen to your boyfriend,' Sarge whispered, his breath reeking of stale beer. 'And keep the hell out of this. You've done enough damage. Now come on, Grace, put that bloody gun down and come home.'

I know now that I should have done what he said. I should have kept the peace. But all I could think about was my mother's letter, her sadness and despair at being kept apart from her child. 'My precious baba', that's what she called me. My precious baba. And the more I focused on those words, the angrier I became. The rage rose inside me like a thick mist. Time slowed down. I could see his face above me but it seemed cracked, like he was falling apart in front of my eyes.

'No. That is not my home. Not any more.'

The voice that came out of me didn't sound like my own. It was harder, stronger.

Then I felt his arms grip mine. He stumbled into me like a sleepwalker. I tried to pull him off but he was too heavy. I heard Isobel shout something then felt a crack on the back of my head and the shock of cold snow on my body as I fell.

And then. Nothing.

PART FOUR

40

Lisa

I sit in the centre of the room and let the hand holding the book drop to my side. The writing had been so vivid, so beautifully evocative of the woods and the cold and the moonlight that it feels like I'm out there. I can still smell the winter air, still feel the crunch of snow underneath my feet. My head sways slightly and I stumble to my knees, letting the book fall on the floor beside me.

As I sit here I try to make sense of what I've just read. Grace and Isobel had been friends. Very close friends. Yet when I'd mentioned Grace to Isobel at the party earlier she said she barely knew her. Still, there is no mistaking who wrote that account. The adult Grace's voice was unchanged from the teenager whose words I've just read. The intensity, the digression of thought – jumping from present to past and back again via a circuitous route, taking in all sorts of byways and vistas – but at the heart of it an integrity, a sense of right and wrong, good and evil, light and darkness. That was Grace all over and it was that innate goodness that drew me to her, that made me open up to her, tell her things I hadn't ever told another soul.

And yet here she was at the age of thirteen planning an act of violence so extreme it called for the inclusion of a gun. Her words were like little explosions scattered across the page. Her hatred of Steve was palpable. But had she killed her father? I shiver as I imagine the deathly silence that must have descended on the woods that night, the fear Grace must have felt.

It's the same fear I am feeling now.

'Joe,' I whisper as I lie down on the floor, curling my knees up to my chest. Please let him be all right. Please let Isobel get my message and come and let me out of here so I can find my baby. Please.

I take my phone out of my pocket and shine the torch at it, hoping, crazily, that the phone has somehow managed to charge itself in the last few minutes. But the screen is still dark.

My eyes are sore and heavy from crying and I tell myself that I'll just close them for a few moments, but soon I'm falling into a heavy darkness that wraps itself round me like a blanket.

I hear a scream.

'Joe,' I call out. 'Joe. It's okay, Mummy's coming. I'm going to be right with you. Any moment now I'll see you and I'm never going away again. I promise.'

'Mummy!'

His voice is agitated. He's somewhere out there looking for me and though I can hear him I can't see him. I try to stand up but something is holding me back, a weight pressing down on my legs.

'Mummy!'

His voice is getting closer, so close I can almost smell his milky scent. My beautiful Joe. As soon as I get to him I'm going to hold him in my arms and never let him go. I shouldn't have run away. I know that now. I should have stayed and faced up to what I'd done, but I didn't and this is my punishment.

Joe's voice is growing fainter and I'm no longer sure which direction it's coming from. Then a loud bang penetrates the air and a noise like a siren starts up, its wail so loud I have to cover my ears. But as I do so I feel something crack me on the back of the head. Pain like nothing I've ever experienced before spreads across my skull. The siren gets louder and louder in tandem with the pain, so loud that it drowns out Joe's voice completely and the white world turns black.

When I open my eyes I'm in the room again. It was just a dream. A horrible dream. My back hurts and as I slowly come to I see that I am still slumped against the door. Panic engulfs me then and I jump to my feet.

I can hear a faint noise outside, a clumping sound that could be footsteps but could just be a tree creaking in the wind.

'Please,' I cry, pounding my fists against the door. 'Can you hear me? Mark, please just let me see him, let me know that he's okay.'

41

I stop pounding the door and listen. It's silent now. Outside I hear the muffled sound of birdsong. I turn round. The room is full of pale-honey light. The morning has come. I see the blanket lying on the floor where Joe dropped it. I pick it up and drape it over my shoulders. It's freezing in here. I sink to my knees and pull the blanket tight around me. I have no idea what to do. I could try calling out of the window again but the silence out there is ominous. There is nobody left here. I've been abandoned.

As the warmth of the blanket envelops my skin I look across and see Grace's journal on the other side of the room where I dropped it. Easing myself across the floor I take it and open up where I left off.

. . . When I opened my eyes I was lying on my back in the clearing. Every part of me was aching: my head, my legs, my arms. Looking down, I saw the shape of a gun imprinted in the snow and smelt the familiar smell of gunpowder drifting on the air. But the gun was nowhere to be seen. After a few moments I got to my feet and looked about for Isobel, but there was no sign of her either. I tried calling her name, but the wood returned my voice as fresh snow began to fall. I followed the line of flakes as they fell from the sky and settled on the ground and that's when I saw it: a patch, the size of a small animal, of deep red blood, staining the snow at the exact spot where I'd been lying. I quickly examined myself for cuts or wounds but I was untouched.

No. No, it couldn't be. I called out for Isobel again as I stumbled through the snow and tried to remember what had happened. I remembered her coming to me as I lay under my doss bag. I remembered her asking me to help. Then I remembered the plan, the plan I'd spent hours perfecting, and I remembered that name, the name of the animal she was planning to run away with, the one she said she couldn't live without.

Steve Markham. She loved him but when I saw him sitting there on the tree stump puffing away on his cigarette I could tell that he wasn't fit to lick her boots. He was a beast, a sneaky-looking fool who had no business being around my Isobel. She couldn't see that though. She couldn't understand that he had violated her. But I knew. I knew from the moment I saw him with his dirty hands wrapped round her. I knew that I wanted to kill him. That had been my plan: to get Isobel to lead me to him, then I'd put a bullet in his head. But all I could remember was approaching the crag, seeing them together. Then nothing. Why couldn't I remember?

As I reached the end of the wood I saw something lying in the snow. It was Isobel's red ribbon. I picked it up and placed it in the palm of my hand. Then I brought it to my face and sniffed it. It smelt of shampoo and flowers, it smelt of goodness. It smelt of Isobel. What

279

had happened to her? Why hadn't I been able to protect her? I was a failure, an idiot, I told myself as I put the ribbon in my pocket and staggered across the road towards the village. It must have been about four in the morning as the sky had that strange silvery sheen to it that only comes in a mid-winter dawn. I knew those things because me and Sarge had spent our life together observing the seasons and the sky, we'd lived in peace, and now I'd brought an outsider into our lives and all hell had broken loose.

And in that moment I remembered and my blood ran cold.

Sarge. He had been there. I'd shouted at him and told him he was a liar but him turning up had stopped me from carrying out my plan. He'd saved me from myself. The blood on the ground wasn't mine and I know now it wasn't Isobel's. She'd got away and dropped her ribbon. It had to be his. What have I done?

The page is damp and dirty and most of the words are obscured by black marks. I try to read on but a loud noise outside makes me stop. I put the book down and get to my feet. I hear the bolt slide back and I rush for the door, my heart thudding wildly. It opens slowly and a familiar face appears.

'Oh, thank God,' I cry, relief flooding through my body. 'Thank God you've come. You have to help me. Mark's taken Joe.'

42

Isobel steps into the room, closing the door behind her. She looks at me, her face strangely impassive.

'Isobel,' I say breathlessly. 'Are you listening? We've got to get out of here. Mark has taken Joe. He came running up here when we arrived and then . . . then I heard this voice singing "Jingle Bells" and . . . and it was dark and then I saw Mark . . . he just ran past me. He took Joe and locked me in.'

I pause to get my breath. Isobel doesn't speak. She just stands there looking at me with that strange expression on her face.

'What's that?' she says, gesturing to the book that is lying on the floor by her feet.

'It's an old diary,' I say, my voice catching in my throat. 'Grace's diary.'

'Grace's diary?' says Isobel, the colour draining from her face. 'Where did you get it?'

'I found it on the window ledge when I was trying to escape,' I say, crouching down to pick up the diary from the floor. 'It was written by Grace when she was holed up in here all those years ago. And it seems you were right. She did kill her father. I can't believe it. I didn't think the Grace I knew was capable of that. But you knew her too, didn't you, Isobel? You were there that night. With Steve Markham.'

'No,' says Isobel. 'No, that's not . . .'

She shakes her head and I'm shocked to see that she's crying.

'He was your boyfriend, I know that,' I say gently. 'And you were planning to run away. It's all there in the diary. I realize this must be a huge shock but . . . you were friends with Grace, good friends by the sound of it. Look, I can understand why you said you didn't know her. You wanted to put all this behind you and that's fair enough. I understand. I just . . . I just can't believe Grace did that. She killed her father.'

Isobel doesn't respond, just stands there shaking her head and staring at the floor.

'Listen, Isobel,' I say, frantic now. 'I need you to help me. Mark has taken my son. I need to get out of here and find them. And this house . . . this house is dangerous. Ever since I arrived here I've felt it, a sense that I'm being watched. Joe even saw someone at the window. What if . . . I don't know . . . what if Grace has been released and she's followed me here? What if it's been a big trap? I mean, she's killed once, she could kill again. We need to get out of here, Isobel. We could be in serious danger. Grace could be watching us right now.'

'Oh, for God's sake, shut up,' cries Isobel, sobbing. 'You've got it all wrong. It wasn't Grace who killed her father. It was me.'

43

I stand there stunned, unable to move or speak. The room is silent save for Isobel's low sobbing and the soft bleating of a sheep in a distant field.

'It all happened so quickly. I didn't know what to do.'

I look down at Isobel. She is staring up at me, her face pink and swollen from crying.

'Grace was . . . Grace was going crazy,' she says, her voice trembling. 'She turned up with a gun and started waving it at Steve, telling him she was going to blow his brains out.'

I nod my head. Isobel's story tallies with what Grace recounted in the diary.

'Then her father came and he . . . he looked crazed too,' she says, her eyes fixed on the ground now, as though seeing the events of that long-ago night laid out in front of her. 'I was so scared. Steve was shaking. When Grace had waved that gun in his face we were both certain she was going to kill him. She had this strange look in her eyes, like she was possessed.'

I remember Grace's words in the diary, how she wanted to kill Steve Markham, to get him away from Isobel for good.

'Anyway, they started arguing,' she continues. 'Grace and her father. It was all getting so heated and . . . I knew that if I didn't stop her then she would come after Steve. We had to get away. We had plans made. A hotel booked in Scotland. Steve's car was back at the village. Oh God . . . this is . . . this is so hard. I was scared, don't you see? I was just so scared.'

'Yes, I'm sure you were,' I say, crouching down next to her. 'What happened then, Isobel? Tell me what you did.'

'I . . . I knew I had to get that gun off her,' she says, looking up at me warily. 'I had to make sure she was disarmed otherwise Steve was in great danger. That's what I thought. I just wanted to stop her. And I wanted Steve and me to get away. Like we'd planned. I didn't mean to . . .'

She pauses to take a breath then continues.

'Grace was so angry, so busy screaming at her dad, that she didn't see me come up behind her,' she says, shaking her head. 'I grabbed for the gun and as I did she swivelled round and . . .'

'And what?'

'She sort of staggered towards me but then she lost her footing and fell backwards, hitting her head on a tree stump,' says Isobel, wiping her eyes with the back of her hand. 'She'd dropped the gun as she fell. It was next to my foot. He was ranting and raving like a madman, screaming at me that I'd killed his daughter, that I was the enemy and he was going to get rid of me once and for all.'

I try to imagine the terror Isobel must have felt faced with someone as unstable as Grace's father.

'He came at me,' she says, her eyes red from crying. 'He was a huge man, tall and broad, a soldier. And I was just

. . . I was just a kid. I thought he was going to kill me. I swear I did.'

'What about Steve?' I say, trying to keep calm. 'Didn't he . . . didn't he try to help you?'

'It all happened so fast,' she says, her face stricken. 'I didn't really know what I was doing, just that I had to stop him, so I . . . I . . . reached down and I grabbed the gun. It was big and unwieldy, but I managed to get a grip on it. Jesus, I'd never held a gun in my life.'

She shakes her head and looks down at the floor once more. After a moment's pause she resumes her story.

'He . . . he went to grab it from me, grabbed me from behind,' she says, glancing up at me. 'I felt his fingers curl round the trigger. He was going to kill me, I was certain of it. So I spun round to face him and . . . and then there was this almighty blast and he . . . he fell down.'

'What did you do then?' I ask, trying to imagine someone as slight and demure as Isobel being capable of shooting a man as formidable as Grace's father.

'It was all a blur,' she says, pulling her knees up to her chest protectively. 'I was panicking so much I thought I might have a heart attack. Steve and I just stood there for what seemed like for ever but can only have been a few minutes. He just kept saying, over and over again, "What have you done, Isobel, what the hell have you done?"'

She stops, closes her eyes and starts to cry again.

'Then we just grabbed each other's hands and started to run,' she says, her voice barely audible through the sobs.

44

'We ran all the way back to the village until we reached Steve's car. Then we drove back to the edge of the wood and sat there, trying to think what to do.'

Isobel's voice cracks again and she takes a deep breath before carrying on.

'I told Steve that I'd go back to the vicarage and tell my father what had happened,' she says, her voice steadying. 'I said I'd tell him that Grace's dad had attacked me and I'd acted in self-defence but Steve grabbed my arm and told me I mustn't do that, that if I did then there was a possibility I'd go to jail. He couldn't let that happen. So . . . so then . . .'

She looks up at the ceiling, closes her eyes, then – as though confessing her sins to some greater being – continues to speak.

'He told me to stay where I was and keep a lookout for anyone coming. If I saw anyone I was to tell them we'd broken down and that the AA were on their way. "Whatever you do, Isobel," he said to me as he got out of the car, "make sure you send them on their way, do you understand?" I nodded my head, though the truth was I could barely hear a word he was saying. My ears were ringing with the aftershock of gunfire. I don't know whether you've ever heard a gun go off at close range?' She opens her eyes and turns to me.

'No,' I say, shaking my head. 'No, I haven't.'

'Well, hopefully you'll never have to,' she says, her eyes welling with tears. 'My head was buzzing as I sat in that car and waited for Steve to return, my heart pounding at every little noise in case it was someone coming to find us. After about forty minutes I heard . . . oh my God, how do I even describe it? . . . I heard this terrible scraping sound. I looked in the rear-view mirror and saw Steve. He was . . . he was pulling the body along the side of the road and that was the noise I was hearing. I still have nightmares about that noise, even after all these years.'

I look down at the ground, remembering the sound of the glass as it sliced into Mark's skin, and I know exactly how she feels. That sound haunted me as I lay on my bunk in that cell, praying for sleep to come and take it away.

'Steve was well built,' says Isobel, her voice snapping me out of my memory. 'He played rugby, went to the gym, all that kind of thing, but Grace's father was a big man alive let alone dead, and it took him the best part of an hour to get him into the boot of the car.'

'Oh my God,' I cry, putting my hand to my chest. 'You had the body in the car.'

'There was no other choice according to Steve,' says Isobel impassively. 'We had to get rid of it otherwise I was going to jail.'

'Where did you take it?' I ask.

She doesn't reply, just stares straight ahead.

'Isobel?' I say impatiently. 'Where did you take it?'

'We didn't have to go far, that's all I'll say,' she whispers, her eyes clouding over.

'Isobel,' I say, my voice trembling. There's something about her tone that is deeply unsettling. 'Isobel, where did you bury the body? I need to know.'

She looks up at me then smiles a strange, resigned smile.

'The lake,' she says, gesturing to the outside with an outstretched arm. 'We put rocks in his pockets, put him in the boat, then Steve waded out with it and tipped it over. The body went straight down.'

I sit there, frozen, trying to take in what she has just told me. The lake? There's a dead body in the lake? I can't take it in. My stomach convulses. I jump to my feet and retch on to the floor.

'I . . . I don't believe it,' I say, wiping my mouth with the back of my hand. 'It's not possible. What about when the police came for Grace? Surely they would have drained the lake?'

'That's what I was dreading,' says Isobel quietly. 'Though, in her manic state, Grace told them she'd left the body in a graveyard. The police spent weeks searching all the nearest churchyards, ours included. My heart was in my mouth when they came to our door. I thought I'd been found out.'

'So how did the police find Grace?' I say. 'Why did they come for her?'

'Apparently she woke up in the woods sometime around dawn,' says Isobel. 'By that time we were long gone but her father's blood was splattered on her clothes. It must have got on to her when he fell. According to the

288

police she told them she'd staggered back to the house after that and holed herself up in this room.'

I look around at the stark white walls and shiver, imagining Grace as a young teenager in here all alone, scared and confused.

'Someone must have noticed she was here alone because the police were given an anonymous tip-off and found her here covered in blood,' says Isobel, her face hardening.

'Anonymous?' I say, frowning. 'But I thought Grace and her father had kept themselves to themselves. Who would have –?'

I stop then, noticing the strange expression on Isobel's face.

'You called them?' I say, my voice shaking with rage. 'You framed Grace for the killing? I don't believe it. How could you, Isobel? You were supposed to be her friend!'

'Friend?' cries Isobel. 'She was never my friend. She was just some misfit who'd attached herself to me. We were never friends.'

'She was sent away,' I say, trying to keep calm as I remember Grace and her small acts of kindness that got me through those dark days. 'She's in prison now.'

'She's not in prison for what happened to her father,' snaps Isobel. 'She was sent to a young offenders' place for that and got all sorts of therapy. What you don't realize is that Grace is mad. She always was. When the police turned up that day she told them she'd killed her father. She was a lunatic.'

'She told them because she was covered in blood and had no recollection of what had happened,' I say. 'She was scared and confused.'

'She was dangerous,' says Isobel, her eyes blazing. 'You forget she'd been brought up by that madman, utterly untamed. After she was released from the young offenders' place she got slung back in prison for all sorts of things: theft, assault, GBH.'

'How do you know all this?' I say.

'I kept myself updated,' says Isobel sourly. 'Googled her name from time to time, that sort of thing. It was in my interest to know what she was up to.'

'But everything that happened to her stemmed from that night,' I cry. 'For being framed for something she didn't do. Grace was a good person. I know that because I spent time in prison with her. I saw her kindness first-hand. Isobel, you have to tell the police what happened. You must.'

'Don't tell me what I must do,' she yells, jumping to her feet. 'I know all about you and what you did to your husband. I saw him on the news the other night, poor chap, begging for his little son to be brought back. What kind of a wife and mother does that?'

'I ran away because I couldn't be without Joe,' I say, my voice trembling. 'I'm his mother. I needed to be with him. You wouldn't understand that.'

'I wouldn't understand?' cries Isobel, her eyes welling with tears. 'Because I'm a cold-hearted, childless bitch, is that right?'

'I didn't say that, I just meant –'

'You think I owe Grace anything?' she says, tears and snot running down her face. 'Getting involved with that girl ruined my life. Do you know what happened three months after that night, eh?'

I shake my head.

'No, why would you,' she shrieks. 'Well, I'll tell you. Three months to the day after he hid that old lunatic's body in the lake Steve went and gassed himself in his friend's garage. They found him after three days. I had to find out by seeing it on the local news. "Mystery as promising young rugby player takes his own life." That was the headline. But there was no mystery for me. I knew exactly why he had done it. It's because he couldn't live with the guilt. He was a good person, a kind-hearted, loving person, and he just couldn't bear to think that he had disposed of a body like that, colluded in someone's death. *He* was a good person, not Grace. And that's why I have no guilt over what happened to her because as far as I'm concerned she killed Steve. She killed the love of my life.'

'I'm sorry,' I whisper. 'I really am.'

'You talk about Grace's life being over,' she continues, her eyes wild now. 'Well, mine was destroyed the day I found out about Steve. My heart was ripped to pieces. And then a few weeks later I found out I was pregnant. Imagine explaining that to your father when he's a vicar. And I wanted that baby. I wanted it so much because it was my only reminder of Steve.'

She starts sobbing. The sound is raw and heartbreaking. I go to her and put my hand on her shoulder.

'Isobel, I'm sorry,' I say gently. 'You've been through the worst possible experience but I know what guilt feels like too. It eats you up inside. You'll never be free until you do the right thing and clear Grace's name.'

'Do the right thing?' she snaps, stumbling to her feet. 'What about you? The runaway mother who slashed her husband's face and . . .'

Her voice is drowned out by the sound of sirens.

'What's that?' I say, my mouth going dry. 'Did you call them? Maybe they've found Joe.'

I rush to the door and start yanking at it. Then I hear Isobel's footsteps behind me.

'Yes, I called them,' she says softly. 'And I also called his dad.'

'What?' I say, turning round. 'Why did you do that?'

'Like I said, I saw you on the news,' she says, sighing heavily. 'You'd been asking me all sorts of questions about Grace and . . . I panicked. I thought you were on to me.'

'On to you?'

'I thought you knew it was me who killed Grace's father,' she says. 'I thought that's why you'd come. I mean, no one would come up here to this dilapidated old place for a holiday. But then I saw your face on the news, heard what you'd done to your husband.'

'So you contacted Mark and told him where I was?'

'Yes,' she says, looking down at her feet. 'I thought I was doing the right thing because he sounded so nice and he said how you had attacked him and that you weren't right in the head. He said he was scared you were going to hurt Joe.'

'I would never hurt my son,' I say, my voice riven with anger. 'Never. He's my world. My life. I came out here because I'd only been allowed to see him for a few hours a week. It was killing me.'

'I can see that now,' says Isobel nervously. 'But I was just so scared that you'd found me out. I thought I was doing it for the best.'

'So you knew Mark would be here when you dropped me off?' I say. 'You knew Mark was in this house?'

She nods her head.

'He told me he would drive up,' she says, her words coming out in fast, nervous bursts. 'I gave him directions to the house and told you'd be out at the carol service and that the door had no lock. He could let himself in. Then when you got back he would confront you and call the police. I had no idea he would lock you up like this or take Joe. I mean it, Lisa, I didn't know he would do that.'

'Mark has spent years trying to scare me,' I say wearily. 'Trying to undermine me, make out I'm mad and stupid and incompetent. That's why I struck out at him that night, Isobel. Because he was abusing me, mentally, and he's been doing it ever since we met.'

'I'm sorry, Lisa,' she says, coming towards me with her hand outstretched. 'I didn't know. And I like you, I really do. It's been good to talk to someone, to finally unburden this . . . this secret I've been carrying all these years. I know I shouldn't have called Mark but I was scared you'd found me out. Yet, the strange thing is that now all that fear is gone. I feel . . . free.'

I go to speak but before I can get the words out there's a violent hammering on the door.

'POLICE! OPEN UP!'

Isobel looks at me with a resigned expression. This is it. For both of us.

45

Harrowby District Police Station

'This way, Mrs Ward.'

The arresting officer, an expressionless shadow of a man with hunched shoulders and a receding hairline, escorts me along a narrow corridor that is lined with interview rooms. My eyes are red and sore from crying and my back aches from the plastic chair I've had to sit on for the last two hours while they interviewed me.

I say 'interview' yet really there was nothing much to say. Mark had been to the station with Joe and told them where I was. Joe had confirmed that he'd been at the house with the big puddle next to it with his mummy and that I'd driven 'for lots of hours' in the car to get there.

Though Isobel is the one who called them, I saw in her eyes those last few moments in the room that she regretted what she had done.

Still, none of that matters now. Rather than anger or fear or bitterness, I feel a deep sense of calm as I walk down the lifeless corridor, a sense that the running is over now. This is where all the pain ends.

'Just up here to the left,' grunts the police officer, and as we pass another series of glass-fronted rooms my eyes are drawn to a person sitting at a desk in one of them.

A slight, elderly man with curly grey hair and a pale thin face looks out at me as I pass. The vicar.

I stop for a moment and our eyes meet. And then something strange happens. He presses both his hands together, as if in prayer, nods his head and smiles at me. It's a warm, gentle smile, one that penetrates my bones and seems to say that everything will be all right. It only lasts a few moments before the vicar turns his head and the officer and I continue along the corridor, but it is enough. It is enough.

'Here we are,' says the officer, stopping outside a blue-framed door at the end of the corridor. 'You've got twenty minutes.'

He opens the door and a familiar face looks up at me. My heart sinks. I'd hoped that Mark might have brought Joe in to see me. But then why would he? After everything I've done.

'What are you doing here?' I say, taking a seat at the small square table.

'I just wanted to see if you were okay,' says Jimmy, leaning forwards, his hands clasped to his chest. 'It's all over the village what happened.'

I don't answer him. Instead I just shrug. What more is there to say?

'We just couldn't believe someone so nice and respectable could be capable of that,' he says, shaking his head. 'Crikey, you think you know a person and then . . . wham!'

'You don't know me, Jimmy,' I snap, irritated at his presence, that it's him sitting opposite me and not Joe. 'We only met a few days ago.'

His face reddens then and he sits up straight.

'I wasn't talking about you,' he says. 'I was talking about her. Isobel.'

'Isobel?'

'Yeah,' he says, 'like I said just now, it's all over the village. It wasn't the daughter who killed the mad soldier. It was Isobel.'

'She confessed?' I say quietly, aware of the officer sitting in the chair behind me.

'Apparently she confessed it to her dad years ago,' he says, leaning closer to me. 'But old Reverend Carter decided to keep it to himself. Probably told her to do some penance, three Hail Marys or something. Oh, hang on, that's Catholicism, isn't it? What do they do in the Church of England world when they've sinned? I'm not religious, see.'

'So what changed?' I say impatiently. 'How did it come out?'

'Well, apparently the vicar decided to grow a pair,' he says. 'According to Val, the woman who does the cleaning up at the vicarage, Isobel and the vicar got into a huge argument the other day, just before Isobel brought you to the pub, and she called him all sorts of terrible things. So bad, Val said she couldn't bring herself to repeat them.'

I think back to Isobel's dishevelled appearance that day, her eyes puffy from crying.

'Anyway, they had another big row last night,' continues Jimmy. 'Isobel stormed off and the vicar must have thought "enough is enough". He went down to the station and told this lot everything. Val's son Dave is the desk sergeant. He rang Val as soon as he came off duty this afternoon and, well, you know what small villages are like, soon everyone knew.'

He lowers his voice to recount the last bit, aware that police officer Dave might get into trouble for his slack mouth.

'So there we are,' he says, shrugging. 'Apparently she's confessed it to the police now too.'

'Yes,' I say, irritated by the brightness of his voice. To him and Val and Dave and the rest of them this is just another bit of juicy gossip, something to chat about at the bar over a pint of Black Sheep and a bag of pork scratchings, but Isobel's lies led to the ruination of an innocent young girl's life.

'Could you take me back now, please?' I say, turning to the officer.

He nods and gets to his feet.

'I'm sorry, Jimmy,' I say, getting up from my seat. 'I need to go now. You understand?'

'Of course,' he says, smiling. 'Like I said, I just wanted to check how you were. I know we've only just met but I like you, Lisa. I care about you. I just wish you'd told me what was happening. I'm sure there's more going on than they're saying in the papers. I would have listened.'

Beside me, the officer clears his throat. Time to go.

'Maybe,' I say, walking to the door. 'Anyway, thanks for coming, Jimmy. I appreciate it. But I do need to go now.'

He nods his head, and as the officer escorts me out I wonder how long it will take for my words to be relayed across the village.

I'm grateful for the silence when I return to the cell. The past few hours have been so full of voices and questions and noise that it's been impossible to think clearly. Now, sitting on this hard bed in another prison cell hundreds of miles from home, I can finally allow myself to return to the night that brought me here.

I'd taken Joe swimming at a new leisure centre that had opened up in Barnet. We'd had such fun that I'd lost track of time so when we eventually got back to the house Mark was home from work. As I pulled into the drive I saw him standing in the doorway, the light from the hallway illuminating his tall, skinny frame. All the exhilaration I'd felt from swimming evaporated as I turned off the engine and heard his voice through the passenger window.

'Do you know what time it is, Lisa?'

I looked across and saw his face, pensive and scowling. Next minute he'd opened the back door and started to unclip Joe from his car seat.

'Oh, for goodness' sake, his hair's still wet,' he cried, lifting Joe out and clutching him to his chest as though rescuing him from a car wreck. 'Surely they have hair-dryers at the leisure centre?'

'We didn't have time,' I explained as I followed him into the house. 'But I got him straight in the car. Honestly, Mark, a bit of damp hair isn't going to harm him.'

'It's December, you foolish woman,' he exclaimed as he marched up the stairs with Joe. 'Freezing cold. God, you don't have an ounce of common sense, do you?'

I didn't respond. Instead I closed the door, put the bags on to the rack in the hall then made my way despondently to the kitchen. Mark had already been busy. The dishwasher was whirring, the washing machine was on a spin cycle. Probably he'd come home from work, seen the dirty pots stacked up in the sink and the overflowing laundry basket in the utility room, and sprung into action. I could imagine what he'd said as he buzzed around the kitchen. 'Christ, Lisa, no wonder I can never find a clean shirt.'

As I stood in the kitchen I felt like I was sinking into an abyss, suffocating under the weight of Mark's controlling ways. I hadn't had a proper night's sleep in months. Joe was teething at the time, waking up every hour or so screaming in pain. I was spending most of my nights pacing up and down the hallway with Joe in my arms, rocking him and willing the Calpol to act fast. The sleep deprivation left me feeling spiky and short-tempered, as though the slightest thing could send me hurtling over the edge. The only time I felt calm was when I went swimming. The water, just as it had done as a child, always made me feel better, like I was floating between worlds, with no cares, no responsibilities, just a wonderful sense of peace. Mark had never understood my love of swimming, of how necessary it was to my well-being. He saw the water as dangerous and unknowable. And the fact that I was drawn to it, needed it, made him distrust it even more. You see, Mark liked to control every aspect of our lives and he hated the fact that when I swam I was free again, wild again, beyond his control.

The events of that evening have blurred slightly, though I remember standing in the kitchen holding a glass of water, trying to wake myself up. Mark had dried Joe's hair and got him ready for bed, muttering loudly how terrible it was that 'Mummy let you get cold and wet'. I could hear his voice in the next room as I stood there and I remember trying to think of something positive, something to cancel out Mark's constant criticisms. I closed my eyes and saw my father standing by the side of the pool holding his arms out to me, a tiny girl of six. 'Come on, Lisa,' he cried, his eyes warm and encouraging. 'You can do it!' And for a few moments I was back at the lido about to swim for the first time. My shoulders relaxed and I felt happiness, pure, simple happiness flood through my body.

But then Mark walked into the kitchen. It all happened so fast. He was taking the glass out of my hands, telling me that I'd been foolish to go to the pool today. That I wasn't fit to look after Joe. That I was stupid, useless, a bad mother. I opened my eyes and looked up at him and in that moment something else emerged from me, some wild, uncontrollable thing. All the rage I'd repressed for so long came hurtling out of me.

I struck out at him, again and again, not even aware that I was still holding the glass in my hands. I could hear him scream but I was beyond caring. I carried on striking at him. The next thing I knew the police were at the door and I was taken away from the blood-splattered kitchen.

I'd never felt anger like that before or since, anger so raw it took my breath away. Yet now, sitting in this tiny cell, my knees pressed up to my chest, I feel it all dissipate. There is nothing left to rage against, nothing to run away from.

EPILOGUE

Lisa

London, 25 September 2019

The brightly coloured room has been designed with children in mind. There's a mural of cartoon characters running the length of the wall, soft yellow beanbags dotted around the floor amid piles of toys and books. This is what is known as a safe space, a neutral place where Joe and I can get to know each other again, away from any distractions. I sit on a beanbag, clutching a cup of tepid coffee in my hands, and watch as Joe pieces together an impressive Lego castle. His little face is focused intently on the task in hand and I feel, not for the first time, that he is barely aware of my presence. Still, these things take time according to my social worker, Lynn. Joe has been through a huge ordeal, his foundations and trust have been shattered. Now it's up to me to be patient, to let him heal, let us all heal.

For absconding with Joe last Christmas I received a suspended sentence on the condition that I attend regular counselling sessions. So for the last six months I have sat in the tasteful but neutral office of Dr Rose Newton, a tiny, birdlike woman with large green eyes that sometimes seem like they are boring into my soul. It took me a while to open up to her, to myself, but slowly, bit by bit, I can feel myself returning to the girl I was before my father died. The girl who believed in magic and happiness and the power that comes from just being herself. Dad was the first person I spoke about to Dr Rose; his presence was everywhere as I described my grief at his death, the empty space I thought could never be filled, until the day I held my newborn son in my arms. It was painful to open up about my grief like that but now I can feel myself slowly letting Dad go, trusting in my own abilities. You could say I'm ready to face life now, ready to be a grown-up. My father was right. I can do it.

I smile as Joe carefully places a turret on the top of the castle. 'Children need to feel secure,' Lynn had told me at our first supervised session at the parent unit. 'They need consistency, boundaries and an understanding that home is home, that it won't suddenly be ripped away from them.'

She was right, I knew that. A loving, stable home is what every child deserves. I was thinking about that as I sat in a prison visitors' room three months ago listening to my friend Grace tell me the story of her life. She is due for release this month, though, as always with Grace, she kept the details of the latest crime to have detained her a secret from me. 'You don't need to worry about me, Lisa,' she said, grinning at me with those stubby, chipped teeth. 'Like I told you when we first met, I'm a survivor.' I knew that. After all, she had been my protector during my time in prison, a wall of steel that the others couldn't penetrate. But I also knew there was a little girl inside Grace who had never had the chance to grow up, never had the comfort and warmth of a proper loving home. That was apparent as I prepared to leave and Grace leaned forward and told me to stick with the counselling and the parenting classes. 'That bairn needs his mother,' she said, fixing her dark eyes on me. 'We all do.' Then she had slipped a piece of paper across the table. It was yellowing and crumpled, and when I opened it I saw it was a letter, written in Arabic. It had been sent to Grace when her case had made the papers again after my arrest. Her family in Iraq had recognized her father's name and decided to get in contact. 'I got a friend in here to translate it for me,' Grace told me in her gruff Yorkshire accent. 'Apparently, my mother died of cancer in 2014. Though they tell me she never gave up hope that she would find me again. Fancy that, eh?' She'd taken the note from me then and placed it in her pocket, a reminder of the home she never knew, the mother she had lost.

The draining of the lake gave the villagers of Harrowby plenty to gossip about. The roads around the house were sealed off while divers excavated the watery grave. As I read the news accounts I knew that Jimmy and Val and the rest of them would be waiting eagerly for a discovery to be made, for the sorry tale of Grace and Isobel and Sarge to come to some sort of resolution. Yet I don't think anyone, not even Jimmy with his overactive imagination, could have predicted what came next.

At Isobel's trial it was revealed that when the divers drained the lake, as well as the remains of Grace's father, Michael Lightowler, they found another body, that of a newborn baby, born just a few months after Michael's death. Investigations revealed it to be the child of Isobel Carter and Steve Markham. At the trial Isobel told how she had given birth to the baby, a girl, at the vicarage early one morning while her father was at the church. After a few minutes she realized the baby was silent and, though she tried to resuscitate her, it was clear that her newborn daughter was dead. Terrified and confused, she wrapped the baby in a blanket and walked through the woods to the house on the lake. Once there, she laid the baby in the boat and rowed out across the water. The transcript from the court makes for heartbreaking reading as Isobel describes how she sang to her dead baby as she unwrapped her from the blanket and dropped her into the lake. 'She was a tiny little thing,' she told the court. 'No bigger than a doll.'

Grace

Yorkshire, 1 January 2020

In my dreams I've returned to this place a thousand times but each time I live out a different version of the story. Sometimes he's alive and well, other times he's just lying there on his back in the snow, his eyes open to the sky and the stars. Sometimes he's nowhere to be found and I run from room to room, calling his name over and over again. 'Dad,' I cry, the word as natural as the air. 'Dad, where are you?'

Now as I stand here, looking at the empty space where the house used to be, I hear echoes of the life I once had, a trail of memories extending behind me all the way back to that mysterious arid desert where men with guns and tanks drove themselves mad with the guilt of their killings.

I put my hand in my pocket and pull out the book that I've kept with me ever since they took me away from here. The book that revealed his secrets, that told me I had a mother and a family and a history. I open it up at the page he had marked with an X and read the words that had haunted him since the day he took me from my mother's arms and brought me to this remote, hostile place in the depths of Yorkshire.

Your love
Oh you with fathomless eyes
Is extreme
Mystic
Holy
Your love, like birth and death
Is impossible to repeat.

And as I read those words, words I've committed to memory now, I realize for the first time that he wasn't thinking about her and the kind of love they could have had, he was thinking about his daughter, the wild little soldier, and when that realization sinks in I finally feel ready to say goodbye.

There is nothing more to see here, just an empty lake and a bunch of old stones. Let the dead rest in peace, I say. I put the book into my rucksack then, lifting it on to my shoulders, turn from Rowan Isle for the very last time. And as I walk towards the woods I feel the wild girl stirring inside me, the girl who has been silent all these years. I see a tiny bairn clutching the hand of a broken man, a stranger who I learned to love, and I realize that this desolate spot in the heart of the Dales made me who I am. He gave me that. As the trees envelop me and a sliver of moon appears in the sky, I remember the words he spoke to me all those years ago: 'The moon is not afraid, Grace.' And with that I feel a remarkable sense of courage. I hear the foxes rustling in the bracken, the curlews circling overhead. All is as it should be. I am heading back to where I came from, to the crags and hills and wide-open spaces. There's nothing holding me back now. I can breathe easy because I know, for the first time in my life, that the only place I belong is out there in the wild.

I'm coming home.

THE NEXT THRILLER BY NUALA ELLWOOD

TAKE MY LIFE

We've all wanted to be someone we're not.

But what if you were caught in the wrong place, at the wrong time, while pretending to be someone else?

Now everyone thinks you killed him . . .

COMING SOON
PRE-ORDER NOW

Acknowledgements

Huge thanks and appreciation to the incredible team at Penguin: my editor, Katy Loftus, for championing this book from the start and being a constant source of encouragement and inspiration; Rosanna Forte for your excellent insight and advice; Georgia Taylor for your tireless and innovative digital and marketing work; and Karen Whitlock for your meticulous copy-editing.

I'd also like to thank my agent, Madeleine Milburn, for being there for me right from the start and for always believing in my work. Thank you, Maddy, for being such a constant source of inspiration and sound advice. You're the best. Thanks also to Giles Milburn, Hayley Steed, Alice Sutherland-Hawes and the team at MMLA for all your support.

Love and gratitude to all the readers and bloggers who have championed my books over the years. I hope you enjoy reading *The House on the Lake* as much as I have enjoyed writing it.

The House on the Lake was written during a period of change and tumult in my life that I couldn't have got through without the support of some very special people. Love and thanks to Fiona, Adam, Siobhan, Daniel, Catherine and Kat. Your kind words and support have meant so much to me.

I want to thank my lovely mother, Mavis, who is the strongest person I know. You introduced me to nature at an early age and ignited a spark that has never waned. Here's to more sightings of our lucky fox!

Thanks also to my father, Luke, for the walks in the Dales that formed the basis of *The House on the Lake*. You have been my guide and inspiration all my life, Dad, and you continue to be. 'Words have value,' you once told me, and yours will stay with me for ever.

This book was inspired by the work of some of my favourite nature writers. Thanks and appreciation go to: Sarah Hall, Robert Macfarlane, Olivia Laing, George Monbiot and the memory of the indomitable Hannah Hauxwell, first lady of the Dales. Also, respect and gratitude to Tori Amos, whose song 'Winter' was pretty much played on repeat as I wrote *The House on the Lake*.

Thanks also to the wonderful writers, publishers and booksellers who have come into my life over the course of writing this novel. To Jane Corry, Emma Curtis, William Shaw, Beth Underdown, Cara Hunter, Simon Lelic, Mel and Richard Drake, Haris Nikolakakis and Irene Sinodinou. I admire you all so much.

This book is about finding out who you really are, reclaiming your true self and coming home. I'd like to thank Arthur for helping me do the same. Always.

Finally, I want to thank Luke, my brilliant boy. Being your mum is the greatest honour of my life and I love you all the world and sixpence.